## Also by MAURENE GOO

*Since You Asked*
*I Believe in a Thing Called Love*

# THE WAY

# YOU

# MAKE

# ME FEEL

# THE WAY

# YOU

# MAKE

# ME FEEL

*Maurene Goo*

**FARRAR STRAUS GIROUX**
New York

Lyrics from "Let Me Back In" by Rilo Kiley included with permission from the band.

Farrar Straus Giroux Books for Young Readers
An imprint of Macmillan Publishing Group, LLC
175 Fifth Avenue, New York, NY 10010

1 3 5 7 9 10 8 6 4 2

fiercereads.com

Library of Congress Control Number: 2017956980

ISBN: 978-0-374-30408-9
International edition ISBN: 978-0-374-31195-7

Our books may be purchased in bulk for promotional, educational, or business use. Please contact your local bookseller or the Macmillan Corporate and Premium Sales Department at (800) 221-7945 ext. 5442 or by e-mail at MacmillanSpecialMarkets@macmillan.com.

*To my parents, with love and gratitude*

*But when the palm trees bow their heads,*
*No matter how cruel I've been,*
*LA, you always let me back in.*

**—RILO KILEY**,
"Let Me Back In"

# THE WAY

# YOU

# MAKE

# ME FEEL

# CHAPTER 1

THIS PAPER PLANE WAS NEAR PERFECT.

Crisp edges, a pointy nose, and just the right weight. I held it up, closing my left eye to aim it toward the stage. Rose Carver and her short-brimmed black hat were in fine form today, a perfect target, her face lit up beatifically by the stage lights. As she went on about junior prom announcements, I grew more focused.

"Clara, aim it at her face."

My eyes swept over to Patrick Keen sitting next to me. He was slouched so far down in his seat that his chin was touching his chest, his long, pale limbs folded into an impossible position.

"That's not how I roll, jerk," I said.

"Yeah, we're here for the giggles, not tears," Felix Benavides whispered from my other side. He looked at me for approval when he said it, eyebrow arched.

Sometimes these two really knew how to kill a joke. Glancing around the auditorium to make sure no teachers were watching, I lifted the plane into my line of vision . . .

"Clara Shin!"

I startled, the paper plane dropping by my feet with a clatter. The voice had come over the speakers. Why was Rose saying my name up there?

I cupped my hands around my mouth and bellowed, "WHAT?" It reverberated off the wood-paneled walls and high ceilings.

Rose rolled her eyes and exhaled into the microphone, making it squawk. "I just said you're nominated for junior prom queen." She held up a piece of paper and stared at it, in disbelief at the words she was seeing.

Patrick and Felix burst out laughing and then reached over me to high-five each other. *Oh my GOD.* "I'm going to *kill* you guys," I hissed. As people swiveled their heads to look over at me, I started to form an idea.

Rose cleared her throat into the microphone. "*Anyway*, the other nominees are—"

I stood up, making the folded upholstered seat bounce loudly as it closed. "Thanks, Rose!" I hollered. She frowned, then squinted into the audience to see what I was doing. I remained standing, then held up my arms dramatically. "And thank *you*, student body, for this honor." I projected my voice as I looked around. I saw a few teachers get up. *Need to make this quick.*

"Thank you for letting me into your hearts. And now, my promise to you: if I get voted prom queen, there will be some much-needed changes made to Elysian High . . ."

Rose's voice interrupted me from the speakers. "You don't get to *do* anything if you win prom queen. It's not like being class president!" she scoffed into the microphone. She would know; she *was* junior class president.

"Regardless!" My voice boomed. "I will promise you all one thing . . . as Queen Clara." I racked my brain for what, the improvisation making me buzz. Then, an idea struck. I motioned for Patrick to hand me my backpack. He tossed it to me, and I reached into the front zippered pocket. "I promise that us girls will not be prisoners to our bodies! We will have equal rights!" Some girls cheered in the audience.

Rose spoke again. "We *do* have equal—"

"So, in the spirit of feminism and equality—THERE WILL BE FREE TAMPONS FOR ALL!" I yelled, releasing fistfuls of my tampons into the crowd. Good thing I had just bought a new box that morning. Yellow-patterned, regular-flow—they flew into the air and landed on the heads and laps of the people in the rows around me. The laughter came in waves, and girls sprang out of their seats to pick up tampons off the floor, some chasing them as they rolled down the aisles. Boys threw them at one another. More teachers stood up to calm everyone down. Rose Carver stomped offstage in a huff.

The disruption and mayhem fed my soul, and I looked around the auditorium triumphantly.

"Aren't you glad we nominated you?" Felix asked, popping a toothpick into his mouth and grinning. Felix thought chewing on toothpicks made him look like James Dean or something.

I shrugged. "It made things interesting."

"Clara."

I looked down the row of seats toward the voice of my young, white homeroom teacher, Mr. Sinclair. I threw him a wide smile. "Hey, Mr. S."

"Hey, yourself. I'm reporting you to the principal, let's go." Because these assemblies were always held during homeroom, Mr. Sinclair was left in charge of me. Lucky him.

Patrick let out a low whistle. "I'll go with you, Mr. S." He winked at him.

Young, handsome Mr. Sinclair, with the chiseled jaw and thick blond hair, rolled his eyes. "Not this time. Clara. Now." He adjusted his tortoiseshell glasses, a nerdy little signature gesture that made everyone in his classes swoon.

I grabbed my backpack and took my sweet time walking by everyone in my row to get to him. The audience was already starting to disperse when I followed Mr. Sinclair down the aisle toward the double doors.

"Nice stunt," Mr. Sinclair said as we wove through the streams of students headed out of the auditorium.

"I live to please."

He shook his head. "Aren't you sick of detention by now?"

"Nope, can't get enough."

"Why can't you channel that smart-mouth into your school-work?"

The May Los Angeles sunshine blinded me the second we stepped outside, and I pulled on my mirrored aviators. "Are you saying I'm *smart*?"

Before he could answer, someone called out my name from behind us. I turned around and made a face. It was Rose Carver.

Tall, graceful, and precise in her movements, Rose walked briskly over to me. Her skinny jeans fit her dancer's legs like a glove, her floral-print blouse was tucked in, and the pixie cut under her hat showed off her delicate features. Rose looked like a long-lost Obama daughter.

When she reached me, I was annoyed that I had to look up at her. "What?" I asked.

Her expression was focused and determined. I could feel the bossiness rolling off her in waves.

I *hated* Rose Carver.

She jabbed a finger into my shoulder. "You need to shut this down."

"Shut *what* down?"

"This whole prom-queen thing. You had your fun. Tampons, *hardy har har*," she said, throwing her head back. Then she focused her laserlike eyes on me again. "Now, drop out of the running and let someone who *actually* cares have a chance to win."

Her condescension was like manna from the gods. I squinted up at her. "You mean, someone like *you*?"

She rolled her eyes. "Yeah, or anyone else, really."

"You're so selfless, always thinking about the greater good," I said with a smile.

Her eyes closed briefly, as if she was harnessing all that impeccable self-control exercised by high-achieving ballerinas everywhere. "I didn't spend *months* as the head of the prom committee only to have you make a joke out of the whole thing." The thought of spending months caring about prom was suffocating.

I stood on my tippy-toes to try to be at eye level with her. "I'm not going to apologize for you wasting your social life on *prom*." Her eyes flashed and I continued, "You know, I was considering dropping out. But you just made me change my mind."

"Clara, Rose. That's enough," Mr. Sinclair said. "Let's go."

I patted Rose's arm before walking away. "See you at prom, Rose."

From behind me, I heard her shout, "You're *such* a child!"

I continued down the familiar path toward the principal's office.

# CHAPTER 2

THERE WEREN'T ENOUGH HOT DOGS AND FLAMIN' HOT Cheetos in the world to satiate Patrick and Felix. After my inevitable detention that afternoon, I met up with them at one of the thousands of 7-Elevens in Los Angeles, this one on Echo Park's main drag—Sunset Boulevard, a few blocks away from Elysian High.

Despite what it means to popular culture, Sunset Boulevard isn't a glamorous street littered with movie stars driving around in convertibles or something. For one thing, Sunset runs here all the way from the beach. It's like twenty-two miles long. It starts at the Pacific Coast Highway, passes by mansions near UCLA, gross clubs and comedy bars in West Hollywood, tourist traps in Hollywood, strip malls with Thai food and laundromats in East Hollywood, juice shops and overpriced boho boutiques in Silver Lake, and then lands here in Echo Park, another quickly gentrifying eastside neighborhood full of coffee shops and taquerias.

When I got to the 7-Eleven, the AC hit me with an icy blast as I stepped inside, the electronic bell chiming. Patrick and Felix were picking out change from their wallets to pay for their hot dogs, and Felix's girlfriend, Cynthia Vartanyan, was there, too. She sat in front of the magazine rack, her skinny, crossed legs encased in sheer black tights, her long, thick black hair tucked into a knit beanie, her fingers flipping through the latest issue of *Rolling Stone*. Of course. She was one of those insufferable snobs who pieced together a personality with obscure music facts.

We didn't get along. One, because Felix was my ex-boyfriend from freshman year, and she couldn't hang with that no matter how many years it had been. Two, my favorite thing to do around her was ask if she'd ever heard of *X* band—a band that was always on the radio. The self-control needed on her end not to go off on some pretentious rant about mainstream music was amazing.

"Hey, kids." I dropped my backpack down next to Cynthia, and she looked up at me with a small, tight smile.

"Please keep your belongings on your person!" barked Warren, the gawky and perpetually greasy-haired clerk.

I opened a bag of Cool Ranch Doritos and popped one in my mouth. "Only if you ask nicely, babe." He flushed but let it go. Warren secretly loved having us hang out here. Once, we ran off a potential robber by throwing candy bars at him and screaming until the guy dropped his switchblade and bolted. There was an unspoken rule from that day on that we were allowed to loiter for as long as we wanted. And that's literally all we did. Hang out at 7-Eleven. My adolescence would end up being represented by a variety of Frito-Lay products.

"What's up, future prom queen?" Patrick asked before taking a huge bite out of his hot dog. Patrick probably ate more calories in a day than Michael Phelps, but he still looked like a Goth scarecrow.

I tossed a chip at his head. "Thanks for *that*."

Felix grinned, his teeth straight, white, and slightly vampiric. "It was a last-minute stroke of genius." Like me, Felix lived for pranks and disruption. Compact and graceful, he was basically a male, Mexican American me, but with much better personal grooming habits. And that's what ultimately killed our relationship—turns out when both people in a couple are stubborn and easily bored, things get tiresome, fast.

And if there was one thing that bonded the three of us, it was the ease of our friendship. There was never any drama or conflict. We existed in a carefully balanced ecosystem of chill—while making sure we kept things interesting, always.

And normally something like running for prom queen would be considered too much work. I looked at Patrick and Felix, who had gotten me into this mess. "You know, this backfired on you guys. I was going to drop out, but then freaking Rose Carver confronted me after the assembly," I said, swinging myself up on the counter by the coffee machine.

"Clara!"

I blew Warren a kiss. "Just keepin' it warm." He harrumphed but continued to organize cigarettes.

Patrick frowned. "What did Overlord Carver have to say?"

"I should drop out since I don't *really* care about winning."

Felix plopped down next to Cynthia and tossed an arm across her shoulders. "Who *does*?"

Cynthia snorted as she snuggled into Felix. "Dorks."

Felix and Patrick laughed, and I let out a brief guffaw. Something about Cynthia's jokes never flew with me, but I knew if I didn't laugh I'd hear it from Felix later. He was always asking me to be *nicer* to her, as if we should naturally be friends by our gender alone. Or by the fact that we've both had his tongue down our throats.

"So, are we gonna do this? Really?" Felix asked.

I nodded. "Yup, good job, bozos. We're in this now."

"All right. I guess we've gotta up our campaign game," Patrick said, tossing the foil hot dog wrapper into the trash. "Signs, slogan, the whole eight yards."

My eyelid twitched. "Nine yards."

He shrugged. Precision was not Patrick's strong suit. He was funny, though—quick to abuse his slim body to make us laugh, and a pitch-perfect impersonator who once made me pee my pants during a school play by imitating the lead's nasal voice, which had vibrated with phlegm on every vowel. I was never bored with Patrick.

I leaned back against the wall. "Can I just be the pretty face of the campaign?"

"Consider us your campaign managers," Felix said, feeding Cynthia some Sour Patch Kids. *Ugh.* While Patrick and Felix brainstormed ways to win me the junior prom crown, I flipped through a celebrity tabloid magazine, making Warren rate all the outfits.

The smell of frying fish hit me the second I stepped into my apartment. Although I had eaten an entire bag of Doritos (topped off with Red Vines) mere minutes ago, my stomach grumbled with hunger.

Nineties hip-hop was blasting, and my dad was in the kitchen, fanning the smoke detector with a dish towel. Our cat, Flo, hid under the sofa, her striped tail poofed like a raccoon's and sticking out in plain view.

"Pai, it smells like all the grease in the world came here to die," I said, flinging some windows open to air the apartment out.

"You're such a poet, Shorty," he said as he tucked the towel into his back pocket and checked the pans on the stove before facing me to ruffle my hair—long, unruly, and growing out of its lavender dye job on the bottom.

"What's for dinner?" I asked. I peered over his shoulder.

"Fried catfish. I found a cool recipe that uses a batter inspired by KFC's secret recipe," he said, adjusting the splatter guard on one of the pans.

I swiped a bottle of some fancy root beer on the counter and took a sip. "Uh, like Kentucky Fried *Chicken* KFC?"

"No, the other one, Kentucky Fried Corn."

Root beer bubbled into my nose as I laughed. My dad hit my back, hard, when I started to choke.

My dad, Adrian, was always experimenting with recipes. As the owner and chef of a food truck, that was pretty much his job. Since before I was born, he'd always worked at various restaurants, starting off as a busboy when he first immigrated here from Brazil ("Adrian" was the Americanized "Adriano"). My clearest childhood memories were the nights when, after his late shift, my dad would pick me up from my babysitter's and carry me home on his shoulders as I dozed off. Finally, two years ago, he had saved up enough money to open his own food truck, the KoBra—a literal and metaphorical merging of Korea and Brazil. My grandparents had made the trek from Seoul to São Paulo, a city with an established Korean immigrant population, where my dad was born. Months before *I* was born, my parents packed up for LA.

The food was symbolic of my dad's upbringing. People were always confused by my dad's Korean face and Portuguese-accented English. It helped with the ladies, though, which was gross.

While it hadn't been a wild overnight success, the KoBra had a pretty loyal following. My dad's dream, though, was to open a restaurant. He was hoping the KoBra could springboard that.

I pulled myself up onto the counter and swung my legs back and forth as I watched him cook. "Guess what?"

"What?" He drizzled some olive oil on a neat row of green beans laid in a cast-iron pan.

"I got nominated for junior prom queen."

He looked at me quizzically, a half smile on his face. "Are you serious?"

"Yeah, Patrick and Felix nominated me, and somehow I'm on the prom court. Which means people get to vote on whether or not I become prom *queen*."

My dad cackled as he opened the oven and slid the pan of beans onto a rack. "You? Prom queen? I would pay good money to see that."

"I know, right? Anyway, I wasn't going to take it seriously until this uptight B literally ordered me to drop out. So I'm going to stay in the game."

He closed the oven and grinned at me as he straightened up and wiped his hands on the dish towel. "Ah, my Clara, always shaking things up." My dad pronounced my name differently from everyone else, *Clahhra* instead of *Clerra*.

"You know it," I said.

"When's prom?"

I shrugged. "I dunno. Probably soon since school's almost over."

"Time flies, Shorty. I can't believe you'll be graduating high school next year. Makes me feel old."

I snorted. "You're like two decades younger than everyone

else's dads." My dad was only thirty-four; he had me when he was eighteen, just a couple of years older than I was right now. Patrick called us the Gilmore Girls.

"You age me, every day," he said, smacking my leg with the dish towel. "Go set the table."

I grabbed some plates and headed over to the round dining table tucked into a small nook in the apartment. Flo finally came out of hiding and rubbed against my legs.

"Anything as epic as my prom-queen nomination happen for you today?" I asked him.

"No." He paused. "Well, actually, kind of."

I pushed piles of bills and mail aside. "Oh yeah, what?"

"Vivian can't work the KoBra this summer—she got an internship at a production company or something."

"Bummer," I said, moving another pile of mail out of the way.

"Yeah, have to find a replacement. *I wonder who?*" His voice took on a singsong quality.

"Please."

My dad sighed. "Worth a shot." Ever since he first started running the KoBra, my dad had been trying to get me to work on it. But the idea of being stuck in a hot, cramped truck for hours on end literally made me want to die. Although my dad had turned his life around from former-punk-kid to man-with-a-dream, I was happy to be kept out of it.

"Good luck, though," I said as consolation. Then a colorful postcard caught my eye.

I picked it up, already knowing who it was from. The front

of the card had a photo of a bustling outdoor market filled with beautiful baskets and textiles. When I flipped it around, the familiar handwriting made me smile. Large, loopy, and scrawled:

M'dearest Clarrrrrrrra,

You MUST come with me on my next trip to Marrakech. It was INSANE. The hotel we stayed at—oof! Like, fountains IN MY ROOM. Tiles were bananas. I got you a few trinkets that will look GORGEOUS on you. Also, hello, the men there are no joke.

I miss you, filha. But see you SOOOOON! Tulum awaits!

XxxXxxxxX
Mãe

The contrast between my mom's life and my own was never more sharply in focus than when I got a postcard from her travels while the smell of frying fish wafted over me. She was a social media "influencer," paid to traipse around cool destinations.

"Why is August so far awaaay?" I whined as I tucked the card into my back pocket. My mom had invited me to Tulum this summer, and ever since I got the invite I had been counting the days, minutes, seconds. Because my mom traveled so much, it was really hard to pin her down. The last time we saw each other, she was in town for *twelve hours* at some launch party for a purse at the Chateau Marmont. I'm not kidding.

My dad made a noncommittal noise, not looking up from cooking. While most people thought my mom's globe-trotting life as an Instagram influencer was glam, my dad had little patience for her. Probably had something to do with the fact that she had left him to follow her dreams. First it was fashion school, which she dropped out of. Then modeling, which my dad persuaded her to quit when she started struggling with an eating disorder. And now it was having four million followers while she traveled the world looking like a babe.

Sometimes I wondered if my dad was so cautious with everything because, if you thought about it, his relationship with my mom was a big failure. And that failure had repercussions that were wide and deep for our family. My dad had been a mess for a while, overwhelmed by raising me when he was almost a kid himself. In my opinion, the level of investment needed to share your life with someone was insane, and knowing the aftermath of how it came crashing down on my young parents? I always viewed it as a cautionary tale.

"Move your butt," he barked, walking by me with the sizzling pan of fish. Placing it on the worn-out blue trivet, my dad glanced over at me. "Did you make sure your passport's not expired?"

"No, but I will tonight!" I said as I sat down at my seat.

I couldn't wait. It was going to be the best two weeks of my life.

# CHAPTER 3

I PINNED ONE OF PATRICK'S HANDMADE BUTTONS onto my prom dress. It was huge, round, and filled with rainbow glitter, and featured a drawing of a tampon with the words VOTE WITH YOUR OVARIES, VOTE CLARA.

We were milking the tampon moment for all it was worth.

It was the night of the junior prom, and the past couple of weeks had been spent hard-core campaigning. There were about one billion other things I should have been focused on as my junior year came to an end, but . . .

Weren't there *always* more important things you could be doing instead? I chose to live *in the moment*.

And at *this* moment, music was blasting in my cluttered bedroom, pink twinkle lights casting the room in a warm glow. I stepped onto the pukey purple-and-brown woven rug that my dad had bought for me when I was ten years old. The reflection in the full-length mirror bolted to my bedroom door startled me, and I covered my mouth. Oh *my*.

I was wearing a floor-length peach satin gown with thin spaghetti straps and a cinched-in waist that I had found at Goodwill. Given that I was a whole five feet two inches tall, I looked like a little girl playing dress-up in her mother's clothes. The dress pooled around my feet, so I stepped into my white platform boots. There, *much* better. My hair was twisted into a bizarre-looking updo with curled tendrils grazing my cheeks. I reached over to my desk—littered with makeup, books, and Sanrio pens—for a tube of drugstore lipstick in an old-lady coral shade. I applied it in two big sweeps.

*Perfect.*

I grabbed my faux-leather jacket with faux-fur trim and tossed it on before heading downstairs. My dad was sprawled across the sofa watching a baseball game in his lucky black Dodgers cap. He looked up at the sound of my clomping footsteps.

"Meu Deus," my dad blurted, nearly falling off the sofa laughing.

"O-M-Deus is the effect I was going for," I said with a twirl. My phone vibrated with a text. Patrick, Felix, and Cynthia were here.

"Enjoy your evening, Father. Wish me luck!" I called out as I grabbed my skateboard by the door.

My dad waved from the sofa. "Good luck, Shorty. Don't stir up too much trouble."

I opened the front door. "I will!"


The first person I saw when we got to the dance was Rose Carver.

She was greeting everyone at the cafeteria door and handing out little slips of paper. Rose looked every part the prom queen— wearing an airy dress in dark blue with fluttery sleeves and a deep V-neck, showing off her sculpted dancer's shoulders. The length was short and her legs were endless in her strappy gold heels.

When I reached her, she held up a piece of paper. Her lips pursed. "*You're* definitely going to need this."

I tilted my head, looking at it for a second before taking it from her. "What bribery are you attempting at the eleventh hour?" When I glanced down, I saw that it was a coupon code for a ride share.

"So people don't drive home drunk," she said flatly, giving me and the rest of my group a meaningful glance.

Cynthia let out a snort of laughter. I smiled. "What a helpful citizen. It shall be a privilege to be your prom queen."

Patrick reached over and took another flyer from Rose. "Just in case," he drawled.

Her deep fuchsia lips turned down. "People *do* drive drunk, you know. It's, like, an actual problem."

"Thanks!" I said cheerfully, lifting up my skateboard before hiding it under my dress to head into the cafeteria.

The rest of prom was mind-numbingly boring, as expected. If I saw another guy dancing along to Bruno Mars in a sexy fashion in front of his date, I would torch him. And for some reason, the theme of our dance was *1001 Arabian Nights*, which I found offensive. It just manifested in colorful scarves draped around the cafeteria and rugs tossed on the floor.

We passed the time by taking Snapchats of people making out or groping one another on the dance floor.

Then it was time for prom queen and king announcements, and the lights dimmed before Rose stepped on the stage. Everything was dark except for a spotlight on her and the flickering LED candles hanging in decorative Moroccan-style lamps. "Good evening, junior class of Elysian High!"

Everyone cheered. Except for Cynthia, who booed. Always the subtle subversive, that one.

"It's the time you've all been waiting for! The prom king and queen announcements!" More cheers. Someone yelled, "CLARA!" I waved from my slouched position.

Rose opened up an envelope dramatically. You'd think this was the Oscars. "Drumroll, please!" she commanded. We thumped the tables with our hands, Felix and Patrick doing it with gusto— making the table bounce.

"Elysian High's junior prom king is Daniel Gonzales! And the prom queen is . . . oh. Clara Shin."

There were some audible gasps and then roaring cheers. I

stood up, pumping my arms in the air before giving Patrick, Felix, and Cynthia high fives. Patrick handed me my skateboard from its hiding spot under the table, and I stood on it with Patrick and Felix on either side of me, pushing me toward the stage. Slowly making my way, I waved my right hand like a beauty-pageant contestant, smiling widely. Daniel Gonzales and Rose were waiting for me, him awkwardly wearing a crown and her glaring at me.

Before I got up onstage, Patrick leaned over and whispered, "It's all ready."

I nodded. "Wait until I say *honor* before dropping it."

Rather than take the stairs to the stage, I hoisted myself up, hiking up my dress enough to get a few catcalls. I flipped my middle finger in their general direction, then walked over to Rose. She placed a tiara on my head, every part of her resisting— like a ghost was trying to wrestle the crown away from her.

She also handed me a pink satin sash, her fingers extended toward me with distaste. Instead of taking it, I bowed my head forward, waiting for her to place it on me. She muttered something unintelligible as she tossed it over my head.

Everyone cheered as I faced the crowd, and I soaked it all in, closing my eyes like a complete weirdo. Then I glanced at Daniel. "Do you have a speech?"

He made a face. "A speech? *No.*"

"Okay, good." I faced the crowd again and stepped up to the microphone. "Dear wonderful classmates. I can't believe I've finally become the queen of your hearts. I've dreamed, nay, *prayed* for this moment since I was a little girl." Several people laughed. Rose cleared her throat loudly behind me. I kept going. "I promise you, that in my reign as queen for the next two hours, I will keep things interesting. Things will *not* be boring." I looked over at Felix by the side of the stage, nodding slightly. "It will truly be an *honor.*"

As soon as the word was out of my mouth, something cold and wet doused the top of my head, knocking my crown off into my hands. Within seconds, I was covered head to toe in blood.

Some people screamed, a few laughed. I blinked, the fake blood dripping off my eyelashes. When I glanced to my right, I saw Felix immediately dart off. Excellent. I smiled, and I could feel the red liquid slip over my bared teeth. My head turned toward everyone slowly, and I raised my arms. The laughter turned nervous.

And now for the finale. Dramatically holding up my crown, I opened my mouth to let out a scream, but before I could, someone shoved me so hard from the left that I toppled over, slipping in the blood.

I wiped off my face and saw Rose Carver towering over me, her gold heels planted on the bloody stage somewhat precariously. *What in the WORLD?* Before I could react, she bent over and snatched the crown from my hand.

She pointed it at me, as if brandishing a sword. "You. Little. *Freak.*" The word was picked up by the microphone, and it reverberated throughout the cafeteria. You could hear a pin drop.

Laughter bubbled out of me, uncontrollable. This was going

*so much bette*r than planned! I knew Rose was uptight, but this was new levels of cray. I pushed myself off the floor, my hands slipping a little. I could see a few teachers headed for the stage. "You're *totally* going to get suspended for that," I said gleefully.

The fireballs in her eyes were growing huge. "You think this is *funny*? Is *everything* a joke to you? You *ruined prom*!"

I rolled my eyes, reached over, and snatched the crown from her. "Get a *life*." I was about to place it back on my head when Rose's hands grasped for mine.

I held on to the tiara, enjoying watching her struggle to stay balanced. But then one of those beautiful heels slipped, and she knocked into me. We crashed onto the floor, me backward, and a sharp pain shot up my back as she fell on top of me with a surprised *oof.*

"Get *off*," I screeched, feeling panicky—being smashed by a five-foot-nine ballerina made of pure muscle was on my top ten list of nightmares. I struggled to push her off.

"I'm *trying*!" she screamed. But she punctuated that by kneeing me in the stomach.

"OW!" I yelled.

"Sorry, I didn't—"

But it was too late. I grabbed a fistful of her short hair. "I'm sick of this!" I yelled. She screamed again, grabbing my wrists. We were both covered in blood, so it was hard for her to hold on to me.

"*Clara! Rose!* Stop this immediately!" Mr. Sinclair yelled, his voice sounding far away.

Someone grabbed hold of Rose's shoulders, but she shook them off, still holding on to me fiercely. My breathing quickened, and my heart pounded so hard that I felt its vibrations in my jaw. "I can't breathe!" I cried out.

"I don't care!" Rose growled as she let go of one of my wrists to take another swipe at my crown. The crown was smushed behind my head at this point, poking my scalp. Everything was starting to hurt, and my panic was rising.

"Stop it! Stop it! *Stop it!*" I screamed. There were a few people onstage now, dragging us apart. Just as I was freed from Rose's death grip, my right foot got tangled up in some cables on the floor. Rose took that moment of vulnerability to lunge toward me again, pulling herself away from a couple of teachers who were holding on to her. Her arms were stretched out, and one of them got caught in the dangling chain on a lantern.

The lantern crashed onto the floor. We both looked at it momentarily before a stage light also came crashing down between us. I froze and Rose hopped back from it. The glass lens shattered and sparks flew—into the fake blood surrounding us. Then the blood caught on fire. *No way.*

People started to scream, and Mr. Sinclair ran over to the flames, taking his blazer off in one swoop and batting at the fire.

An English teacher named Ms. Leung ran up to the mic and cried, "Everyone remain calm but slowly start making your way to the exits in an orderly and—"

The stampede of feet and people screaming drowned out the rest of her words.

I was headed down the steps when the dark blue curtain hanging to my left burst into flames. I jumped back and yelled, *"Good God!"*

Someone pushed me toward the stairs. "Hurry, you idiot!" Rose screamed from behind me.

We both scrambled off the stage with the teachers behind us, including Mr. Sinclair, who had left his blazer up onstage, now a little ball of fire surrounded by burning fake blood.

I took one last glance before being rushed out of the cafeteria, the cool night air hitting my face at the same time I heard the sirens.

# CHAPTER 4

THE PRINCIPAL'S OFFICE WAS FAR ENOUGH AWAY FROM the cafeteria that it didn't smell like smoke. Instead it smelled like stale coffee and a barfy cinnamon pumpkin Yankee Candle.

I sank deeper into the green fiberglass chair facing Principal Sepulveda. She frowned from behind her desk. "Clara, you're getting blood all over my chair."

The chair squeaked when I sat up straighter, another smear of blood appearing as the sleeve of my jacket rubbed the armrest. I looked at her with a shrug. "I think it's a lost cause. You can hose them down later, right?"

"Or you can just sit like a human being," Rose muttered next to me. She was perched on the very edge of her seat, her back straight, chin held up high, and her ankles crossed like royalty.

A very bloody royal. There was a smear of blood on her cheek, bloody handprints on her neck, and her dress was an abstract study in blues and reds.

"Shut it, you two," Principal Sepulveda snapped. "I don't want to hear anything out of your mouths until your parents get here." The stern tone was at odds with her appearance—she was wearing a fleece vest over a thin floral-print nightgown. When the fire department had called her an hour ago, she had been home in bed watching true-crime shows.

The fire was out now; luckily the firefighters got to it before it spread beyond the cafeteria. Everyone had gone home, but Principal Sepulveda had shown up with guns blazing and had trapped Rose and me in her office. Mr. Sinclair sat in the corner, trying hard to stay awake. She wanted him there as backup, I guess.

"Principal Sepulveda," Rose started with that bossy tone of hers, "wouldn't it make more sense to discuss this on Monday? We've had quite the scare." What the heck, who *talked* like that. Did grown-ups really fall for this act?

"No." The word sliced through the air like a knife.

I smirked. "Nice try."

Rose ignored me, looking down at her cuticles. Oh, so *now* she was above it? Where was all this poise when she was losing her mind attacking me onstage? When I looked at her, resentment oozed out of my pores—she was the reason for me being stuck in the principal's office at midnight. I couldn't believe Rose had gotten me into this crap again.

Because in ninth grade, Rose Carver got me my first suspension.

It was the first time I had smoked. As I nervously lit up the cigarette in the bathroom stall, I heard someone come in and froze mid-puff. A second later, the door I'd forgotten to lock slammed open—and there was Rose. She ran out to tell on me before I could stop her. First cigarette, first suspension.

After that I had a reputation for being someone who got into trouble. At first it worried me—did I want to start high school with this label? But it stuck before I could really do anything about it. My teachers had low expectations, and I, well, I went with it.

It was easy and almost always more fun than actually trying. I saw old friends from middle school get sucked into that rigid college track. The more we drifted apart, the closer I got to Patrick and Felix, who were way more on the same wavelength as me.

And Rose? She was the epitome of all this high school drudgery. Everything about her rubbed me the wrong way: her inability to chill; her uptight, follow-the-rules compulsion; her stupid narc tendencies; and her need to get ahead in life. So, whenever I could, I made life very untidy and chaotic for her. Where I saw an opportunity to poke and irritate, I did. Like the time I coordinated a flash mob during her first dance competition. Or the time I added sugar to all the lettuce in the salad bar where she got her lunch every day. Any punishment handed to me was always worth it.

An eternity went by. I was dozing off with my neck bent at an impossible angle, my knees tucked under my long dress, when the office door flew open.

"Rose!" An elegant black woman ran over to her. She looked exactly like Rose except shorter, with long, wavy hair that was perfectly styled even in her harried state. Rose clearly got her height from her dad, a tall and ruggedly handsome black man with a little bit of dignified gray in his black hair.

"Are you okay?" Her mother grasped her by the shoulders, then widened her eyes. "Oh my *God*, why are you covered in blood?" She looked over at me. "Why are *both* of you covered in blood?"

"It's fake, Mom. I'm fine, it's not a big deal," Rose said, with that arrogant self-confidence that usually drove me mad. Right now, however, I actually appreciated it. I hoped that it would get us out of this.

But her mother wasn't fooled. She raised a thin, arched eyebrow, and her words came out measured and careful. "Not. A. Big. Deal?" For the first time ever, Rose was visibly uncomfortable and squirmed in her seat. Her hands stayed clenched.

Before anyone could react, the door opened again, and my dad's cap-covered head popped in. *Yessss, time to bust out of this joint.*

"Come in, Mr. Shin," Principal Sepulveda said, waving at him.

"Call me Adrian," he said before stepping in reluctantly. My dad had gotten into so much trouble as a kid that he hadn't graduated high school. So he never felt comfortable having to set foot on a high school campus.

He did a double take when he saw me. "What happened to *you*? Are you okay?"

"It's fake blood," Mrs. Carver said before I could answer. Bossy genes in full effect.

The adults stood around us awkwardly.

"So . . ." Rose's dad started, clearing his throat.

Principal Sepulveda stepped around her desk and leaned against the edge of it, arms crossed and facing all of us. She was a tall woman who used to be an athlete—even in a nightgown she was an imposing presence. "Your daughters caused quite a scene at the prom tonight."

"Is the cafeteria okay? How bad is the fire damage? Did anyone get injured?" Rose's mom asked, her voice in professional lawyer mode. Joanne Carver was kind of a big deal around LA because she had been the prosecuting lawyer in a big police-beating case a few years back. She'd also been featured on the cover of *Ebony* magazine and was named one of *People*'s Most Beautiful People. So there was that.

"Well, Mrs. Carver, the fire was contained, and it was only the stage that was damaged. And, thank God, there were no injuries. No thanks to these two."

My dad glanced over at me. "So what happened, exactly?"

Principal Sepulveda wagged a finger at both of us. "Why don't *you two* let us know what happened? From Mr. Sinclair's account, it was very confusing."

From his corner, Mr. Sinclair began to stand, kind of crouching there and holding up a hand, like he was a student asking for permission. "Uh, I think it was because Clara won prom queen."

"You *won*?" My dad whipped around to look at me.

I shrugged.

"Yes, she *won*," Rose interrupted. "And it was a joke. She went up there on a skateboard and gave a *speech*. I mean, who *does* that? And *then*! The best part: one of her lackeys dropped a bucket of blood on her head."

My dad let out a snort of laughter. Principal Sepulveda shot him a reproachful look, and he turned the laugh into a cough.

Rose's mom threw her hands into the air. "So what, Rose?" At the same time, Rose's dad looked over at me. "Oh, like *Carrie*?"

Betrayal flashed across Rose's face for a second as she looked at her mom. "So *what*? Mom, she made the entire thing a *joke*."

"Well, Rosie, it's not exactly the most important thing in the world," her dad said with exasperation.

Rose's voice shook with emotion. "It's important to *me*!"

The room grew silent, and I shifted in my seat. Rose's *feelings* about prom were seriously cramping my prank style. In the many years I'd known Rose, I'd never seen her so rattled before.

"Okay, so then what happened?" her mom asked more gently. Rose stubbornly set her jaw.

Pivoting slowly on his sneakered heel, my dad looked at me. Pointedly.

I sighed, clomping my boots down onto the linoleum floor with a loud thud. "This nutjob attacked me."

My dad rolled his eyes. "Clara, give me a break."

"It's true! Tell them, Mr. Sinclair!" I twisted around to look at him in the corner.

He cleared his throat. "Well, it does seem like Rose started the fight."

Mrs. Carver stared at Rose. "Is this true?"

Rose looked straight ahead at a spot on the wall and nodded without saying anything.

"Yeah, you *know* it's true," I said. "She literally tried to take this stupid crown off my head and then we ended up . . . I dunno, fighting and stuff."

Mrs. Carver looked at me. "Can you clarify that?" Dang, no wonder Rose was always so precise in her language. And even though I tried to remain cool, being the object of Mrs. Carver's attention was like having the Eye of Freaking Sauron on you.

"We fought."

"Physically?" she asked, her voice a little more high-pitched this time.

"Yup. Your daughter sure knows how to fight dirty."

My dad poked me. "Watch it." He looked over at Rose's parents, his face a mask of deep shame for having me as a child. "Listen, I'm sure it was all Clara's fault. She pulled that *Carrie* stunt to provoke people, which is exactly what happened. She can take full responsibility."

"What!" I exclaimed.

But Mrs. Carver was already shaking her head. "No, Rose is to blame, too, for losing her cool." She turned to Rose again. "We're having a little *discussion* later."

Principal Sepulveda raised her hands. "*Both* of the girls are at fault here. Clara, you pulled another crazy stunt that was not only . . . disturbing, but dangerous, with the fake blood. Which happened to be *flammable*." My dad dropped his head and shook it. Principal Sepulveda looked over at Rose. "Rose, you started a fight. And all those things added up to almost *burning down the cafeteria*. You are both suspended for a week."

"Suspended?" Rose cried, jumping out of her seat. "I can*not* be suspended! This is ridiculous!"

"YOU. STARTED. A. FIRE!"

Principal Sepulveda's booming voice startled us, and I let out an involuntary nervous laugh. Everyone's heads swiveled toward me.

My dad stared at me with an unrecognizable stony expression. Something had transformed since he walked in—his typical loose, relaxed demeanor had solidified into something tougher, more stern. "This one isn't going to learn anything from another suspension," he said calmly.

Pardon? *This one?!* I opened my mouth to respond, but he held up a hand. "Quiet. Not another word. You're going to pay back the damages for the cafeteria. And you're going to do it by working the KoBra. *All summer.*"

"WHAT!" This time it was *my* turn to jump out of my seat. "There's no freaking *way*. What about Tulum?" I sputtered to my dad, standing directly in front of him.

But Pai shook his head, resolute. "This is what a *punishment* is. All your wages from this summer will go toward paying back the school."

Before I could respond, Mr. Carver snapped his fingers together, the sound reverberating through the room like a firecracker. "Wait! The KoBra? You mean the Brazilian Korean food truck?"

My dad blinked. "Yeah. That's the one."

"Are you the owner?" Mr. Carver asked, excitement propelling him as he stepped across the room toward us.

"Yeah, hi. Adrian Shin," my dad said, holding out a hand. Mr. Carver shook it firmly. He was so tall that my dad looked twelve next to him.

Mr. Carver couldn't stop grinning. "Jonathan Carver. Call me Jon. Amazing! Man, I love your food. I used to work downtown, at the bank building on Sixth, where you'd come by."

My dad's face lit up. "Oh wait! Yes, I recognize you. Kimchi pastel?"

"You got it!" The two laughed like old golf buddies.

I made a face. "Can we bromance later?"

Mr. Carver looked at me, and then a shrewd expression came over his features. "Adrian. Do you think Clara will need an extra hand this summer?"

My dad's lopsided grin, which usually charmed everyone around him, sent a legit chill down my spine. "Yeah . . . she could *definitely* use a hand." They both looked over at Rose, who was fanning her face.

She stopped and stared at them. "What?"

Her dad pointed at her. "If Adrian is cool with it, you're also working for the KoBra this summer."

Rose froze. "Huh?!" she screeched, arms outstretched.

"You heard me. You've been busy with summer school and internships since sixth grade—it's time you learned how to work a good old-fashioned summer job. Minimum wage." He looked for confirmation at my dad, who nodded.

Rose's mom looked like she was going to protest, but Mr. Carver sent her some spousal-telepathy signal. She nodded her head slowly and said, "That's a great idea. *All* the money you two earn will go to paying back the school. How does that sound to you, Principal Sepulveda?"

I was too stunned to speak. *What* was happening? Principal Sepulveda and our parents talked in a huddle, and Rose and I just stood there, helpless to our fates.

"Am I still suspended?" Rose asked, hands on her hips. "Hello?"

But they were absorbed in their conversation. I kicked the chair I had been sitting in, making it wobble but not fall over. Everyone ignored me.

The grown-up pack finally broke up, everyone looking satisfied. Principal Sepulveda pulled on her jacket. "All right, girls. Your parents have convinced me to hold off your suspensions since there are only two weeks left of school. *If* you work all summer to help us pay for the damages, we can revisit this in the fall when school starts."

Rose looked relieved, but I wasn't. "Just give me the suspension! Leave me out of this UN deal!" I cried.

Principal Sepulveda chuckled. "It's going to be an interesting summer, Clara."

I looked helplessly at my dad, whose grim expression wasn't changing. He turned his back to me and headed toward the door. When I looked over at Rose, our eyes met. I scowled, and a spark of hate ignited in her eyes before she swept out of the room with a flourish, her skirt twirling around her.

This is some *nonsense* you've started, Rose Carver. Ready your body for the worst summer of your life.

# CHAPTER 5

MY DAD GROUNDED ME FOR THE LAST TWO WEEKS OF school. I was *forbidden* to see Patrick and Felix outside of Elysian. They found that hilarious. I'd go to school then head straight home.

"What about Tulum?" Patrick had asked when I told them about my summer sentence. I swear he was more invested in my Tulum trip than I was. Patrick and Felix were kind of enamored of my mom. My mom's life was, in general, #goals. Sometimes the only thing that got me through high school was knowing that a life like my mom's was possible. Although she technically lived in São Paulo, she was barely home—never staying in one place long enough to get bored or bogged down by complicated relationships. If someone's *life* could be a role model for us, it was hers.

I had assured Patrick there was no way my dad would hold me to this for the entire summer. He would cave, because that's what he always did. Especially this year, when I wouldn't get to see my mom as much as I usually did. Despite her schedule, my mom always made sure to show up for my birthday and the holidays. And I always got to visit her twice a year, usually in New York or some other big city. But last Christmas she was sick and stuck in Thailand, and I hadn't been able to make it out to visit her during spring break because of a visit from my grandparents. So there was no way my dad could make me skip yet another visit with her.

With this in mind, I played along with the punishment. While grounded, I didn't sneak out, especially since my next-door neighbor Mr. Ramirez would have snitched on me in a second. Mr. Ramirez basically lived by his front window. He was the first person to catch me drinking, with a boy over, and sneaking out of my bedroom window. I thought people like him only existed in 1950s suburbs.

So the last two weeks of school was Netflix and chill. Literally.

And every single day that passed was filled with more dread than the day before because I knew it brought me closer to my KoBra prison sentence with Rose. Even though I was sure this entire punishment would end prematurely, the thought of spending *any* time with her made me want to puke.

*   *   *

40

The first Monday of summer break, I woke up to the blinds snapping open and sunlight flooding my room. "Bom dia, daughter!" my dad announced cheerfully, sipping from a giant thermos of coffee.

"No!" I yelled, throwing my pillow at him.

He knocked it out of the way with a soft punch. "Yes."

When my eyes adjusted to the ungodly amount of light, I saw my dad holding up a KoBra T-shirt and a matching cap. I groaned. "I'm not wearing that."

"I'm sorry, do you think you have a *choice* in the matter?"

In this light, my dad looked like a merch-wielding devil-angel—the sunlight haloed around him majestically.

"What time is it?" I grumbled, grasping for my phone on my nightstand.

He took another sip. "Six a.m. We have to replenish our ingredients today, so it's an early one."

Ugh.

After dragging out my morning routine for as long as humanly possible, I met my dad downstairs in the kitchen, where he was making fried-egg sandwiches.

"So, I can't believe you're actually making me do this." I set my elbows onto the kitchen counter, my feet kicking at the stool rung.

He cracked an egg over a cast-iron skillet, and it sizzled loudly. "Believe it."

"You're being so weird. Since when do you punish me?"

Pai looked up from the stove and leveled his gaze at me. The

41

seriousness of his expression unsettled me. "You know, Shorty. That question itself is kind of a problem, don't you think?"

"No," I muttered while taking a sip of the milky Masala chai that my dad made. It was usually the only breakfast I had— Indian tea made with spices in a stained and chipped Dodgers mug as big as my head.

"It's a problem because *I am your dad*." He leaned against the counter. "Something happened while I was in that principal's office. Rose's parents? They acted like parents. And I was . . . embarrassed."

The tea burned my tongue, and I put it down. "That's nuts."

"No, actually, it's not. I know I was a little punk in school, but I had my reasons. My parents and I—the gap between us was, like, catastrophic. You and I, Clara? We don't have that problem. There's no good reason why you should get into so much trouble. The only reason is that I've been slacking, trying not to be overbearing like my parents were. But it's clearly backfired. I've been getting my act together for the KoBra, but not with you."

My dad talking like this made me feel itchy, and I looked beyond him, at a spot on the kitchen wall.

He plopped an egg sandwich in front of me. "I'm not slacking anymore. And it's starting with breakfast. Eat up." I wrinkled my nose and lifted the corner of the whole wheat bread. Sriracha mayo.

I sniffed. "Fine." With every gulp, unease filled me in

incremental doses. My dad's moment of enlightenment didn't bode well for my plan to get out of this punishment. Pai had told me he would e-mail my mom, but I hadn't heard from her, so it was most likely an empty threat. Or she didn't believe him. They didn't get along, and I knew my mom thought my dad was kind of a nag.

Once I finished the dishes, we headed out. My dad was locking the door when Mr. Ramirez's curtain flicked open and his face peeked through. "Good morning!" I said loudly. He cringed and closed the curtain.

"Remind me to bring him some food tonight as a thank-you," my dad said with a sly grin as he shut the screen door.

"Yeah, I'll be sure to poison it."

We headed down the steps and said hello to the occasional neighbor on the way out of our complex. It was small, holding only twelve units arranged around a courtyard.

"Good morning, Adrian!" Mrs. Mishra called out as she watered her roses in a lavender Juicy Couture sweats combo. She glared at me. *"Clara."*

I glared back at the little old Indian lady. "Mrs. *Mishra.*" The hose got an extra glare. A couple of years ago she had seen me making out with my boyfriend and drawn that same exact hose on us.

My entire apartment complex was basically a bunch of old-people narcs. Good thing there were only a few things that would actually piss my dad off: boyfriends in the apartment, drugs, and being a jerk to elders. Being a jerk to jerks was sanctioned, but old people were off-limits. My dad asked for very little, and I was pretty good at avoiding any of his major no-no's. So this sudden, very strict grounding and his forcing me to have a summer job was something new. I hoped it wasn't an alarming trend.

It was still early enough in the morning that there was a chill in the air. Our summers were brutal scorchers that lasted until Thanksgiving, but the evenings and mornings were almost always cool no matter how hot the day. I hugged my sweatshirt tighter around me as I kept in step with my dad. The parking lot where the KoBra lived, called the commissary, was a few blocks away from our apartment, and Rose was going to meet us there.

We walked down our hilly street filled with duplexes, old Craftsman homes, and small apartment complexes like ours. Just a block down, we hit Echo Park Avenue, one of the main drags in our neighborhood. Palms and mature jacaranda trees lined the street where the beginning of commuter traffic passed by. A coffee shop was already bustling with hipster moms pushing strollers. Right across the street was a little liquor store in a strip mall where two workers were changing shifts for the day—the one off duty getting into his ancient Toyota Corolla, the car protesting with a groan when it started.

While we were waiting on the corner for the light to turn green, a homeless white man sporting a full head of snowy hair and wearing a soccer jersey walked up to us.

My dad held up a hand. "Jerry, I don't have cash today."

Jerry cackled, his blue eyes flashing with good humor before he spat onto the sidewalk. "Maybe not you, but Clara here?"

I shook my head. "I wish. I'm about to spend my entire summer working on this guy's food truck."

"Bummer," he said. Jerry used to be a bike messenger in the 1960s. One too many concussions brought him to our neighborhood streets, but he claimed he loved the "yokeless life."

My dad promised him some food when we were done at the end of the day, and we crossed the street. A couple of blocks later, we passed by my favorite fruit stand, a rainbow-umbrella-adorned cart run by a middle-aged Latina woman named Kara who sliced fruit, then tossed it with lime juice and chili powder. Fruit crack, basically.

"Bom dia, Adrian," she said with a wink.

He winked back at her. "Buenos días, Kara."

I rolled my eyes as we walked past. "You're like freaking Mr. Rogers of Echo Park."

"That reminds me, been thinking of getting a cardigan."

I stopped in my tracks. "WHAT?"

My dad kept walking, pulling on his mirrored Wayfarers. "No, Shorty, they're cool now."

I kicked a purple jacaranda blossom. "Cool for grandpas like you."

"When are you gonna learn that I'm just innately cool?" He had the nerve to do a little spin. My dad used to be a break-dancer back in the day; it's how he got my mom's attention. With his sweet moves.

My feet flew as I walked ahead of him. "New rule: you must always walk five feet away from me."

But that only got me to the commissary quicker—and waiting for us, standing in the middle of the parking lot holding a giant Starbucks cup, was Rose Carver.

# CHAPTER 6

"RIGHT ON TIME, ATTA GIRL!" MY DAD BELLOWED, raising his hand for a high five.

Rose awkwardly held up her hand, and he slapped it with gusto. Then she swept her eyes down to her feet, looking away shyly. God. Everyone crushed on my dad. It was so offensive.

We didn't greet each other. I looked at her outfit, though— sweat shorts over a black bodysuit. She caught me looking at her and said, "What?" Then she adjusted her hair. "Because of this *punishment*, I have to squeeze in a barre in the morning."

"Whatever that means," I said with a yawn.

My dad interrupted us. "Okay right, shorties, here's the deal. Today's going to be KoBra 101. We're gonna go over all the basics, and you'll also shadow me to get a feel for what a normal day is like. Understood?"

I nodded at the same time Rose replied, "Yes," in a nice, clear voice. Teacher's pet until the end.

My dad spread his arms wide. "This mild-mannered parking lot is actually what we food truck people call a commissary. It's where we park our trucks, plug in for the night, dump out our oil, clean up the trucks, refill our ice, and even keep some of our food in the industrial kitchen back there." He pointed to a small concrete building in the corner of the lot. The rest of the lot was closed in on three sides by tall pine trees. Although I had never formally worked the KoBra, I'd visited the truck and the commissary plenty of times. With all the truck stuff dumped out here, it was kind of gross, but I always liked it anyway—it felt tucked away from the rest of the city.

"Rose, can you find the KoBra?" Pai asked, arms crossed.

Setting this up like a pop quiz was wise. Rose's eyes lit up as she inspected the four trucks parked neatly against one of the walls of trees.

She instantly zeroed in on the black one. My dad nodded. "You got it. Let's go over and introduce you to her."

I *hated* when my dad gendered the stupid truck. To retaliate, I called my boobs Brock and Chad, which my dad hated with equal fervor.

We walked over, and Rose's mouth dropped open slightly.

The truck was painted a glossy black, and an illustration of a coiled snake sat beneath pink neon letters that spelled out THE

48

KoBra. The headlights were painted to look like menacing eyes, and the grille was a mouth. Gleaming gold. The first time I'd seen it, I felt an intense wave of secondhand embarrassment very specific to kids with parents who tried to be cool.

"Wow," Rose managed to utter.

My dad beamed. "Isn't she just completely rad?"

*No, Pai, you are* not *innately cool.*

"Very . . . eye-catching!" She was good, that one.

"If you want your eye to catch gonorrhea," I muttered. The truck only seated two people, so we got into Rose's car to trek to a few different markets to pick up produce: onions, parsley, garlic, green onions, red pepper, tomato, and pear. The KoBra did supply pickups Mondays and Fridays and kept most of the ingredients in the commissary kitchen before we prepped on the truck. Thank God that on most non-supply days we started prepping around nine a.m.

"Couldn't we get this stuff from like, Vons?" I asked as we stopped at one of the markets in East Hollywood's Thai town. It was a tiny one, owned by a woman listening to a loud Thai talk show on the radio while ignoring us.

My dad pressed a bunch of green onions to his chest in mock horror. "It's all about keeping it local and *authentic LA.* Vons . . . whose daughter *are* you?" He was always saying stuff like "local" and "sustainable" and a plethora of other foodie words that I liked to parrot back at him while munching on Flamin' Hot Cheetos.

Then we hit up Korean and Salvadoran butcher shops for cuts

49

of beef rump and various pork parts. We even went to an Indian market in Atwater Village to pick up spices. It was tedious and never-ending.

Rose, on the other hand, couldn't get enough. She was fascinated by every store, every stop. Taking notes in a little notepad.

"Have you ever been to Los Angeles, California?" I asked her as she marveled at the row upon row of teas at India Sweets & Spices.

She threw me a withering glance. "God, Clara, will I *ever* be as cool as you?"

My dad called us back to the car before I could respond, letting Rose have the last word.

After we'd gone to every single grocery store in the county, we went back to the commissary. We had about an hour and a half before our first stop of the day—a bustling coffee shop in Silver Lake. "Okay, shorties. We're going to actually *make* food now. You ready?" my dad asked us. He was wielding a large butcher knife and wearing a KoBra apron.

Rose pulled out her notebook again. "Yes." But she started taking these weird shallow breaths. Probably some, like, control exercise that Sheryl Sandberg or someone recommended in order to be bossier. Before I could make fun of her for it, my dad looked at me pointedly. I made a face. "I don't need *notes* for this."

I waited for Rose's snippy retort, but she was staring down at her notebook, her mouth moving silently as she read. Well, well, well, Queen Carver actually felt unsure about this. I, however, felt fully confident. The quicker I figured all this out, the quicker I could get it over with and prove to my dad that I had learned my lesson and blah blah. Tulum was still very much a possibility.

The KoBra had two main dishes:

- Picanha (beef rump) grilled on skewers (in the Brazilian style of churrasco) in traditional Korean galbi marinade
- Lombo (pork loin) grilled churrasco-style with a spicy vinaigrette sauce (similar to pico de gallo)

There were also various pickled veggies (very Korean) that you could add as a side, homemade beverages like lime caldo de cana (sugarcane juice with lime added), and a kimchi-and-cheese-stuffed pastel—a traditional Brazilian pastry. That was my personal favorite.

It was all delicious, actually.

"Okay, so we already have the meat on for lunch," my dad said, pointing at the skewered pieces of beef roasting over the small grill. In addition to the grill, the truck had a griddle top, two burners, and an oven. There was no AC in here, so the truck's roof had windows for ventilation, and my dad had installed a fan in the corner. And, as expected, the truck was already turning into a mini greenhouse. I felt a drop of sweat roll down my forehead, and I glared at Rose, because everything was her fault.

The picanha would be sliced off as it was cooked so that the pieces served were never stale. My dad continued, "But we're going to prep the meats for tonight."

He had us prepare the galbi marinade for the beef: mixing

together soy sauce, sesame oil, sugar, loads of garlic, sesame seeds, Korean chili powder, onion, ginger, and thin slices of pear. "You get me the ingredients and I'll mix," I ordered Rose.

She put a hand on her hip. "Excuse me?"

"This is my dad's truck; I have seniority."

A throat cleared right behind me. "Excuse *me*?" my dad asked.

I closed my eyes. This was going to be a pain in the butt every step of the way.

"You two are *equals*. There's no *seniority*, you kidding me?" My dad tapped the rim of my hat so that it fell over my eyes.

Rose grabbed a metal bowl and whisk. "You probably know where everything is, so doesn't it make sense for *you* to get the ingredients?"

"She has a point there," my dad said, not able to hide his glee.

Once Rose finished blending everything together, my dad placed the beef rump in a giant metal bowl, then poured the marinade over it. "This is for later. We already have some marinated meat for the next stop. I'll leave this here until after this stop, and we'll come back for it and start roasting. It needs at least three hours to marinate." He sealed the bowl shut with plastic wrap, then took it to the giant commissary fridge.

He believed in making the marinades fresh, the day of. "It would probably be more flavorful if we made a large batch and kept it for a long time, but I like the freshness of the marinade in contrast to the roasted meats. It's different," he said as he handed me the ingredients for the vinaigrette: onions, tomatoes, parsley, vinegar, olive oil, and bell peppers. Rose was jotting all this down, her cap and apron impeccably placed. She looked like she was attending the Harvard of food truck schools.

"May I please make the sauce?" I asked her, waving a wooden spoon in front of her.

She shrugged. "Sure, I'm fair."

Gritting my teeth, I mixed the ingredients in yet another large metal bowl. From what I could tell, everything in the KoBra was made in a giant metal bowl—the kind that older Korean ladies, ahjummas, use to make vats of kimchi. My dad's Korean-ness always came out in these stealth ways that I don't think even he noticed.

Last were the pasteis. These had been my favorite, ever since I was a kid. They were deep-fried hand pies—half-moon shapes with crinkled edges for the KoBra's version. Traditionally, in Brazil, they were stuffed with various meats like ground beef and chicken, or cheese and veggies, and sold on the street. My dad put a twist on tradition by stuffing them with kimchi and cheese. When my dad had first made them a few years ago, I was seriously grossed out. *Kimchi* and *cheese*? In a pastel? But once I had taken a bite of the melty, crispy goodness, I was a convert. And now, it was what the KoBra was known for.

The pastry dough had been premade by my dad. He put his hands on his hips. "Are you guys going to fight about who rolls out the dough?"

Rose and I looked at each other.

"You can do it," I said magnanimously.

Rose smiled, tight-lipped with dead eyes. "No, after you."

"No, you."

My dad sighed and took off his cap. "You're trying my patience here. Rose, your turn."

Ha! I hated rolling out dough—whenever my dad made pies I skipped that step. It was always so hard to make it a nice circle shape without the delicate edges falling apart on you.

Rose drew a deep breath and took the rolling pin from my dad. He guided her a bit as she rolled out the dough on the metal countertop, then cut out circle shapes with a metal ring the size of a dessert plate. She messed up at first—the dough breaking off when she rolled it out. I could sense that she was keeping her immense frustration under wraps, but her teeth practically bit holes into her bottom lip. She eventually got it right, but you could tell it kept bothering her. Jeez.

My dad let me have the honor of tossing handfuls of shredded mozzarella into each circle. After that, I laid thin strips of kimchi on top of the cheese, adding a small cube of butter at the end before folding the dough over. My dad popped the pasteis into the oven, where they would bake for a bit before being deep-fried.

In an hour everything would be ready, fresh and piping hot for the customers.

"Not so bad, huh?" my dad asked with a grin, tossing a dish towel at me.

I shrugged, deliberately missing the towel and letting it fall to the floor by my feet. Rose picked it up with the end of her fingertips and tossed it into the sink.

"Butt-kisser," I muttered. My dad shook his head and settled into the driver's seat.

# CHAPTER 7

USUALLY, THE KOBRA HAD TWO TO THREE STOPS A DAY, and it was in business every day of the week. During the school year, when my dad had Vivian and other part-time workers, he would have days off. But this summer, it was just the three of us, and we'd each have to work at least five days out of every week.

On weekdays, the first stop was always from ten a.m. to two p.m. and, depending on the day, we'd either go to a coffee shop or some workplace, like an office park or movie studio. Our evening shift began at five p.m., and we usually stopped at various bars or events in the city, like farmers markets or festivals. Fridays and Saturdays were always coffee shops in the day and events at night. Sunday evening was the only time the KoBra took a break.

Although it was Monday, my dad decided to keep it to one stop because so much of today would be taken up by our training.

I rode with Pai in the truck and Rose met us at the location, a coffee shop called Wildfox, which was completely packed in the middle of a weekday. Everyone was on their laptops, and no one looked like they were over the age of thirty. "Does anyone in this town work anymore?" I grumbled as I pulled on my cap.

Rose almost elbowed me putting on her KoBra shirt over her body suit. "It's called *freelancing*."

"And it's called *sarcasm*, you humorless bag," I snapped.

*"What?!"* Rose yelped.

My dad stepped between us. "Are you two going to get your act together, or do I have to kick you guys to the curb?"

Rose immediately straightened, properly chastised. I snapped my gum. "Fine."

Before we opened the order window, Pai pulled out his phone and took a photo of Rose and me for the truck's Instagram account. He tried to make us smile, but we refused.

"You two," he said, shaking his head. "By the way, we document every stop, so I'll give you guys the passwords to our social media accounts." The wheels started turning for all the weird stuff I could do with this power.

My dad pointed his phone at me. "Don't even think about it. I'll be reviewing every post and have the ability to delete at any given moment."

"Do you have guidelines?" Rose said, pulling out her little notepad again.

I scoffed. "How complicated could it be to take a photo?"

He jabbed a finger into my temple. Very Korean. "Rose, I'll e-mail you everything you need to know, no worries."

She beamed and my dad rubbed his hands together. "All right, this is the real thing, you guys. Girls. Ladies. Whatever. Clara, we're going to handle the food. Rose, you'll handle the orders."

"By myself?" Rose asked, her voice abnormally fearful.

He smiled at her, and her expression changed to adoration. Barf. "Don't worry, I'll come over and help," he said, chucking her playfully under the chin. She floated off to the order window.

Before I could gloat about getting kitchen duty, my dad said, "After thirty minutes, you'll switch." Then he popped open the windows. Just like that, without any warning. Rose's eyes grew wide, and I knew she was equally surprised.

There was already a line. Rose nervously smoothed down the front of her shirt then glanced at my dad—waiting for permission, it seemed. "Go ahead and ask what they'd like," he said, nodding encouragingly.

She leaned over the counter and spoke loud and clear. "Hello, what would you like to order today?"

I laughed. "You sound like a robot."

Another poke in my temple from Pai. "Knock it off, Clara. Get ready to prep." He pushed me toward the food prep counter, which was on the opposite side from the windows.

A nebbishy white guy in round tortoiseshell glasses ordered one lombo and one pastel, which my dad repeated loudly to me. Rose fumbled with the cashbox, dropping wads of cash onto the floor. "Oh God!"

My dad swept it up and handed it to her before she could even reach down. "You're fine, Rose," he said with a wink. She smiled but still looked rattled taking the next order. Dang, she really was nervous.

The nervousness seeped into me, too, suddenly. Why was I in this stupid predicament? Sweating over a stove, worrying about people's dumb lunch orders when I should have been floating on an inflatable unicorn in a swimming pool. I took a breath, then started to prep the ingredients—my dad would put everything together later.

Things were going smoothly until the orders started coming in quickly. Really quickly. And a harried Latina girl with thick black bangs and a nose piercing put in an order for five different plates and ten pasteis.

Sweat pooled under my cap, and one thick lock of hair kept tickling my nose as I rushed to get all the ingredients together. "What the heck, is she catering an *event* in that dumb coffee shop?" I cried, opening the jar of pickled daikon radishes.

"You guys made an extra lombo order instead of picanha!" Rose hollered, her voice panicky and on edge. The three of us were so smashed into that small space that I felt her breath on the back of my neck as she yelled.

Pai was plating another batch of pasteis. "That's okay, you can—"

"Just *deal* with it!" I yelled back, at my wit's end. I lifted up a hand as I said it, and the latex glove that I had been pulling off flew into the air. I swiveled around to see where it had landed, and when I did, I was standing face-to-face (or to be more accurate, face-to-neck) with Rose.

The kimchi-coated glove was plastered to her cheek.

I burst out laughing at the same time that someone outside yelled, "Yo, where my pasteis at?"

"Coming right up!" Rose called out as she peeled the glove away from her face.

*"Coming right up!"* I mimicked in a high-pitched voice. I couldn't help it; my stress levels were off the charts and my resentment had failed to die down over the course of the day. In fact, it was increasingly fueled.

My dad was handing out food through the pickup window. "Clara!" he barked in warning.

"Can't you just do your *job*?" Rose snapped. "You're such an incompetent clown."

Without thinking, I whipped off my other glove and threw it so hard at her face that it made a satisfying *smack*.

She gasped and clutched her cheek.

My dad stepped between us again. "I swear to God I am going to kick you both out of here unless you calm down. Can you manage to grow up for three seconds and do that?"

Rose nodded, taking a deep breath, smoothing down her shirt

again. It was like rubbing the shirt gave her magical calming powers. "Sorry, Adrian," she said with a little smile.

He looked at me, arms crossed, his forearm tattoo of my birthday written in Gothic font obnoxiously displayed.

I tilted my head back and rolled my eyes as deeply as humanly possible. *"Okaaaay."*

Rose went back to taking orders and me to cooking and assembling them. I had just finished wrapping the pasteis up in foil when Rose bumped into me as she reached for the cashbox.

We glared at each other but didn't say a word, feeling my dad's eyes on us. But when I turned to hand the pasteis to my dad, Rose stepped back again and her shoulder knocked my head, shooting a jolt of pain straight through my skull.

I grabbed my head. *"Watch* it, clumso!"

*"You* watch it!" As she said it, Rose swept her arm and knocked over a bowl full of vinaigrette onto the floor.

We both froze. My dad turned at the sound and cursed. "Are you kidding me right now?" His voice did this funny squeaking thing.

"Sorry!" Rose said as she reached over to grab a towel.

I picked up the bowl. "Has anyone ever told you it's annoying when girls say sorry all the time?"

She threw the towel on the floor where it landed with a wet splat. "That's *it*. I've tried to be the bigger person here and let you act like a little jerk to me. But you need to be put in your *place*!"

Something about Rose's anger really gave me life. I let out a brittle laugh. "This isn't Elysian. You have *no power* here."

Her face was inches away from mine. "We'll see."

The guy who was ordering at the window clapped his hands over his head. "Fight, fight!"

"PARE!"

We all stared at my dad. He shook his head. "I mean, *stop*. That's it. You guys are not only acting like kids, you're affecting business!"

And within seconds, we were both pushed out onto the sidewalk and the KoBra's door was locked against us. I pounded on it, but my dad refused to open it.

"PAI!" I yelled. "You're being a total fascist!" I kicked the door and stalked off, throwing my cap onto the ground as I walked away.

Rose followed behind. I was steaming but didn't know where to go, and I was annoyed that Rose was following me. "Can't you go to your *car*?" I seethed as I walked rapidly down the sidewalk. She didn't respond, but I could still feel her on my heels. Where had she parked? God!

"Too good to talk to me now?" I asked while glancing behind me.

She looked at me, then huffed with frustration. "Will you, like, turn into a toad or something if you stop talking for more than one minute?"

I glared at her. "Don't be jealous of my charisma."

She just made a repulsed face.

I continued walking and clenched my jaw. "You do realize that this entire thing is your fault? That if you hadn't lost your mind at the dance we wouldn't be in this mess?" We passed by a group of hipster dudes who laughed at my raised voice. I flipped them off.

I could almost hear Rose's eyes roll. "If you hadn't felt the narcissistic need to pull a prank at junior prom and make it all about yourself, then we wouldn't be in this mess."

I stopped walking and turned around to face her. "Narcissistic? I was *entertaining*. It was a selfless act—someone needed to spice up that dance."

She scoffed and walked right up to me, her posture challenging. "I've known you since middle school. You are a classic narcissist. Inflated sense of self-importance? Check. Need for attention based on some issue with your absent mother, clearly? Check."

I felt an uncontrollable anger rising up—something that I usually had a grip on.

"And, here's the kicker, you have absolutely no empathy for others. Never wondering if the stuff you're always pulling might *actually* hurt other people. Like, did you know Kathy Tamayo really wanted to win prom queen? That her little sister recently got into a car accident and was badly injured and maybe this would have been a nice thing for her to win?" Her voice was louder now.

I felt a brief flash of guilt before anger took over again. "How was I supposed to know that? And it's not *my* fault her sister's hurt or that she didn't get enough votes! It was supposed to be a *joke*!" I was yelling at this point.

A sharp whistle interrupted me. "Girls, can you move along?" I looked over and saw a man leaning out of his shoe repair shop. He had an annoyed expression on his face.

"*You* move along, sir!" I snapped back but then stomped off, leaving Rose standing on the sidewalk behind me.

A bus ride later, I was home, and I headed straight to the bathroom, my heart pounding and my hands clammy. I splashed my face with cold water, trying to wash myself of Rose's self-righteousness. Who the heck did she think she was? Like she was just *so* kind and never self-serving! What a load of utter crap. And how was I supposed to know about Kathy freaking Tamayo and her sister?!

Guilt pooled inside me—insidious, unfamiliar, and very unwelcome. I holed myself up in my room and started reading an old John Grisham novel that I had read so many times the cover was creased beyond recognition. Then I blasted girlie Motown and settled deep into my pillows, Flo curling up into a ball comfortably on top of my head.

But when I found myself reading the same paragraph for the fifth time, I tossed the book aside, making Flo growl deeply and jump off my head.

"Excuse me for living, Queen Licker of Butts," I muttered as I pulled out my phone. I went to Facebook and took a deep breath. In the search bar, I typed "Kathy Tamayo." When I got to her profile page, I saw photos of her in a sparkly silver dress at junior prom. I scrolled down farther and saw a link for a crowdfunding page for her sister, Jill. The photo accompanying the link was of a little Filipino girl, maybe ten or so. Shiny black hair, big smile with dimples. I bit down on my lip. For Pete's sake.

I clicked on the link and read about the car accident that had injured Jill a few weeks ago. And then I read about the medical bills.

Good thing I had memorized my dad's credit card number a long time ago. I donated thirty dollars on the site. Then I scribbled a note on a piece of notepad paper and slipped it under my dad's door.

*Pai, I owe you $30, you'll see a random charge on your credit card.*

# CHAPTER 8

MY DAD HAD US TAKE THE NEXT TWO DAYS OFF. I WAS excited about it until I realized he wasn't going to talk to me. He didn't make Mr. Ramirez check in on me, and he didn't make me breakfast.

I went out with Patrick and Felix, but I couldn't enjoy it. I'd never gotten the silent treatment from my dad before.

I tried to butter him up with pizza and ESPN Classic, but he ignored me and went straight to bed. *Without eating dinner.* The only time my dad skipped meals was when he had mad diarrhea. And even *that* didn't stop him sometimes.

On day two of silent treatment, I wore clown makeup and an orange wig, then waited for him to come home, sitting on the sofa in the dark. I knew things were serious when he didn't react and instead walked straight up to his room. My dad did not kid around with clowns.

I called my mom the second night of the deep freeze, needing sympathy from someone who would understand.

I had to FaceTime because my mom refused to do anything else. When she picked up, raucous laughter rang out before she could say hi to me. The video on the phone was wobbly and I winced. "Mãe!"

"Clara, one sec!" I heard her laughing, the camera on her face but also moving wildly. I turned my head away to avoid feeling nauseated.

Finally, she steadied the camera on herself—all tousled hair and perfect brows. "Hey, filha, sorry. We're in the middle of this shoot for Whimsy."

"What's Whimsy, and where are you?" I was already annoyed at not having her full attention.

A flash of sunshine from the window behind her blinded me for a second. "Whimsy's a new online styling service, and I'm in Brooklyn!"

"You are?" I felt myself cheer up, just knowing she was in the same country as me. "For how long?"

"Leaving in a couple of days, actually. Have this trade show in Italy."

I flopped down onto my bed and stared at the dusty yellow light streaming through my threadbare curtains. "Oh, this little ol' thing in Italy."

She laughed, her teeth white and recently veneered by some

fancy dentist who sponsored it when she live-Storied the procedure. "We'll go together one day and stuff ourselves with pasta."

My eyes closed, imagining a day when I wasn't stuck in LA all summer, desiccated as the plants.

"So what's going on?" she asked, interrupting my brief daydream of eating gelato in a cobblestoned alley.

"Pai's pissed at me."

"Uh-oh. What did you do?"

"Why would you assume it was *me*?"

Her sharp bark of laughter made me cringe. "Give me a break, Clara."

I couldn't help but smile. "Well, my first day on the truck with Rose didn't go so great."

"I can't help but think that might be an understatement."

It was hard to fool my mom because we were so similar. Every time I tried to gloss over something or play it cool, she called me out instantly. "We just got into a fight. What else is new? Rose and I have never gotten along."

"You're going to have to, though. You're working with her all summer, right?"

Flo decided this was the perfect time to hop onto my chest, her sturdy paw digging into my boob painfully. I winced but let her stay there because I was always at her mercy. "Yeah. But don't worry! I'm going to try and make it to Tulum, no matter what."

A low voice on the other end interrupted before my mom could respond, her gaze drifting somewhere to the left of her phone. Suddenly, Brooklyn seemed light-years away.

"Clara, I have to run. But don't worry about Adrian; you know he always gives in. Wear him down!" With that, she gave me, or the phone rather, an air-kiss and was gone.

I went to bed that night still feeling unsettled and craving a giant bowl of spaghetti.

Thursday morning I was woken up by blinding sunshine again. I squinted and saw my dad taking a sip of coffee next to the window.

"You have fifteen minutes to meet me downstairs, Shorty."

Relief pulled me out of bed at record speed. My dad was waiting for me with an avocado toast and tea in a thermos. Not my favorite breakfast, but I didn't complain. I was just happy that he was talking to me again.

He pulled on his shoes, a pair of pristine black Nikes with neon green stripes running down the sides. "Okay, today we're doing two of our regular stops. Rose is meeting us at the first stop. And I swear to God, Clara, if you two don't figure out a way to work together, I'll have a bigger punishment in store."

I bit into my toast. "Yeah, yeah." I hid my excitement at being back on speaking terms with my dad, the bread covering my smile.

After prepping the food, my dad and I headed to Pasadena, which was just northeast of us. But to get there, you had to take the Western United States' first freeway, the 110. Pretty cool, except the lanes were about as narrow as a bicycle and the on- and off-ramps were two feet long and often set at ninety-degree angles to the freeway.

And this time, I was driving.

"This is, like, terrifying," I said, my sweaty hands clutching the steering wheel.

My dad patted my shoulder. "You're good. I taught you how to drive this freeway last year."

"Yeah, in a normal car, not the KoBra!"

"Nah, you got this." If only his confidence in my driving skills was at all warranted.

We finally got off Murder Freeway and arrived at our destination in one piece: an office park filled with grass, big shady trees, and depressing 1980s architecture. "Oh, so this is where your youth goes to kill itself," I announced as we pulled in.

As we parked the truck alongside the curb by the lawn, I caught some movement out of the corner of my eye: an Asian guy my age or so standing on the corner, holding one of those arrow-shaped signs that advertise a business. It said JAVA TIME and had a hand-painted illustration of a mug of steaming-hot coffee.

I wanted to look away from the secondhand embarrassment of it, except I couldn't. This guy was *good*. He was tossing the thing up in the air and catching it behind his back. Then when he got sick of *that*, he did a backflip and held the sign up with his *feet* while doing a handstand.

"What in the world is *that* guy putting in his 'java'?" I asked with a snort of laughter.

My dad followed my gaze, then grinned. He jumped out of the truck and hollered, "Yo!"

The guy caught the sign in the middle of spinning it around the top of his head like a helicopter propeller. "Hey, Adrian!" he called out. He trotted over to us—his step light, his body agile and bouncy. Like a Labrador. He and Pai exchanged an elaborate fist bump involving fingers wiggling, slapping, and some weird elbow tapping. Okay, bros, we get it.

Then he glanced over at the truck, and I almost choked.

Upon closer inspection, the Labrador was *very* good-looking. Not my type at all—I usually fell for guys who looked a little malnourished and tortured. This guy was the picture of health and vigor: broad-shouldered with the lean yet muscular build of a runner, thick hair cut short with a few wavy locks flopping into his eyes, high cheekbones, and the nicest skin you ever saw on a male—he was practically *glowing*. He was like the photo you would find when looking for a stock image of "happy handsome Asian teenager."

"Hey, you must be Clara!" he exclaimed, walking over to the truck with a giant, toothy grin. His very sharp canines seemed to glint against the sunshine. I blinked.

Smile still firmly in place, the Labrador deftly placed the sign against his hip and held his hand out. "I'm Hamlet Wong."

I stared at his hand then looked up at him. Who in the world our age *shook hands*? I held up my hand in greeting instead. "Hi. Your name's Hamlet?"

"Yeah," he answered, unfazed.

"Why would your parents do that to you?"

My dad, who was standing behind Hamlet, shook his head. "Clara."

I feigned innocence. "What! It's an honest question!"

Hamlet shrugged. "Oh yeah, I understand. My parents, uh, liked the idea of naming me after a prince." He laughed loudly, startling me.

My incredulity was genuine. "A Danish prince who no one else in the entire world is named after?"

Before he could reply, Rose popped up next to me, magically. She must have gotten here before us. "Hi, I'm Rose Carver," she said as she held out her hand. Her smile was dazzling. Why was I not surprised when they shook hands.

Hamlet's eyes lit up even more than the lit-upness they already were. "Oh wow! I didn't know there was a new employee!"

My dad leaned in the doorway to the truck. "Well, these two are working the KoBra this summer as punishment."

"Really?" Hamlet's eyebrows practically rose into that amazing hair of his. "What'd you guys do?"

I looked at Rose. "Let her tell the story. She's really unbiased, like Fox News."

She did this little head flip—if her hair had been longer, it would have whipped my face. "We got into an argument and almost . . . well . . ."

"You attacked me. And we almost burned the school down," I said flatly.

Hamlet did a little surprised hop, raising a fist up to his mouth. "No *way!*"

Rose made a face at me. "Don't *exaggerate.*" Then her eyes flitted over to Hamlet—a split second of self-consciousness. "We didn't burn it down! And anyway, we only fought because she pulled this prank at junior prom—"

"What kind of prank?" Hamlet's head swiveled toward me and his eyes sparkled. "I really love prank stories."

I frowned. It was like the time a lady pointed at my bloody-bunny T-shirt and said, "I *love* creative shirts." The truly earnest made me so uncomfortable. I muttered, "I reenacted the end of *Carrie.*"

Confusion clouded his features. This guy's emotions were closed-captioned on his face. "What's that?"

"What's what?" I asked, almost just as confused.

"What's *Carrie?*"

My jaw dropped. "What! You don't know what *Carrie* is? Jesus, do you live under a rock?"

He shrugged. "I grew up in Beijing."

Rose shoved me, getting closer to him. "Wow! When did you move here? Your English is flawless."

I tsked. "That's so racist."

She bit her lip, mortified. "Oh! No, I didn't mean . . ."

Hamlet laughed and held up his hands. Two nice, strong-looking hands, with elegant fingers. "No, no, it's fine! I moved here in sixth grade. I've had time to get pretty good."

Rose tilted her head and smiled. "Cool! I'd love to talk to you about that experience one day!"

For Pete's sake.

"Oh, for sure! But I actually have to run—starting my second shift," he said regretfully, picking up his sign. "It was great meeting you guys. I'm sure I'll see you around this summer then?" Was it my imagination or did he hold my gaze a bit longer than necessary?

He ran off, leaving us with a clear view of my dad. Pai was grinning. "Oh, you girls."

"What!" Rose blurted, spending an inordinate amount of time tucking her hair into her cap. She glanced at me. "Do you think he was offended when I made that comment about his English?"

But I wasn't paying attention. Instead I watched Hamlet run toward a coffee kiosk under a big shady tree. He whipped off his shirt, tugging it from the back of his collar. My mouth went dry. He was bare chested and glorious for a full two seconds before pulling on a white polo shirt, a navy apron, and a matching cap. Then he served someone coffee.

"What in the world?" I asked out loud, pointing at Hamlet.

Both my dad and Rose looked to where I was pointing. Noticing us, Hamlet waved and yelled, "Jack-of-all-trades!"

Before I could stop myself, I laughed. My dad smirked at me, and I threw a towel at him.

# CHAPTER 9

THE MORNING AND LUNCH CROWD AT THE OFFICE plaza was pretty mellow, and we managed okay. That is, when Rose and I didn't have to talk to each other. She handled the customers, and I was in charge of the food again. Then we swapped. My dad helped, and other than a few little missteps (oops, leaving oil smoking on a pan for too long and giving someone a twenty-dollar bill instead of a five), the first stop went smoothly.

Every once in a while, Hamlet would holler jokes, and he even came over with iced drinks for us. At every contact, I felt his gaze linger on me for a half second longer than necessary. Hm. Was this dweeb crushing on me? But I pushed the thought aside; I had *no* desire for a food truck summer romance. I just wanted to get this over with, no strings attached.

We wrapped up the Pasadena stop and headed back to the commissary for a break before our next stop, a bar in Echo Park where we'd catch the happy hour and evening crowd.

After cleaning up the truck, Rose sat down in the passenger seat and pulled out a thick AP biology book.

"A total beach read," I said as I locked up the cabinets holding our supplies.

She responded without looking at me. "Since I'm not going to summer school, I'm taking night classes at the community college for credit. Is that okay with you, nosy?"

"Your boring life, not mine."

She put her earbuds in and propped the book on her knees.

My dad was handling some bookkeeping and social media updates, so I had time to grab an ice cream from the liquor store across the street.

Much too freaking soon it was time for us to get back to work, and we arrived at the bar just as the sky turned a pale peach. There were a ton of people there already. It seemed like once you became an adult, your life revolved around the next glass of rosé.

Parking the truck, I pulled on my cap and apron, then turned on the griddle. Rose parked next to us and hopped into the truck, pulling out the cashbox and the iPad Square.

My dad opened the order window, then turned to us. "Ready to roll?" he asked, looking at both of us sternly.

"Yup," Rose answered, with her patented future president smile.

I held up my plastic-glove-covered thumbs.

Things went smoothly for a while—I realized that working in the KoBra was almost like a finely choreographed dance. Because the space was so small, the three of us had figured out a way to stay in our little spheres. It helped that I was so short; both my dad and Rose were able to reach for things above my head, and I was able to duck easily under various limbs to get what I needed.

Just as I was in the zone, concentrating on skewering some beef onto a stick for the picanha, I heard a familiar peal of laughter. My skin prickled in recognition.

"Felix, get me a pastel, yeah?"

Cynthia and Felix.

"Yo, isn't this Clara's dad's truck?"

And Patrick.

I shuffled over to the dark corner farthest away from the truck's windows. Of all the people to run into! My dad walked over to me to reach for the picanha plate. "Clara, what are you doing? Get the two pasteis orders plated."

"Shh, Pai. My bozo friends are out there. I don't wanna deal with them right now," I whispered loudly.

But the truck was small, and Rose had the hearing of a bat. She popped her head out the window, practically on tippy-toes, so half her torso was hanging out. "Hey! Are you guys *Clara's friends?*" she shouted out.

"Shh!" I hissed, shrinking farther into my corner.

I heard Patrick's voice again. "Rose?" Confusion and disbelief.

Rose waved. "Hi, guys. Didn't you hear? Clara and I are working the KoBra this summer."

In fact, they hadn't heard. They knew I had to work, but I had left out the part about Rose. I didn't even know why. Sometimes I simply didn't want to deal with the Patrick and Felix peanut gallery. It could be a lot.

"She's right here," Rose said with a smile, looking back at me. Like an obvious cartoon villain.

Handing my dad the two pasteis, I reluctantly walked over to the window, mouthing *You're dead* to Rose.

When I looked out, my heart sank. It wasn't just Patrick, Felix, and Cynthia. They were with a few other people we partied with. No doubt they were using their fake IDs to get into the bar tonight. Pangs of jealousy and resentment flared again.

"What's up?" I asked, not a care in the world.

Patrick and Felix were grinning, and Cynthia looked pleased to see me in a compromising position for once. She held on to Felix's arm with less possessiveness than usual, her denim jacket tied around her waist.

Felix tapped the top of his head. "*Sweet* hat, Clara."

"You look *adorable*," said Cynthia with a giggle.

"Better than your ratty Cubs one," I said easily to Felix. "Which I still have, by the way." I didn't even look at Cynthia, but I felt her glare. You simply couldn't out-jerk a jerk like me.

"Save the socializing for after-hours, children," my dad said, handing an order out the window. "Clara, back to the kitchen."

Heat crept up my neck. Patrick widened his eyes at me and cocked his head to the side, telepathically signaling, "Come out here."

Every part of me wanted to toss my cap on the floor and join them—preferably by jumping out the window in a swan dive into the line of people.

But I couldn't. I ignored him. "Have fun at happy hour, kids," I said before stepping back to my station.

A crappy mood settled over me. Every single thing Rose did made me want to scream. I tried to zone her out, concentrating on cooking. When we got an order for a vegetarian option—a grilled eggplant in place of lombo—I tossed some thinly sliced Chinese eggplant into a skillet.

Suddenly, Rose was all up in my space. "Did you cook pork in this pan beforehand?"

"Yep."

"Clara! You can't do that! Some vegetarians are really picky about that! And pork is actually *forbidden* by some religions and cultures."

I watched the eggplant sizzle in the oil, bubbles popping. "What they don't know won't hurt them. They'll just have to wonder why their food is suddenly more delicious. Hint: pork."

Rose gasped. "Clara, I'm serious!"

"I know you are, and I don't *care*." I grabbed a bunch of scallions and chopped them. Aggressively. "If I had to use a new pan for every freaking vegetarian order, I'd be behind and washing pans constantly."

"But it's *the rule*!" Rose said. "Adrian went over this our first day. Right, Adrian?"

My dad turned from the pickup window. "What?"

I threw the knife onto the cutting board with a clatter. "Are you *kidding* me right now? You just *narced* on me to my *dad*?"

Rose blinked. "What? I wasn't—"

"Yes, you were! It's not enough you got me suspended freshman year, you have to hover over me in *my dad's truck* after you got us into this mess?"

A flash of anger passed over Rose's face. "I didn't *know* you would get suspended! And also? YOU WERE SMOKING! You do something wrong and then you freaking blame it on *me*? You have some real issues with misplacing blame. Hint: LOOK IN THE MIRROR."

Rage that had been building inside me since prom reached its freaking boiling point. I thought of ninth grade, of how that suspension had put me on a specific trajectory before I even had a chance to figure myself out. "Screw you, Rose. You don't know me. *At all*."

My dad stepped between us. "Hey! Both of you, cool it. Now."

Rose's shoulders slumped for a second before she took off her cap. "Hey, Adrian, I'm sorry, but I don't think I can do this. Thanks for giving me the opportunity."

Before my dad could say anything, she placed the cap on the

counter and left the truck, walking down the street, away from the bar crowd.

"What a drama queen."

My dad looked at me, hard. "You have so much to learn, Shorty."

Behind us, the eggplant burned.

# CHAPTER 10

THE NEXT DAY, I WOKE UP TO MY ALARM. NOT MY DAD.

Hm. Still in my pajamas with toxic morning breath and cuckoo hair, I crept over to his room and knocked on his door. Nothing. "Pai? Are you still asleep?"

Still nothing. I was about to knock again when someone tapped my shoulder. I jumped about a mile.

"Morning, Shorty." My dad held out a mug of tea.

I took it and smiled. "To what do I owe this princess treatment?"

He ran his hand through his hair and yawned. That's when I noticed he was still in his pajamas, too. A worn-out Clippers T-shirt and flannel pants. "Well, there's a change of plans. You and Rose are running the truck without me today."

The tea scalded my tongue. "Huh? Are you sick?"

"Nope."

"Uh, do you have a meeting?"

"Nah."

"Then what?"

There was a mischievous gleam in his eye that chilled me. A gleam that I've inherited. It never means anything good.

"It's a test."

I stopped drinking my tea. "No."

"Yes."

"FATHER!" I yelled.

He pointed at me, at once stern and ridiculous with his spiky hair and giant threadbare T-shirt. "You and Rose need to figure out how to get along. Not just put up with each other and work, but to *actually get along*. Rose is cool, and I want you to see that."

I exhaled loudly. "Okay, Dr. Phil. But Rose quit, remember?"

"I talked to her parents and they convinced her to give it one last try. Actually . . . a one-week one-last try."

I shook my head like I had water in my ears. "Pardon me?"

My dad already had one foot in his bedroom. "Yeah, the test is for one week. Good luck today, see you later!" He rushed inside and locked the door.

I banged on it. "No way!"

His voice was muffled. "Rose is waiting for you at the commissary. You guys know the drill by now. I'm not concerned about mistakes, I just want you to make it work, or a fall suspension, and you'll be grounded for the *entire* summer!" He paused. "Text me *only for emergencies.*"

"The only texts you'll get from me will be barnacle photos!" My dad had severe reactions to images of things with a lot of holes or bumps clustered together, like barnacles and seedpods. This revulsion/fear, called trypophobia, was always my Hail Mary when my dad was being a jerk. Like today.

"So what are *you* going to do all day?" I hollered through the door.

"Today, I take the day off. The others? Work on the restaurant hustle, handle business to get things started," he responded, his voice sounding far away and much too relaxed.

"Well enjoy your day off with *barnacles.*"

By the time I reached the commissary, seven photos and gifs of barnacles had already been sent to my dad. He didn't respond—but I kept them going. I wanted him to live in abject terror. I was *not* into Strict Adrian.

Rose was already there, of course. Leaning against the KoBra, in a white cotton tank and powder blue shorts, her feet in dainty brown sandals. She looked at me through her tortoiseshell sunglasses, arms crossed. "I actually thought I liked your dad," she said in greeting, voice dry.

"Well, even cool dads are actually just *dads* in the end. Lameness guaranteed at some point."

Rose straightened up. "My parents were going to make me quit the dance team if I didn't finish this job." Given that she'd been captain since freshman year, I knew that was a big deal.

We were quiet for a second, neither of us sure where to start. And then we both started talking at once.

"So your dad e-mailed me the social media info—"

"My dad wants us to stick to—"

We both stopped talking. I would have laughed except Rose Carver was like the antidote to mirth. I walked toward the commissary kitchen. "Well, let's start by looking at the food supplies. Today's a grocery-run day."

After a quick survey, we realized we were short on meat, so we needed to head to Koreatown before our usual stop at the office park.

"Should I drive, then?" I asked as we both stood in the truck. Politeness clipped my words.

She shrugged. "Sure, seems to make the most sense," she said as she buckled herself into the passenger seat. Because I couldn't stand to make the fifteen-minute drive to K-Town in silence, I turned on the radio. It had been so long since I listened to the actual radio that I had to fiddle around a bit to find a station that wasn't offensive—something that was playing oldies.

After a few seconds, Rose asked, "Can we listen to NPR?"

I bristled. "Um, no?"

"Just because your dad owns this truck doesn't mean you automatically get to make executive decisions."

"I do when it involves listening to freaking NPR."

"Yeah, because wow, how super *uncool* to pay attention to what happens in the world."

I yanked the steering wheel hard as we turned left onto Vermont. "You said it, not *moi*."

"Forget it, you're such a brat," she huffed, rolling down her window and turning her head away from me. We didn't talk the rest of the ride, which was *fine by me*.

Driving through K-Town in a clunky food truck was no joke. No matter what time of day, traffic was always jammed, and my usual weaving, raging style was seriously cramped by both the cars and the unwieldiness of the giant truck. I didn't really mind; it was always fun to people-watch in traffic since K-Town was one of the few neighborhoods in LA where people actually walked.

There were professionals in business wear; teenagers in giant headphones and backpacks; grandmothers clutching hands of toddlers and children. All within the shadows of the skyscrapers and strip malls pushed up against one another. Koreatown was an LA neighborhood that told the city's entire history through its architecture—from 1920s apartment buildings with art deco iron lettering on top of the roofs to the neon, layered storefronts that arrived loudly in Los Angeles via Seoul.

I felt at home here, not only because I'm Korean American, but because it was a blend of old and new LA. I related to this future version of America that wasn't tidy but layered, improvised, and complicated.

We arrived at the butcher where I had to use my preschool-level Korean to order the beef rump and pork loin. The butcher grumbled under his breath the entire time, and I suspected he was criticizing my bad upbringing as he heaved slabs of meat over the counter.

Back at the commissary, we worked on prepping the food like my dad had showed us—marinating the meats, making the sauces, cooking the rice. Rose reluctantly let me take the lead with food since I had a bit more experience than her. But she watched every move I made with hawk eyes, memorizing everything I was doing like an android. It was annoying, and I felt self-conscious.

"Got that properly downloaded?" I grumbled as I washed my hands.

"It's not exactly brain surgery," she said, but I noticed that she still had that little wrinkle of concentration between her eyes.

I started the truck. "I can't believe my dad actually trusts us."

Rose rolled down her window and pulled on her sunglasses. "Well, he knows *one* of us is responsible."

"You are a delightful conversationalist, you know that?"

She didn't respond and we didn't speak until we drove into the office park.

And there was Hamlet, tossing that sign up in the air. This time wearing a dark green baseball cap, white T-shirt, and very well-fitting navy shorts. No socks and sparkling white sneakers.

"Hey, Hamlet!" Rose waved at him from the window before we even parked.

He waved the sign in return. "Hey! You're back!"

She glanced at me, her smile disappearing then reappearing as she turned back to him. "Yup! Actually, it's just Clara and me running the truck for a week."

"Whoa, really?" He walked over to us, the sign still held up high above his head. "Did Adrian go somewhere?"

*Yep, going to let Rose handle this question.* Ever the politician, she smiled and chirped, "Oh, no, he thought we were ready to try this on our own. You know, trial by fire and all!"

He threw his head back and laughed. Heartily. Like someone had told a joke, except no one had told a freaking joke.

Rose hopped out of the truck to walk up to him. As they talked, I rolled my eyes and put on my KoBra shirt and hat.

Then I heard an exclamation from Rose. "Wait a second, are you on Arcadia Prep's debate team?" She was pointing at his T-shirt, which said, in a big nerd proclamation: ARCADIA PREP DEBATE. She grasped his upper arm in excitement.

I stuck my head out the window.

He dropped the sign and grasped both *her* arms. "Yeah! Wait, you're that captain from—"

"Elysian High!"

And for some reason that elicited a huge bear hug from Hamlet. I felt a stirring of jealousy that startled me. Pardon, why was I jealous about this?

But watching the two of them lose their collective mind over recognizing each other from dorky-ass debate club definitely made me feel funny inside.

"You were *so* awesome at the semifinals this spring!" Hamlet said with both his hands held up in front of him in this bizarre way. I kept staring at him. Who or what was he reminding me of . . .

Rose *giggled*, and he looked at her with this toothy grin, his canines glinting again.

Canines.

Yeah, still reminded me of a Lab. His hands were held up in front of him, torso-height. Waiting for his treat.

Why did I find him attractive?

Watching the two of them wax poetic about debate club made me realize that I was being a total loser getting jealous *purely* because Rose was flirting with him. That was it.

I opened the order window and whistled sharply. "Rose! When you two debate dorks are done, maybe we could actually get to work?"

Rose glared at me, but Hamlet, of course, was unfazed. In fact, he trotted over to the truck. All that was missing was a Frisbee in his mouth. "Hey, Clara." He fixed his big eyes on me, dark lashes contrasting sharply against his skin. "So you guys go to the same high school, right?"

I slammed the cashbox onto the counter. "Yup."

"Not on debate team, though?"

"Literally would rather die."

He guffawed. If dogs could laugh, their laugh of choice would be the guffaw. "So, what are you into, then?"

I looked at him, cocking my head a bit. "Why?" I could see Rose stalking toward us, clearly annoyed that Hamlet was talking to me.

"Why not?" And there was something so matter-of-fact and weirdly intimate about that, almost a challenge. Daring me to be earnest in my answer. It didn't help that he was looking straight into my eyes with unnerving openness.

"I'm into walks on the beach, cupcakes, and kittens."

He laughed again, that guffaw. His incredibly straight, white teeth gleaming. "You're so funny."

I pressed my lips together, holding back laughter and a cutting remark. Because, to be honest, I had no idea how to react. Who *says* that?

"No, but really. You don't do anything?" he asked.

It was a rude question, but the way he asked it was so genuine. Or confused. Or something. And I felt like there was this giant spotlight on me that I wasn't ready for. Nobody ever asked me *what I did* at school. I was the class clown. Good for a laugh, and the leader of my merrymen, Patrick and Felix. But in the truck, all of that felt little. Not important.

"We have a customer coming," Rose said, shoving me away from the window.

I wiggled my fingers at Hamlet. "Bye."

He blinked. "Bye!" Then he bounded over to his spot on the corner.

Rose glanced at me. "Looks like someone has a crush."

I almost dropped the pitcher of water I was holding. "I don't have a crush!"

She shook her head. "Who says I'm talking about *you*?"

# CHAPTER 11

SOMEHOW ROSE AND I MANAGED TO GET THROUGH our entire first day without a single fight. There was an incident where I hit her head by accident and she hit me back, but that was fine. I could tell it was just instinct.

Also, we were both *exhausted*. Running that truck with just the two of us was no joke.

At the end of the day, we both lurched out of the truck, one of the commissary lights flickering on and off in the dark lot. Rose lifted her arms and stretched them above her head like a little ballerina cake topper.

I rubbed one of my Docs onto my bare leg, scratching a mosquito bite I'd somehow acquired while inside the truck for eight hours. "Maybe since we didn't kill each other today, my dad will come back tomorrow."

Rose pulled out her phone, not even looking at me, the light of the screen making her face glow eerily. "Yeah."

All right, then. I gritted my teeth and was about to start my walk home but stopped when I saw a couple of guys walk by—shrouded in shadow, walking slowly, appraising us as they did so. I stared at them. *I see you*. And they kept walking. When one of them looked back at me, I kept my gaze steady. Creeps.

I sighed and turned around. "Do you have a ride home?"

She tried to look nonchalant, but I saw her glance down at her phone again, agitated. "Um, yeah, I mean my mom was supposed to be here."

"So you're gonna wait here alone?"

"Aren't you going to walk home alone?" she immediately countered. Her bravado would have been more convincing if she hadn't checked her phone again.

I pulled my sweatshirt tighter around myself. "Yeah, but this is my neighborhood, I know how to deal." I paused. "Plus, my dad makes me carry pepper spray."

Rose pulled something out of her shorts pocket and held it up. Mace.

I laughed. "LA kids."

"We know all varieties of pervs," she said with a wry smile. I smiled back, and then we looked away from each other.

I could hear her take rapid shallow breaths again. And this

time I wasn't so sure if she was breathing like that to get control—it didn't seem in her control at all.

"I'll wait with you, then." Before she could respond, I crouched low to the ground, my feet flat, my butt just an inch or so off the cement, pulling out my phone to avoid looking at her.

"How are you sitting like that?" Rose asked, bending over to look at my feet. "You're using your ankles as a seat!" She tried to copy me, but when she reached a certain depth, she fell over, landing on her butt.

I tsked. "See, even though you can touch your head with your toes, only Koreans can do this squat. It's called the kimchi squat for that reason." Obviously, any human could do this squat, but I liked goading Rose.

She scoffed. "Give me a break. You're making that up."

"Try it again."

Rose squatted down, but had to balance on the balls of her feet, so her butt was still a good foot off the ground rather than the near-hovering mine was doing. I could sense her concentration, her thighs strained in the awkward position.

"Ha! I've found the one thing Rose Carver can't do."

She stayed balanced. "We'll see about that." Looking down at her feet she said, "Also, it's true, I really didn't think you'd get suspended."

I almost fell over. "Are you *apologizing*?"

She laughed, an unexpected response that further startled me. "No, actually I'm not. Hasn't anyone told you that it's annoying when girls apologize all the time?"

"Good one."

"Also, don't think I'm stupid. I know that's why you've hated me and made my life as awful as possible since then," she said.

I shrugged, still crouched. "You deserved it."

"I admire your endurance."

"Thanks."

There were a few seconds of silence, a gusty wind kicking in. Rose steadied herself, and I looked at her. "That was only the first time I smoked, you know?"

That little wrinkle between her eyes showed up again, and she shook her head.

"This is lame, but I only did it because I decided I wanted to *rebel*." I didn't know why I was even saying this. It was like something needed to fill in the gap between being annoyed at someone for narcing and my relentless poking over the years. "A few weeks before that, my parents had this huge fight about me. As you've noticed, my parents aren't together anymore. My mom travels a lot for her job, so my dad's got sole custody."

Rose nodded.

"Anyway, my mom wanted me to take a break from school to travel with her, and my dad flipped. I was really pissed. I wanted to be with my mom, but, I don't know. I also knew it wasn't right, really? Anyway. The smoking. It was something I could control."

The wind made the trees around us creak. "I'm sorry, that sounds stressful," Rose said after a few seconds, giving me a tiny smile. "I know I apologize a lot. But maybe it's not a bad thing. Maybe it's considered a bad thing because it's something girls do a lot. Maybe it's actually something nice that keeps the world humane. It's a gesture."

Huh. I nodded. "Yeah. It's not always bad. And . . . thanks, I guess."

Headlights flooded the lot.

"Rosie! Sorry hon, Jessie's snake went missing!" Rose's mom yelled out the driver's side window of the sleek luxury SUV.

Rose sprang up, graceful as ever even on the verge of falling over. "Oh my God, Pizza went missing?" she yelped. "Did you find him?"

Her mom's hand fluttered out the window. "Kind of."

Disturbing. I got up, too. "See ya."

"Where are you going?" Rose asked.

I looked around. "Home?"

"We can give you a ride home," she said stiffly, the headlights shining behind her, her figure a silhouette.

"I live six blocks away; it's fine."

She shrugged. "Okay, but don't say I didn't warn you."

Uh, ominous much? I knew this walk, nothing would happen to *me*. As I skirted by the car, Mrs. Carver honked and I nearly flew out of my skin. Rose's mom stuck her head out the window again. "Get your butt in this car, Clara!"

I scrambled over and hopped into the back seat.


My dad's feet greeted me when I walked into the apartment— bare and propped up on the sofa arm. The rest of him was hidden under a fleece LA Galaxy blanket, his hands and phone sticking out. There was a lump near him that was, unmistakably, a comatose Flo.

I slammed the door shut, making Flo yowl and causing our clock from the dollar store to rattle. It was orange and plastic and uggo beyond belief, but my dad had a fondness for it. I knew he liked it precisely because it was ugly. My dad had a sick need to adopt and foster rejected and unwanted things. We'd been at the register when he spotted it in the sale bin. In case it wasn't obvious, the sale bin at the dollar store was seriously like the crème de la crème of sadness.

What a pair we made.

"How's my darling daughter?" he called out from his reclined position, not even lifting his lazy head.

"Wonderful." I grabbed a carton of mint chocolate chip ice cream from the freezer. But there was only a small scraping left—with a fine layer of frostbite on top. "Pai! Can't you be on top of ice cream duty *for once*?" I said as I emptied it into the sink.

"You only talk to me to yell at me?"

Our stupid faucet had the water pressure of a gentle breeze, and it took forever for me to rinse out the carton before tossing it into our recycling bin. "Yeah, that's what you deserve."

Pai sat up on the sofa and looked at me, his arms draped over his bent knees. "So, it went just as terrible as I suspected?"

I leaned against the sink and looked at him. "Contrary to popular belief, I'm not *totally* incompetent."

"Good to know. So you guys did okay? You didn't text anything but barnacle photos."

Heh-heh. "You're welcome. And yeah, it was *fine*. I don't know what you thought was going to happen."

"Oh, I don't know. Maybe a *fire*." Flo wriggled out from the blanket and stretched before making her way over to me.

I bent down to scoop her up, kissing her white-dipped front paws. "Well, there was just that small grease fire."

"What!"

I laughed, making Flo squirm out of my arms. "You're off your game."

My dad harrumphed, settling back into the sofa. "Don't forget to tally how much you made in the Google doc." The KoBra had a Google doc shared between Pai, Rose, and me. Whoever was in charge of cash was supposed to fill in the day's total profits.

"Rose handled the money, so she's going to do it."

"Well, good job, Shorty. I'm proud of you for not killing each other and not burning the truck down."

"Such high expectations." I picked some cat hair off my shirt. "I feel like Rose has some issues that might explain why she's so annoying."

Pai adjusted his reading glasses and looked a little concerned. "Like what?"

"I dunno. Something. She's a little too stressed out all the time. And holding herself to some impossible standard." I yawned. "Anyway, I'm gonna take a shower. I smell like a walking barbecue."

As I headed upstairs with Flo close at my heels, my dad shouted out, "How was Hamlet?"

I stalled on the stairs. What was with everyone and Hamlet? "He's fine, why?"

"Just curious." The silence that followed was so heavy with insinuation that you could cut it with a pastry knife.

# CHAPTER 12

HAMLET GREETED US WITH ICED LATTES A FEW DAYS
later when we were back in Pasadena.

It was already ninety degrees out, and I grasped the cold drink
gratefully. "Thanks."

Rose looked at the cup he was holding out with mild trepidation. "Um, thank you. But did you use whole milk?"

Hamlet glanced down at the drink, assessing it. "Yeah. Uh-oh,
are you lactose intolerant?"

"She's delicious intolerant," I said before taking a nice, long
swig from mine.

Rose shot me a dirty look. "I'm a dancer. I have to watch what
I put into my body." She looked back at Hamlet apologetically.
"But it's okay! I can just drink it." When she brought the straw

to her lips, it was almost in slow-mo, her reluctance clear in every micromillimeter of movement.

I grabbed it out of her hands. "For Pete's sake! *I'll* drink it. Hamlet, please make her something else." Sometimes Rose was such a contradiction—a bulldozing boss one minute, and someone fretting over hurt feelings the next.

But then, look at who was the object of her worry.

Hamlet's strong shoulders shrugged in his form-fitting mint green T-shirt. "Not a problem. Why don't you tell me what you want?" As the two walked over to his coffee cart, I watched them with irritation.

My phone buzzed in my pocket. It was a text from Felix: **Pool today?**

FOMO seared through me. Last summer, I had spent almost every day poolside with Felix and Patrick, reading crappy magazines at a community pool no one else seemed to know about. It cost two dollars for the day and always had hot lifeguards. Summer was usually sweaty make-outs, sunscreen, and sneaking into air-conditioned theaters.

Now it was about Rose Carver and grilled meats.

I had leveled down hard-core.

**Working** 😩

Felix texted back: **Ditch it**

Normally, I would. But when I glanced up at Rose and Hamlet, two earnest little citizens, I didn't feel like it. There were actual consequences with my dad if I ditched this time. And I needed to do a good-enough job to make it to Tulum.

**Can't. Don't get sunburned on your scalp again.** 🔥

I slipped my phone into my back pocket and tightened my apron. Time to get this party started.

When Rose got back to the truck, she was holding an iced black coffee.

"You live a joyless existence," I said as I stirred the rice in the pot, making it nice and fluffy. There was nothing worse than matted-down rice. She ignored me and sipped her drink in one long, loud drag.

The office park run went astonishingly well. I slipped easily into the cooking zone. Soon I knew how to get the lombo to the perfect crispness level and how many pickles to scoop out so that the juices didn't run into the rice. I was surprised by how little I hated this. Rose chatted easily with the regulars and grew adept at both taking orders and getting the food out at the pickup window.

When we were getting ready to wrap up the stop, Hamlet moseyed over to the truck again.

"Slow day?" I asked as I wiped down the counters.

He smiled, his eyes crinkling in the corners as he propped his arms on the low counter where people could place their plates to eat, cradling his chin in one hand. "Yeah."

He was just looking at me at this point. I stopped and stared at him levelly. "So, are you a gymnast or something?"

"A gymnast?" An adorable puzzled expression appeared on his face for a second.

"Yeah. You do all those flips and stuff."

A grin stretched across his face, quick and easy. "Oh! No, I used to do a lot of martial arts and stuff as a kid. But now I mostly box."

Totally out of my own control, my face flushed. I found this inexplicably hot. "Who boxes anymore?" I sputtered. "I mean, like men from the 1970s wearing sweatpants maybe." What *are* you saying, Clara.

But this made Hamlet crack up. Head thrown back and everything.

Rose popped up next to me, outta nowhere. "Where do you train?"

"At this gym in Chinatown."

"Cool! Do you compete?"

A little modest shrug. "Yeah."

To my surprise, Rose scrambled out of the truck and hopped over next to him on the pavement. "Show me some moves!" She held up her fists comically, a huge grin on her face.

It was cute, and I wanted to barf.

Hamlet laughed and stepped toward her, hands reaching out. "Is it okay if I touch your arms?"

*WAS IT OKAY TO TOUCH HER ARMS.*

She nodded, keeping it cool.

"Are you right- or left-handed?"

"Right."

He adjusted her arms so that her right fist was held up to her cheek and her left was in front of her face, positioned a little to the left of her nose. "Okay, keep your arms up like this at all times, protect that nice face." His voice took on an authoritative tone, and I resisted the urge to fan myself.

Even in this awkward new pose, Rose looked graceful. Then he adjusted her stance a little bit. I wanted to look away, but I couldn't.

"So, strike out at my hand with your left fist," he held up his right hand, palm facing out. "But take a small step with your left foot forward as you do it."

In one pretty, fluid motion, Rose gently punched, her body moving toward him.

"Awesome! That was good, but you can *really* hit me, you know," he said.

She made a face. "No way!" He assured her that it was fine, and while skeptical, she hit him harder the next time.

"Yes!" he cried out, giving her a high five. She was glowing. Brownie points via hot dude: a heady cocktail for Rose Carver, I'm sure.

I watched them go back and forth for a while, getting grumpier with every second, with every bit of physical contact between the two of them.

To squash down this unpleasant jealous feeling, I turned away and wiped down the griddle.

After a few minutes, Hamlet called my name. Argh. I looked out the window, and he motioned toward himself and Rose. "Do you wanna try?"

No. "No."

Rose rolled her eyes. "Come on! It's fun! Plus, you get to punch a dude."

Well. That was actually enticing. My hesitation was enough. Rose ran inside the truck and dragged me out. I stood in front of Hamlet, my arms crossed. He looked at me, head to toe, and I blushed. *What the heck, Clara. Chill!*

"So, you saw what I showed Rose, right?" He stepped forward but stopped, hesitating. "Um, do you need me to . . ."

Feeling extremely stupid, I held up my fists like Rose had. "Like this?" He nodded, and I was disappointed when he didn't adjust them for me.

"Okay, Clara. Hit me."

I looked at his face, so open, so encouraging. A sheen of sweat on his forehead, his high cheekbones. And I got incredibly self-conscious. My limbs felt clumsy and heavy, and I couldn't figure out how to move my feet properly as I reached out to punch him. When my fist hit his open palm, it was weak and sloppy. It didn't make the satisfying smacking noise that Rose's punch had.

I dropped my arms to my sides. "Cool. That sucked."

"No, it didn't! It was good!" Hamlet exclaimed, walking over to me. "Here, just spread your legs out a little more . . ." His voice trailed off and he kept staring at my feet. But I saw a blush creeping up the back of his neck. "Um, sorry, I mean . . ."

He was dying. I was dying.

Making a fool of myself in front of cute dudes was literally the opposite of my brand, and every molecule of my being was on fire right now. "Thanks, but we have to go anyway." I ran inside and hopped into the driver's seat. "Rose!" I barked as I started the engine.

She threw me an exasperated look, then shut the metal awnings that covered up the order and pickup windows. When she slipped into the passenger seat, I honked and yelled, "BYE, HAMLET!" Rose waved out the window. As we drove away, I saw Hamlet toss the sign up in the air in the rearview mirror, as if sending us off.

"What a total dork," I said.

Rose scoffed. "Clara. Who do you think you're kidding?" I opened my mouth, but she reached over and turned on the radio, cranking NPR. Loud. Then she sat back with her arms crossed. I was still so flustered by the whole boxing thing that I didn't bother fighting her.

We stopped by the commissary for prep and a little break as usual, then headed toward our next destination, a farmers market in Echo Park that was one of our weekly stops. The market was tucked behind a row of historic buildings, and it was starting to bustle. I parked the KoBra next to a few other trucks: a classic taco truck, an udon bowl truck, a grilled cheese truck, and a boba truck.

We parked and nervously started setting up—the air tense and both of us quiet in our own little corners. This would be the biggest crowd we'd served so far.

"Hey, are you Adrian's girl?"

I glanced out the window and saw a young white woman sporting a bandana and blond pigtails. "Yeah, hi. Clara."

She wiped her hands on her gingham-print apron before reaching out to shake mine. "Hi, Clara, I'm Kat, the owner of Gouda Done Worse."

Oh *my*. No, Kat, you gouda NOT done worse.

Keeping a smile plastered on my face, I shook Kat's hand. "Hi, Kat."

Kat grinned at me, and her eyes swept over the truck. "Adrian told us that you'd be manning the KoBra today. Pretty impressive."

Before I could respond, another blond girl who looked exactly like Kat stepped down from Gouda Done Worse. "Hi, Clara! I'm Kat's sister, Sarah!" Twins.

And then a man-bun-sporting Middle Eastern guy popped his head out from the udon truck. "Oh heeeey, it's the KoBra's heir!" For Pete's sake. Yet again, it was like *Mister Rogers' Neighborhood* up in here.

After some introductions with Rose, I realized very quickly that my dad had prepped everyone beforehand—there was this forced oh-so-casual nature to how they were all checking up on us.

And it was nice, because it got busy, fast. The truck grew hotter as we hustled our orders for a while. Then a familiar voice called out, ringing through the noise in the truck.

"Surprise, Rosie!"

I turned around to see Rose's parents and a little kid, who I could only assume was her brother, at the order window.

"Hey!" Rose said with a huge smile. "What are you guys doing here?"

Rose's dad's voice boomed into the truck, and to everyone within earshot. "We're here to see our gorgeous daughter at her first real summer job!" I could hear Rose's mom laugh.

Rose dropped her face into her hands, but she was still smiling when she looked up again. I wiped my hands on my apron and walked over to the window. "Hi," I said with a wave.

"HI, CLARA!" The kid waved back. "I'm Jessie!" He was wearing a Pikachu hat. And was about two feet tall with a lisp and missing front tooth. Basically, the cutest kid alive.

"Hey, Jessie, what do you guys wanna order? This is usually Rose's job, but she seems to have turned into a robot momentarily."

Jessie's eyes widened. "Wait . . . no, not really, right?"

I shrugged. "I dunno, we'll have to see if she reboots."

"Like when Grandma uses Windows."

I burst out laughing and nodded my head. "Yes, exactly like that."

Rose's mom smiled at me from under her large, stylish straw hat. She was wearing a breezy caftan cinched at the waist and strappy gold sandals—like she belonged in a fashion magazine spread titled "Look chic during your farmers market run!"

"Hi there, Clara. May we please get one lombo, one picanha, and two pasteis? Also, two lime sugarcane juices?" she asked.

"I want my own juice!" Jessie pleaded.

Rose's mom looked down at him. "Excuse me?"

He gulped. "I mean, please can I have my own juice?"

"Yes, you may. One for you, one for me. Daddy's going to drink water," Rose's mom said while pulling some cash out of her wallet.

I gave her some change. "Thank you, it should be ready in a few minutes."

Jessie came up to the window on tippy-toe, and Rose's dad lifted him so that Jessie was eye level with me. "Nice to meet you, Clara." Then he held out his hand.

I took the sticky little hand in mine and shook it solemnly. "Nice to meet you, too, Jessie."

Rose stuck her head out the window. "I can't hang out, unfortunately. I have to work."

Rose's dad winked. "Got it, Rosie. We're here to support you in this new chapter of your life. Even if it is a punishment."

It was almost farcical except it was *sincere*.

"Okay, okay," Rose said before blowing her family a kiss and helping the next customer.

The Carvers sat at one of the picnic tables scattered at the market and eventually left with waves and cheerful good-byes.

I watched them walk away into the crowds, swinging large baskets full of produce. "Are you guys for real?" I asked Rose. We had a break from customers so I sat on the floor and took a swig from my water bottle. It was boiling in the truck.

Rose wiped her brow and adjusted the little oscillating fan so that it was aimed directly at her face. "Are you being a jerk?"

I pulled my shirt away from my chest, airing it out a little. "No, for once in my life, I'm being sincere. Your family is pretty cool to show up. Plus, Jessie's rad."

"Jessie can be 'rad' when he's not being a little know-it-all."

"Pardon me?" I held my hand up to my ear. "Did . . . did *you* call someone a *know-it-all*?"

Rose tossed an ice cube into her mouth and crunched it, making me cringe. "Believe it or not, I am *not* the worst in my family. Know-it-allness is a shared trait among the Carvers."

"Well, you definitely seem like a family of total brains."

She crunched the ice again, making my arm hairs stand on end. "Let me just say this one thing to explain the Carvers: we have a weekly dinner pop quiz."

I stopped fanning myself with my shirt. "Are you serious?"

"Yeah. About the week's news, like *Wait Wait . . . Don't Tell Me!*" She noticed my blank expression. "It's a weekly quiz show on NPR."

"Of course."

"Anyway, yeah. Every Friday evening, we invite some person over, like a city council member or teacher or something, and we do the quiz with my parents as the hosts."

I snorted. "Wild Friday nights with the Carvers."

She laughed. "I mean, I know how it sounds. But I actually like hanging out with my family." Her fondness was apparent in how she perked up when talking about them. Again, I felt a pang of curious jealousy. Rose's family kind of seemed like my worst nightmare. Or maybe it was the worst nightmare in some narrative about myself that I wasn't sure was totally accurate.

Another ice cube crunched in her mouth and I pointed at her. "*Don't!* That sound is the worst thing in *the entire world.*"

Rose rolled her eyes but tucked the ice cube into her cheek so that it bulged out. "Well, I'm sure my family seems super boring compared to your like, cool-dad life."

I made a face and fanned myself with a napkin. "Cool-dad life, oh my God."

"It's true! Your dad is so awesome."

"Please don't get a crush on him."

Her mouth dropped open slightly. "I won't!"

"Good." I took another sip of water.

Her eyes lit up. "Hey! Also, not to be a creep, but I found your mom online through the truck's Instagram account. What is her *life?*"

Whenever people found out about my mom, I wasn't sure what to feel—pride? Embarrassment? In most cases, I feigned ambivalence. So I shrugged. "Oh, she's a social media influencer. Or something."

Rose mulled that over. "That's her job?"

"I guess."

"How do you get a job doing . . . that?"

The words flew out of my mouth before I could stop them. "Extreme narcissism."

Her eyes widened in surprise and I laughed loudly. "Just kidding. She's really good at social media. And looking good in clothes. And . . ."

"Having good taste?" Rose ventured. I looked at her sharply for signs of sarcasm, but she seemed genuine. A sly expression crossed her face. "I mean, she must. She hooked up with your dad."

"ROSE!"

She cackled and the awkwardness quickly dissipated. I fanned myself with a paper plate and asked, "Are both your parents lawyers? I forget."

She nodded. "Yeah. My dad has his own law firm. My mom's a prosecutor. She got kind of big a few years ago when—"

"That police-beating case."

Rose raised her eyebrows. "Wow. You know about that?"

"It was all over the news, hello."

"Says the girl who hates NPR."

"I didn't say I *hated* NPR. It just doesn't exactly pump me up for work."

She smiled. "Okay, whatever. Anyway. My mom became this community figure. She got to meet Michelle *Obama*."

"I'm not even kidding, that's a life dream of mine," I said, my voice high with excitement.

"You and every human being who isn't garbage," she said. "Anyway, so that's my mom. She was on the cover of magazines; people wanted to interview her. And then there's me."

I frowned. "What about you? You're basically Joanne Jr."

She shook her head firmly. "I wish."

"Whoa. Rose Carver doesn't think she's good enough? What are the rest of us subpar humans supposed to do now? Might as well give up and jump off a cliff."

She crossed her arms. "I'm serious."

"So am I! You're basically on track to become the president of the United States of America."

I could tell she was pleased by that for a second. "The point is that there's a lot of pressure on black girls to be *better* than everyone else anyway. And then add to that the fact that my mom is who she is. You don't even know how aware I am of how I look and act *all the time*. I don't have the luxury of rolling out of bed and acting like a little jerk like you do every day."

"Thanks."

"You know what I mean. Like, I can't just run errands wearing cruddy sweatpants and not do my hair."

I squinted at her. "I understand what you mean, but you would still look like a celebrity doing a coffee run in *Us* magazine."

Someone rapped on the window. "Hey, are you guys open?"

Rose hopped off the counter and smoothed her hair back from her forehead. "Hi there, what would you like to order?"

Reluctantly, I dragged myself back up to the griddle, but before I turned it on, I made a sugarcane juice with less sugar and more lime, and filled it with ice until the plastic cup frosted over.

"Here," I said, holding it out to Rose.

She startled, then took it from me. "Oh. Thanks, Clara."

"And keep doing what you do. The first woman president has to happen in my lifetime, or I'm going to light this entire planet on fire."

Rose laughed, her teeth straight and perfect, and I turned back to the griddle to hide my own smile.

# CHAPTER 13

"TODAY'S TEA HAS A LITTLE SOMETHING EXTRA FOR you. To celebrate your last day of manning up."

I took the mug from my dad. "You mean womaning up. But thanks." When I took a sip, my eyes widened. "Oh yum, horchata hybrid?"

My dad tapped the tip of my nose. "Bingo, Shorty."

Horchata was my favorite, and my dad usually added it to chai on my birthday. Today was the last day of me and Rose running the KoBra together, so I suppose he thought a celebration was in order.

But the difference between how I felt today and how I felt a week ago was so drastic that I myself couldn't really understand it. Instead of dragging myself out of bed and being filled with dread on my walk to the commissary, I was actually—excited? Looking forward to it?

Maybe it was because I knew we had passed the test with flying colors. My dad would definitely cave and let me go to Tulum, I was sure of it. I was in such a good mood that I cheerfully waved at two surly middle school girls walking by me. "What's her freaking problem?" one of them bitched to the other. I laughed.

As always, Rose was waiting for me at the truck, already prepping.

"Morning," I said as I climbed in. Rose glanced up from where she was wiping down the oven.

"Morning!" she greeted back. Then she stood up and wiped her hands on her apron nervously. "Um."

I kept looking at her when she wouldn't go on. "Yeah?"

She turned around and grabbed something off the counter and shoved it at me. "Here. In case you're hungry."

It was a small plastic bag filled with fresh fruit tossed with chili powder. "I know you really like that one fruit cart," she said nonchalantly.

Aw, Rose. So awkward at gestures of friendship. Taking it from her, I said, "Thanks. Do you wanna share? This is a lot of fruit."

She shrugged and tugged at one of her delicate gold heart studs. "Sure." I grabbed a couple of forks and handed one to her.

We ate the fruit in silence—one mango slice and melon piece at a time. Finally, I spoke up. "So, my dad says that since we did better than he thought we would, he wants us to keep going with limited supervision. So, three days out of the week we'll be working alone." I glanced at her, gauging her reaction. Maybe she'd hate it?

But her face remained relaxed and she nodded. "Cool."

"So you're okay with it?"

She shrugged. "Yeah. I mean, even if it means our reward for surviving our punishment is the extension of that punishment."

I laughed. "True. Well, I think he's been excited to have some more time off the truck. He's taking this business course at the community college, and he wants to focus on the business side and getting his restaurant started. Finding investors and space and stuff. We can handle more of the day-to-day in the truck."

"Oh cool! I didn't know he wanted to open a restaurant?"

I nodded, wiping some chili powder from the corner of my mouth. "Yeah, it's his big dream. The KoBra is the first step toward it."

"That's so awesome!"

"Calm down, future Mrs. Shin."

Normally, that would have pissed Rose off—normally, that would have been my intention. But she snort-laughed instead, then coughed and looked down at the fruit. "Wow, that's spicy."

"Oh, you probably got a pocket of chili powder." I moved some of the fruit around until I found an area without too much of it. "Here."

"There's only coconut left?" She made a face as she poked around.

"Stop complaining, you ingrate." The words came out of my

mouth before I could stop them. Before she could react, I said, "Sorry, that came out wrong. I mean, actually it came out how I meant it. But I guess I don't need to say exactly what I feel all the time."

She looked down at the bag of fruit for a second before lifting her head to respond. "That's okay." Then she grinned. "Man, we're so good at this friendship thing."

I almost choked on my mango, laughing. "Yeah, we should do tutorials on it."

"Put it on YouTube."

"Bring on guests to show them how to awkwardly compliment each other."

We were both giggling so hard at this point that we had to put our fruit down. I kimchi squatted because my legs lost their strength and Rose joined me.

"Hey! You're doing it!" I said, pointing at her flat feet and balanced butt.

She twirled her arms up in the air, like a squatting showgirl.

"I practiced. Did you think I was gonna let *you* be able to do something that I couldn't?"

I pushed her over.

We got to the office park, and I honked in greeting to Hamlet, who saluted us, tucking his sign neatly under his arm.

As had become ritual, once we parked, Hamlet jogged over to us carrying a couple of iced drinks—a mocha for me and an iced coffee for Rose. "Thanks!" I said, taking mine with a wink. He blushed slightly. In return for our usual drinks, we gave him a plate of whatever he wanted.

"So, when are you going to throw Hamlet a bone?" Rose asked as we prepped.

My nose scrunched. "How did you know?"

She looked at me with a hand on her hip. "What? That he likes you?"

"What? No," I sputtered. "You said, throw him a *bone*. I mean, how did you know he's a Lab . . . ah, never mind." I fumbled with the cashbox, trying to remember the padlock code and messing up twice. I cursed and smacked the box with the palm of my hand.

She took it from me slowly, as if taking a bomb away from an unstable person. "Well, what *I* mean is that it's obvious he likes you. Are you into him at all?"

I squinted out the window into the sunny courtyard, watching him make a drink with gusto. Tossing cups into the air, whistling, grinning. Eyes sparkling, charming everyone's pants off.

Except mine. No, my pants were firmly on.

"He's not my type." I brushed by Rose and turned on the grill.

She laughed this smug little laugh that ended with a condescending shaking of the head. A specially patented Rose Carver kind of laugh.

"What?"

"So your type is not *that*?" She pointed out the window. Where Hamlet's thick black hair shone in the sun, arms tanned and flexing as he reached for a gallon of milk. And when he glanced up at us, his eyes crinkled into a smile before his toothy, white grin broke out. He waved.

Rose and I looked at each other and started cracking up. He cocked his head to the side, curious but smiling.

Labrador.

"He's adorable, and you know it," Rose said as she organized the cash—large bills under the tray, change and small bills sorted on top.

I leaned against the counter and pulled my hair up into a sloppy ponytail, a few strands escaping and falling loose around my face. "Like I said, adorable is not my type."

"Let me guess—you like 'em *naughty*."

"Ew. Who even says 'naughty'?"

Rose waved a hand in front of herself, lips pursed. "You know what I mean, bad boys. Like, high school Mr. Rochesters."

"Who?"

"Don't act obtuse."

I pulled the container of vinaigrette out of the refrigerator. "Oh, but actually I *am* obtuse."

"Clara!"

Something about Rose's exasperation delighted me. Always. I stirred the sauce with a wooden spoon, breaking apart bits of parsley, the scent of vinegar filling the truck. "And no, I'm not into Mr. Rochesters. One, I like men who aren't controlling-old-uncle types. Two, I'm not into brooding, either."

"So, what then? What's your issue with Hamlet?"

I placed the bowl of vinaigrette in the small fridge under the counter. "I don't have an *issue*. He's just—I mean, he's *your* type. Eager beaver overachiever."

She was quiet long enough for me to get nervous. *Did* she like him? A little bit of dread pooled in my stomach because even though I didn't take flirting with Hamlet seriously, the thought of not having him as an option bummed me out. Not to mention the fact that I actually liked being on nonhating terms with Rose. And I didn't know if I had the energy to be mortal enemies again. Especially over a *dude*.

But after a few seconds, Rose shrugged and smiled. "He's cute, for sure. But he's made it *so clear* that he likes you. I've got some pride, okay?"

I smiled tentatively. "Are you sure? Because, you should go for him if you want."

"Thanks for the permission," she said with an eye roll.

"It's not permission! Jesus, I'm just saying—"

She threw a dish towel at me. "I said no! He likes *you*! And honestly, the lady doth protest too much . . ."

I snatched the towel off the floor and waved it at her. "Can you not talk like that? I'm embarrassed for you."

Rose spent the rest of the afternoon speaking like a Shakespearean reject to every customer. Touché, humorless one.

Later that evening, we were closing up the truck when Rose's phone rang. "Hey, Mom," she said when she picked up.

A few seconds passed before she exclaimed, "What? Tonight? But I'm not ready!" I heard her mom's muffled voice. "It *is* a big deal! I'm not ready." They spoke for a few more seconds, with Rose's voice so quiet I couldn't catch the rest of the conversation.

After she ended the call, Rose pressed her forehead against the wall and started taking those shallow breaths again. I approached her tentatively, "Hey, are you okay?"

She nodded. "Yup." But then she kept her eyes closed.

"Rose. Seriously, are you all right? Sit down." I took her arm and pulled her over to the driver's seat.

I crouched down by her and just watched her, unsure of what to do. She seemed seriously freaked out, and I knew friend duty involved making her feel better, but *how?* I was about to tell some terrible joke when she looked up at me.

"I'm fine," she said, sounding embarrassed.

"Are you sure?"

She nodded. I wasn't sure if she wanted to talk about it, but it seemed like we should. I filled a cup with water and ice and handed it to her. "What do you have to do tonight?"

She took a sip before answering. "Thanks. And it's not a big deal." Which was *literally* the opposite of what she had said to her mom.

"You seemed upset." Understatement of the year.

Again, she didn't answer right away, and I picked at a spot of dried sauce on the counter. After some silence, she said, "Well, it's that we're going to have a senator over for dinner."

"What!"

"It's really not a big deal. She's friends with my dad and might write a letter of recommendation for me. I just, I didn't know I had to have dinner with her tonight." Rose picked at her nails again.

"Oh. I mean, *for me*, having dinner with a senator would be a big deal, but small potatoes when you're a Carver, I guess," I said.

She scoffed. "It's *not* small potatoes. I have to impress her tonight is *all*." Her voice was raised now. "This letter of recommendation is for an internship in the *governor's office* next summer! Only the most important internship of my freaking life!" She got up and paced back and forth in the truck, fanning herself off with her hand. "And I'm about to get home and have about five minutes to get this nasty grease smell off of me and be prepared to be informally interviewed!"

I glanced at the clock in the truck. "Well, how about I drive you home instead of to the commissary? I can handle closing up alone today. That should buy you some time?"

Rose stopped pacing. "Really?"

"Yeah. This sounds like a ridiculous dinner, but important nonetheless."

She laughed. "Nonetheless, huh? And you have the nerve to call *me* a dork?"

I started the truck. "All right, all right. Buckle up. We're about to weave through the 110, baby."

She opened the window and cleared her throat. "And thanks. I really appreciate it."

I raised the volume on the radio. "What?!" I shouted.

She shook her head.

"TELL ME WHAT YOU SAID RIGHT NOW! LIKE SHOUT IT!"

"YOU ARE SUCH A LOSER!" she shouted back as we hit the road.

# CHAPTER 14

ON SATURDAY, MY DAD HANDED ME A PLATE OF EGGS Benedict drizzled with a sriracha hollandaise sauce. "So, I have some last-minute plans. I'm going out of town. Do you think you can handle the truck all weekend?"

I shoved a forkful of runny yolk and English muffin into my mouth. "Sure. Wait, you're leaving today?"

"Yup." He glanced at the clock. "In like, an hour in fact."

"Where are you going?" I asked as I added more sriracha to my eggs.

My dad plopped down on the stool next to me with his own plate of eggs. "Santa Barbara. Wine tasting."

I almost choked. "What? Who *are* you? Diane Keaton?"

"Yeah, I'm Diane Keaton. Surprise."

"Wait a second." I looked at him suspiciously. "*Who* are you going with?"

He cut his egg in half, the yolk oozing out onto the wilted kale and muffin. A giant forkful of egg went into his mouth, and he didn't answer.

"Pai!"

Many seconds later, he took a gulp of coffee and looked at me. "I'm going with Kody."

My brain quickly flipped through the Rolodex o' women from my dad's life until it stilled on one. "Kody the . . . ?"

"The drummer."

Kody was a Filipino American babe with a Patti Smith haircut and a raspy smoker's voice. My dad had dated her a couple of years ago, though, so I was confused. "Kody the drummer? Didn't you guys break up?"

He expertly cut the rest of his eggs, crisscrossing his slices so that each piece was perfectly bite-size. "Yeah. But we grabbed coffee last week and . . ." He shrugged. "You know how it goes."

"No, I don't. I'm a child."

A snort of laughter sent a piece of egg flying across the counter at me. I swiped it off my forearm. "Gross! If all these women only knew how disgusting you are at home."

I said "all these women" because, well, my dad had all these women. Which I understood—he was thirty-four and not hideous. I never made a big stink about it. Even so, he tried not to introduce me to too many girlfriends. "Don't want you to get attached," he always said. I think he might have learned that from watching sitcoms about single dads or something. The only thing that annoyed me was when he made jokes about being a hot commodity at PTA meetings. You'd think he was Don Draper waltzing into classrooms full of harried mothers desperately feeding him baked goods. And in what universe did he go to PTA meetings? Please.

My dad shifted uncomfortably on his stool. "Well, to be honest. I've been seeing Kody for a couple of months now."

"Really?" I racked my brain for when they could have had dates in the past two months. It seemed like my dad was home a lot in the evenings, so when did this happen?

As if reading my mind, he said, "She's been helping me out with restaurant stuff. Since before you guys started working on the truck."

"You sly dog."

He made a face. "Gross," he said, throwing the word back at me. I laughed. He looked over at me, nervous again. "So, Clara. I think we're a little serious? Kody and I."

Whether it was the words or the tone of my dad's voice, I didn't know, but my stomach flipped. "Oh, okay." I looked down at my eggs and tried to keep any trace of weirdness out of my voice.

"Yeah. Like, maybe more serious than anyone else in my entire life."

I glanced up then, my eyebrows raised. "What? No way."

"Yes way."

And the tells—the tiny pieces of egg, his foot tapping on the stool bar, his impeccably shaved jawline—were suddenly clear. He *was* serious.

"Pai! Why would you want to settle down now? This is like, your prime of life!" I held my fork up in the air for emphasis.

He laughed. "Okay, *sixteen-year-old daughter*. In case you couldn't tell, I was forced to settle down a long time ago." I blinked. Because even though my dad never, ever complained about being a young dad, I always wondered about his regrets. How his need to keep abandoned, sad things might apply to me, too.

Pai kept talking. "Anyway. Kody's older than me by a little bit, and she's thinking about the future, too. The crowd's starting to settle down."

Every week there was a new wedding invitation or baby announcement in the mail. Our refrigerator was crowded with them. Script fonts letter-pressed into thick paper announcing some hip wedding or a giant newborn's face, its hands in mittens and its face always froglike and never cute. I guess I always thought that phase of my dad's life was over. The thought of Kody and him getting married one day . . . having a kid? It was too much for my brain to handle.

I changed the subject. "Well, be sure to drink a lot of merlots or whatever it is people do."

He laughed. "Thanks. Aren't you excited to have some privacy for once?" He paused, holding *his* fork in the air for a second. "Privacy for reading books and finishing your knitting home alone, that is."

"Ha ha." I took a sip of tea. "You know I don't know how to read."

He pulled his Dodgers cap down over his eyes. "Well, just knitting then."

I smiled. He wasn't saying it, but this was a big step. Precafeteria fire he was cool with leaving me alone for a night or two. But post-fire, he had been more watchful than he had ever been in my life. Leaving me alone was a gesture—to show that I was regaining his trust.

My dad and Kody headed off for Santa Barbara shortly after. "Enjoy those tannins!" I yelled from the balcony, standing barefoot on the metal railing as I leaned over and watched them drive away.

After working the KoBra that day, I had the evening free. I picked up my phone to see what Patrick and Felix were up to. But my fingers hovered over the screen, and I ended up texting Rose.

**Let me guess: you're brushing up on constitutional law tonight?**

She immediately texted back: **Ha. Are you enjoying the heroin den?**

**You took the joke too far**

**Too accurate?**

**Yeah I draw the line at doing drugs that require accessories for them**

I waited a second before typing: **How did the dinner with the senator go?**

I was searching for a senatorial-looking emoji when another text popped up. Mãe.

**No Tulum???** 🤮 😟 😡 🌴 ☀️ 🍹

Shoot. I guess my dad did tell her. I texted back immediately: **I'm working on it! We're doing good on the truck—he'll cave.**

**K k got it. Make your eyes like this** 😍. **Your dad's a sucker for that kinda stuff.**

I wanted to agree, to LOL, but I realized my mom didn't actually know Pai at all anymore. Current Pai was no longer the doormat of the past. Then I noticed the barrage of texts from Rose updating me on the senator dinner. She was excited because it went well. I had settled into the sofa and was texting with her when someone knocked. Flo jumped off my lap and ran over to the entrance, her nose poking at the space under the door.

"Clara!"

Felix? What in the world.

I dragged myself to the door. "What are you doing here?" The words were out of my mouth before the door fully opened.

He was spiffed up—his thick hair tousled just so, smelling good, and wearing his tightest black jeans. "You're coming with us." I saw Patrick's car idling on the curb.

I nudged Flo out of the way with my foot so she wouldn't escape. "What? Where?"

"Some party. Come on, we barely see you anymore. I'll give you five minutes to get ready."

"What, I don't look good enough?" My arm swept over my ripped white tank top and knee-length sweat shorts.

He raised his eyebrows and shot me a wolfish grin. "You always look good, babe."

"God." Felix was full of moves, and two years ago I had fallen for *all* of them. "Give me a second." I ran upstairs and got dressed in record time. I remembered to grab my cell as I was headed out the door, sending Rose a text: **Want to do something fun for once?**

"So then if you think of it that way, Tom Cruise is basically a *wizard*, transcending time and space."

I stared at the guy in front of me, then wrapped my hands tighter around the warm bottle of beer I was holding. Rose and I had been talking to this conspiracy theorist about Tom Cruise at this house party for a solid five minutes.

The guy licked his lips nervously, his fair skin getting paler by the second. "So actually, if Cruise—"

"I have to pee," I said, handing my drink to him as I grabbed Rose by the arm.

"Wow, I thought people got more stable once they graduated high school," Rose said as we headed out of the living room toward the kitchen.

"Paranoid people exist at every age," I shouted to be heard over the live band. Patrick had some sort of sixth sense for parties with a high ratio of hot dudes in bands. It had been hard to persuade Rose to come out, but I promised her cute boys and she had met us fifteen minutes later. Too bad we had been stuck with Tom Cruise Whiz.

It was stuffy in the apartment, so we went searching for some air through the kitchen. It had terrible fluorescent overhead lighting that was a harsh contrast to the cave feeling of the living room. Rose and I skirted by a group of girls in various denim cutoffs and cropped tanks while a tall man in a felted hat lectured them on something or another. They looked bored to tears, some of them even on their phones.

As we walked by the opining guy, I slipped into him, knocking his beer into his pinstripe shirt. "Watch it!" he yelped as he jumped away from me and wiped at his shirt furiously.

"Oh no. So sorry," I said, holding up my hands apologetically. The group of girls scattered immediately. *You're welcome.*

Rose laughed. "That was some good sabotage, Shin." I resisted the urge to create further disruption, my prank itch temporarily scratched.

"Thanks, Carver." I found a sliding door that led us out onto the balcony, which was miraculously empty. Taking a deep breath of fresh air, I asked, "Are we a buddy-cop movie now?"

Rose took a sip of her Diet Coke, which I had managed to find for her deep in the recesses of the refrigerator. "Carver and Shin. We need to have like, moments of culture clash."

"I'll teach you how to use chopsticks while you fumble and curse the entire time," I said as I leaned against the railing.

The sliding door opened then. Felix.

"Hey. You guys hiding out here?"

I shrugged. "This party is full of the most unbearable dudes."

Felix plopped down into a dirty plastic chair. "I know. Found out it's some band's apartment."

"Figures."

"But Patrick's interested in some guy, so I think we're stuck for a while." He clinked his bottle on Rose's can. Patrick and Felix had been surprised when I told them Rose was coming, especially because they had always been integral to Project Make Rose's Life a Living Hell. But despite the initial awkwardness, everyone was being civil.

I leaned against the balcony railing and looked over at the CVS parking lot that was adjacent to us. "Isn't Patrick's new boyfriend going to have a problem with that?"

Felix laughed. "Define 'boyfriend.'"

I took a sip of beer. "Speaking of significant others, where's Cynthia?"

"She had to work tonight."

My stomach rumbled. "Let's go visit her!"

Felix rolled his eyes. "She can't give us free food."

"Where does she work?" Rose asked.

I interrupted Felix before he could answer. "Why not?!" Cynthia worked as a server at a burger place whose theme was literally "island stuff." And getting us the occasional free meal was one of her finer qualities.

"Her new boss is a total dick." He glanced at Rose. "She works at Island's."

"Well, I'm starving and this party sucks. You guys want to go find some food?"

Felix shrugged. "Sure."

I looked over at Rose, who downed the rest of her drink. "Okay," she said as she wiped off her mouth. I liked Game Rose.

A few minutes later, we left Patrick at the party with the dudes and headed out toward Sunset, where I could practically smell the tacos. My favorite truck, Cielo Tacos, was only a few blocks away. On the way over, Felix spent the entire time talking about Cynthia and the fight they'd just had. I tried my best to be attentive, but honestly it took every ounce of willpower not to just say, "Dump her already." They had the same fight every week: Felix wasn't spending enough time with her. When in reality, his life pretty much revolved around her every move. It was tedious. If this was what being in a serious relationship was like, count me the eff out. Rose was being nice and making the occasional sympathetic comment so that I didn't have to.

A line had already formed at the truck. As I pulled out my wallet to see if I had enough cash, a guy approached me with a flyer in hand. "Food truck competition this summer!" he said cheerfully.

"No thanks, man," Felix said with a wave.

But I grabbed it. "Thanks."

The glossy card read *AUGUST 11—ANNUAL LA FOOD TRUCK COMPETITION* in hot-pink scrawl, the text laid over a photo of swaying palm trees. Under it:

*The biggest competition in town! Winner takes home $100K. ALL trucks eligible, sign up on our website. Or just show up and enjoy some choice foods and local music.*

Whoa. 100K?! Pai thought opening a restaurant was far off—like after I was married with children far off. Maybe it could be much sooner.

"What's that?" Rose asked, poking her head over my shoulder to read the flyer.

I handed it to her. "There's a food truck competition in August and—"

"ONE HUNDRED THOUSAND DOLLARS?" she screamed.

People were staring at us, so I stepped in closer to her and snatched the flyer out of her hand. "Dude, have some *chill*."

"Your dad *needs* to enter this!" she said, her voice back to normal decibel levels.

I started to nod but was struck by an idea. "What if we entered the KoBra but didn't tell him? It would be the *best* surprise if we won!"

Skepticism wrinkled her forehead. "Don't tell him? At all?"

"Yeah!" I was getting excited at the idea of hitting my dad with this kind of killer surprise. "Can you even imagine getting a check for that kind of money?"

Rose nodded slowly. "I mean, that would be so cool. And honestly, we're good at this now."

"I have complete faith in us," I said firmly.

That's when I noticed Felix staring at me. Arms folded, eyebrows raised. "What?" I asked, my arms also crossed over my chest, the tanned limbs protecting me against his judgment.

"It's just . . . wow. I've never seen you care about your dad's truck before."

Embarrassment flared through me. Felix always had this way of pointing out when people were trying too hard or being uncool. I had never been on the receiving end of it before.

"So?" I pushed by him to order my tacos.

"Nothing, jeez!" He held his hands up, all "Hey, now!" I hated when he did this. Made me feel like I was overreacting when he had clearly set me up for it. Typical boy gaslighting crap.

I folded the flyer in half and tucked it into my back pocket.

When I got home that night, I opened the laptop I shared with my dad. The apartment was dark except for the blue glow of the screen.

Folding my legs under me, I knelt down on the living room rug and stared at the application form I had filled out, the cursor hovering over the Submit button. A nervous flutter in my stomach made me pause. But then I imagined Pai's reaction when we won. How I could do something for my dad, for once. Fast-forward his dreams.

I clicked the Submit button.

# CHAPTER 15

ON MONDAY MORNING WHEN I GOT TO THE commissary, Rose was lying down on the hood of the truck, sunglasses on, limbs splayed. "Good morning," I said, tapping her foot with an iced coffee I'd bought for her.

At glacial speed, she sat up with a groan. "Morning."

"What's wrong?" I handed her the drink.

She took the world's longest sip before answering. "I just had a two-hour barre this morning."

"*Two hours?* That means . . . you've been awake since, like, four a.m.?"

"Yup." She swiveled her long neck slowly, touching her ear to her shoulder, then dropping her head back to stare up at the sky. "I want to die."

"Why do you do this to yourself?"

Bringing her head back up, she took off her sunglasses and looked at me. "I love it, I guess."

What was it like to love something so much you woke up at four a.m. on your summer break to do it?

We got into the truck and buckled ourselves in—me in the driver's seat as usual. Rose glanced over at me. "Oh, I forgot to ask at the party. I heard you talking to Patrick about a trip to Tulum?"

I steered the truck toward the freeway. "Yeah, a vacation with my mom."

"Adrian's letting you go?"

As we waited for the light to turn green on the ramp, I drummed my fingers on the steering wheel. The morning was already hot, and I couldn't tell whether the dampness under my arms was from that or from the mere mention of Tulum. I stared at the little sign that said ONE CAR PER GREEN. It felt unnecessarily aggressive today.

When the light turned green, I stepped on the accelerator with force—making the truck lurch forward. A couple of metal bowls rolled around noisily in the cupboards. "Not exactly. It's still more than a month away, though, and I have plenty of time to prove my worthiness. He'll have to let me go."

Rose didn't react.

I took a breath. "I never get to see her. They don't get along, and I know my dad uses any excuse to undermine our relationship. He doesn't approve of her life choices."

Rose raised her eyebrows. "What? I doubt he tries to undermine your relationship. I mean, he's raising you; maybe he just feels protective?"

"I know, but . . . it's complicated."

A few loaded seconds passed. Rose was one of those people who could never feign indifference; her do-gooderly intentions emanated from her pores. She said, carefully, "When did your parents get divorced?"

Divorced. That was an interesting way to put it. "They were never married. My mom left my dad when I was four." The words came out before I could stop them. "I mean, she didn't just, like, *leave* with a suitcase overnight. It was a mutual decision for them to separate."

"Oh! Wow. That's a long time ago."

Weaving through traffic, I glanced at my rearview mirror before replying. "She and my dad met in high school—that's when she got pregnant, actually. They were both eighteen."

"Yeah, your dad looks way young."

"He is. They met in Brazil. Making my dad Korean Brazilian. American? Not sure. A lot of things. He was born there, his parents emigrated from Korea back in the day. My mom's also Korean Brazilian."

Rose nodded. "Hence the KoBra's fusion menu."

"Right. Hence. Anyway, after my mom got pregnant, my parents decided to move to LA. More economic opportunity, fresh starts and all. They thought they'd get married and raise me here. As an American citizen."

"Their families were cool with that?"

"Not exactly. My mom's parents pretty much disowned her. My dad's didn't love it, but they couldn't do much since my parents were both eighteen by then."

"Wow."

We drove through downtown, passing a solid line of bumper-to-bumper traffic on the opposite side. "Yeah. Dramatic. So they moved here, I was born, and then . . ." I trailed off, gripping the steering wheel. "Then, my mom went back to São Paulo before they ever got married."

I kept my eyes on the road, but I could *feel* Rose's stare. "She . . . moved back to *Brazil*?"

"She couldn't handle LA. I mean, it was a different country, and she was a teenage mom. Could you blame her for freaking out?"

Pity unfurled from Rose like ribbons. "I guess not," she said quietly. Even though I knew that Rose Carver, even if she got pregnant this very second, would stick to whatever plan she made until the end. But eighteen-year-old Mãe was not Rose Carver.

"How often do you see her?" she asked.

Our exit was coming up, and I pulled the truck into the right-hand lane. "It depends. She has to come to LA now and then because of her job. So that works out—I've seen her more in the past few years than ever. But it's been like six months, so I *really* want to go to Tulum."

"Six months! Holy crap. I can't imagine not seeing my mom

for that long," Rose said. Then she touched my arm. "Sorry. Not judging."

I pulled the truck onto the off-ramp. "No worries, I didn't take it that way. I know my family's not normal."

She laughed deeply. "*No one's* family is normal."

I drove into the office plaza. "Get out of here, your family is so blessedly normal."

After I parked, Rose got up and stood next to me. "Thanks for sharing that."

I took my seat belt off and fiddled with it for a second. "Um, you're welcome. And, hey. That was fun at the party. I'm glad you came out." We had worked together on Sunday after the party but hadn't talked about it yet.

"You're welcome," she answered primly. We made eye contact and cracked up.

"I mean, really I should thank you," she said. "As you can tell, I don't go out that much. I just spend so much time with my family. I forget I can go and have like . . . *friends?*"

I shook my head. "Sad."

"More fodder for our YouTube channel."

"You really need to stop saying things like 'fodder.'"

After counting out the change in the cashbox, Rose opened the order window. She glanced outside, then did a double take. "Whoa. Look at Hamlet today."

I peered over her shoulder. He was doing his usual embarrassing acrobatics with the sign. But he was dressed up. Wearing slim-fitting navy pants, a light blue button-up, and a gray-and-white striped tie. A tie. In ninety-degree weather.

"Who died?" I wondered out loud.

Rose elbowed me. "Rude. Also, he's wearing blue, not black."

"Yeah, but . . . why would you wear that?"

Before she could answer, Hamlet dropped the sign onto the grass and jogged over to the coffee cart. He ducked down away from view and then popped back up, holding two drinks.

I found myself smoothing back my hair as he walked over. Something about him looking so snazzy made me feel like a bag lady.

"Hey, Hamlet," Rose said cheerfully, taking her drink from him. I reached for mine, too, and my fingers brushed against his. "Thanks."

"You're welcome," he said, his eyes meeting mine for a second. I blinked and took a huge gulp of my iced mocha.

Rose looked at us, eyes twinkling. Oh no. She took a sip of her drink. "So, you look nice today."

Hamlet looked down at his outfit and put his hands on his hips. "Oh. Yeah? Thanks."

"What's the occasion?"

He looked up at me first, then looked back at Rose. "Well. Funny you should ask."

My mouth went dry.

"One second!" he said, then ran off toward the coffee cart again. Rose and I looked at each other in confusion.

He came back with his hands held behind him. Rose and I stared. After an eternity, he cleared his throat. "Clara."

Rose's eyes widened when she looked at me. I choked on my mocha. "Yeah?" I finally managed to squeak out.

He whipped out a bouquet of flowers and held them up toward the order window. "Will you let me take you out on a date this weekend?"

For a second, all that existed was that bouquet of light pink roses. Fragrant, extravagantly wrapped in pink-tinted cellophane, tied together with a thin white grosgrain ribbon.

Then I felt a poke in my arm. I blinked and looked up to see both Rose and Hamlet staring at me.

There was no way. I mean, this was *Hamlet*. No matter how cute the dude, he was *not* someone I would date. Like ever. I opened my mouth, ready with some kind of nice but firm rejection, when Rose kicked my ankle, out of Hamlet's view. Her eyes were threatening to murder me.

Jesus.

Hamlet was starting to sweat. He wiped his forehead with his crisp shirt sleeve. And that little gesture softened something in me.

"Sure." The word slipped out so easily that I almost gasped. I accepted the bouquet of flowers.

Nervousness instantly gave way to pure sunshine and rainbows. Hamlet grinned, his sharp canines sparkling. "Okay! Awesome! Here's my number!" He slid a scrap of paper over to me. It was creased and soft, as if it had been sitting in his pocket for a week. "Let me know what day works for you!"

Someone coughed loudly behind him, and Hamlet turned around to see a line of customers. "Oh! Okay, see you guys later!" Then he high-fived the guy behind him and ran off to his coffee cart.

I held the bouquet in my hands and glared at Rose. "Not a word."

She laughed and started taking orders.

# CHAPTER 16

BY SATURDAY AFTERNOON, I HAD BITTEN MY NAILS
down to nubs. Hamlet and I had agreed to have dinner, and for
some reason I was nervous.

*Nervous for a date with Hamlet Wong.* Like, what was happening, universe? One, I'd been on many dates. No big deal. In
my experience, guys hardly took the time to swipe on deodorant,
so why in God's name should *we* sweat it? I barely bothered
shaving my legs.

Two, this was Hamlet. I wasn't even into the guy. Biggest
dork I knew second to Rose, and he's crushing on *me*, therefore
this date would already begin with my having the upper hand.

And yet.

Because Rose and I had the day off, it was one of my dad's

solo shifts on the truck, and I was whiling the morning away in front of the TV with Flo grooming herself in my lap. Continuing my life's goal of watching every episode of *Supernatural*, the show that would not die.

My phone vibrated with a text from Rose: **What are you wearing tonight?**

I looked down at my sweats cutoffs and black tank covered in Flo's hair and Doritos crumbs.

**Probably what I'm wearing now**

I took a selfie with Flo and sent it to her.

**Is that the same tank top you wear every single day?**

**How dare you this is my weekend tank**

**Isn't Hamlet taking you somewhere nice? You need to wear something cute for once in your life.**

**Cat hair necklace doesn't qualify as cute?**

**Sure, if you want to die alone.**

**That pretty much is my dream**

I cackled and ate another handful of chips while she took a few seconds to text back.

**Do you want help picking out your outfit?**

**Just say it—you're bored and need something to do**

**Actually, I'm wrapping up this meeting for the Future Leaders of Los Angeles and could head over after grabbing some clothes from my house.**

Shaking my head, I texted back: **Come over then**

\*   \*   \*

Rose arrived on my doorstep holding an armful of clothes.

"What *is* all that?" I asked as she stepped inside.

"Clothes befitting a first date," she said, her voice muffled by the pile in her face. She kicked off her strappy cobalt blue heels and dropped the clothes onto an armchair, making Flo jump.

At the sight of Flo, Rose let out an ungodly squeal and dropped to her knees. "Look at the kitty!" she said in a voice I had never heard come out of her mouth before.

Flo stared at her from under the coffee table, not blinking, her striped tail flicking to the side.

Rose beckoned her with clucking sounds, holding out her fingers. "Come here, kitty!" She glanced up at me, as I stood dumbfounded. "I wish we could have a cat, but my brother's allergic."

I watched her as she continued to cluck and make kissy noises. "So clearly this is the first cat you have ever seen in your entire life."

"Ha-ha." She stood up reluctantly after Flo made no move to come closer. Instead Flo sat there like a stone, staring at some random spot between Rose and the sofa.

I riffled through the pile of clothes. "Did it ever occur to you that you're like seven feet taller than me?"

"It did. That's why it's mostly dresses."

I held up a frothy mint green dress with white polka dots on it. "I see. Also, I'm not a cartoon mouse."

"Listen, anything's better than your situation right now." Rose gestured toward me with fluttery hands. "And that dress is super flattering on."

"I don't care if it magically gives me a Kardashian butt, this dress isn't my style."

Rose grumbled as she pushed me aside to look through the dresses. "You're incredibly stubborn. It's fun to be around." She held up a black dress with lace sleeves. "Try this one."

I appraised it skeptically. It was short and looked like it would be super tight around my thighs. I didn't mind my body, liked it in fact, but I also knew that I didn't want to spend all night worrying about thigh bondage.

"Just try it on!" She tossed it at me with exasperation.

I took it with a scowl. "Fine."

I was pulling off my tank when she yelped and spun around. "Clara!"

"What?" I tossed the tank onto the floor and pulled the dress on over my head. "Are you seriously squeamish about seeing me in a bra? Aren't you a dancer?"

Her back still turned, she answered with her hands on her hips. "Yeah, but I *know* those girls and we're in a changing room. Give me a little advance warning, I don't like to see random people's body parts all willy-nilly!"

I stuck my arms through the sleeves, my face hidden within the folds of the dress. "I'm not a *stranger*. Haven't you ever had *girlfriends* before?" When I popped my head out, I saw Rose turn around with a strange expression. "What?" I asked.

She shrugged. "I haven't."

"Haven't what?"

"Had girlfriends." She looked down at her nails, her snobby arched eyebrows at odds with her words.

I let that settle over me, thinking back to the Rose Carver I'd known since middle school. She was always in charge of stuff, in lots of organizations . . . but had there ever been a best friend or a group that I could actually connect her to?

When I thought about it, when was the last time *I'd* had a best girlfriend? Veronica Souza in sixth grade. We drifted apart when she went to private school in seventh grade, and soon after I had befriended Patrick and Felix. "I haven't had a 'bestie' in forever, too. Been hanging with my goons for too long," I said, tugging the skirt of the dress over my thighs.

She nodded. "They were nice." We both knew they weren't "nice," but I let the generic compliment pass. "The thing is, I kind of tell my mom everything. So I've never really needed a best friend."

Again, we both knew that was a weird statement, but I didn't bat an eyelash. "I can see that."

"I know you think I'm weird."

"Well, of course." I held up my arms, showing her the dress.

"That looks good on you," she said.

I looked down. The dress actually fit me pretty well and was comfortable despite the tightness. "Yeah, it's not bad."

Rose wouldn't let me get away with trying on just one, though. She even had me match shoes and hair styles to different outfits. I honestly couldn't remember the last time I had leaned in so hard-core to girlie stuff like this, and it was fun. I felt a giddiness settle into me and actually found myself saying, "That's so cute," about a freaking tube of lip gloss.

Finally, we settled on the perfect dress. It was a loose, short navy blue tank dress made out of comfy jersey material that felt like my favorite old T-shirt. Because the style was meant to show a peep of your bra, Rose made me trade my ratty black one for a bright lacy fuchsia one I had buried deep in my dresser.

I plopped down onto the sofa from the exhaustion of our makeover montage. "I'm starved."

"Not done yet."

When I glanced over at Rose, she was holding some kind of kettle-looking thing with a long chord. "What is *that*?"

"A portable steamer. I'm going to steam your dress." She hung the dress up on a sturdy curtain rod. I opened my mouth to make fun of the portable steamer but shut it. At some point, the mocking grounds were just too fertile, even for me.

"Should I order a pizza?" I asked while watching her meticulously steam the dress.

She glanced at me over her shoulder. "Oh. Um, is that okay? I wasn't sure if I was invited to eat here."

"Huh? Invited? You're already here." It hit me then, the depths of Rose's friendship void. Had she never just hung out, with no plans or schedules? "If you don't have anywhere to go, that is."

The steamer sputtered its last bits of steam and Rose shut it off. "No, I mean, I have plans later but not now."

I was confused by that answer. "So . . . yes, you want to get pizza?" The discomfort continued to weigh down the room.

"Sure." Phew. The most awkwardly earned pizza ever.

After I ordered through an app on my phone ("You have a Domino's *app*?" she asked. "I'm VIP," I answered, a fact that drove my dad and his fancy-pizza feels crazy), we sat around my living room, Rose spending most of the time trying to lure Flo over to her. Some progress was being made. Flo was now lying a foot away from Rose, licking her paws.

"When is Hamlet picking you up?" Rose asked as she lay on her belly, her hand reached out toward Flo, holding a small pile of treats. Flo sniffed the air for a second, her eyes focused on Rose, but the magical cat moment left as quickly as it came.

"I forget."

Rose looked up at me. "What! You don't remember what time?"

"Yeah, it was evening-ish."

"Oh my God." She sat up and pushed a lock of hair out of her eyes. "Check right now what time."

"It's fine! It's only like noon."

"First, that is alarming because it's two p.m. Second, what if you're wrong and he's picking you up in like thirty minutes?"

The doorbell rang, and I scrambled off the sofa. "Pizza time."

"Or it's Hamlet because your date is actually now."

I laughed. "You're nuts." It was the pizza, of course.

We settled around the coffee table with paper towels instead of plates. I folded a slice in half and took a huge, cheesy bite, watching Rose nibble hers, eating the pepperoni off her slice first.

"Are you nervous?" Rose asked as she held out a bit of pepperoni toward Flo. Flo bolted over and sniffed it, taking a little lick. Rose looked ecstatic when Flo took it from her, but then frowned when she just dropped it on the rug and walked off.

I laughed. "Don't take it personally. She only likes her own boring cat food, kibble from Costco. The finest palate." I took a large gulp of soda. "So, yeah, I am a *little* nervous about this date."

"I'm always super nervous before first dates," she said, picking up the abandoned pepperoni and wrapping it in a paper towel. "Sometimes normal, perfectly nice guys turn into total jerks on dates."

Wouldn't have taken Rose for a dating expert. "Do you go on a lot of dates?"

She shrugged, her shoulders lifting slightly. "Kind of."

"For someone with an Awkward Friendship YouTube channel, that's surprising."

Her eyebrows arched. "I might be awkward with girls, but I've got the whole boy thing *down*."

"I guess it helps when you look like *you*."

Rose took a sip of Coke. "Thank you." That was so very Rose Carver of her, but there was something refreshing about her just accepting a compliment. I had a hard time doing it—my girl-instinct was to deflect it, something that I was always working against.

"Are you dating anyone now?" I asked.

She sighed—the long-suffering sigh of a woman in hot demand. "Not dating, but seeing like three guys. I dunno, they're kind of . . . whatever."

"*Three?* Damn."

"Like I said, they're all whatever. But I like to keep my options open. I refuse to date anyone seriously right now."

"Distractions you don't need?"

She nodded. "Exactly." Eschewing the bottle of sriracha, Rose reached for the Tabasco instead and doused her slice of pizza with it. Legit. Before taking a bite, she looked over at me, suddenly shy again. "Have you had a boyfriend before?"

"Yep."

"Like, a lot of them?"

"Yep."

"How many?" Rose was so riveted that she didn't notice Flo slowly making her way toward her.

I thought about it for a second. "Um, I don't know, five?"

"FIVE? You've had five boyfriends?!"

"Don't judge!"

"I'm not! I'm just impressed." Flo sniffed Rose's foot. Rose still didn't notice. "I think I remember some of them . . . you were with Leo Nguyen this year, weren't you?"

A shudder passed through me. "Unfortunately. I found out he didn't brush his teeth."

Rose screamed, sending Flo shooting off to the kitchen. "Gross!"

"Yeah, I don't even want to . . . I mean, we made out so many times . . ."

She laughed so hard that she choked. I pounded her back and handed her a drink.

"Thanks," she gasped, waving her hand at me. "Anyway, wow. Totally gross."

"Agreed. So, what about you? Have you had boyfriends? I don't remember any rumors of you dating anyone at Elysian anyway." It was strange to know someone for so many years and not know them at all, I realized. The bulk of my Rose Carver knowledge was like the news feed of someone's life—only the obvious, visible stuff.

"Not really? I date guys, but never longer than a few weeks at most." She looked around for Flo, who was now lapping up water at her bowl in the kitchen. "I've never liked anyone enough. I like them at first. But something happens when I spend more time with them."

"You're over it?"

"Exactly. I don't know . . . when they like me too much I stop liking them?" Suddenly Flo plopped into Rose's lap. Rose's eyes grew wide, and she froze.

I raised my eyebrows. "See, Flo gets you. You only start liking them when they stop paying attention to you."

Rose laughed and pulled Flo to her chest, which made her yowl and jump out of Rose's arms—flouncing away with a swish of her finicky tail. "So . . . five guys. You didn't like any of them enough to keep them around longer than . . ."

"Six months," I finished for her. "My longest relationship. With Felix Rafael Benavides, believe it or not."

"Oh, I remember when you guys dated. You were like our high school's Brangelina."

I snorted. "Please. He wishes he were Brad. Anyway . . . yeah. I dunno, when it gets boring and too real, I bail. Who needs that? We're in high school."

"But you like boys enough to keep wanting them around," she said with a waggle of her eyebrows.

I waggled mine back. "Well, *yeah*." We both laughed.

"I can't even imagine liking a guy enough to call him my boyfriend, so you're preaching to the choir," she said, taking a sip of her drink. She looked at me. "But you know, why is it that we're supposed to feel bad about this part of our lives? Like, if we don't have a boyfriend, we're loser weirdos. If we date too much, we're 'sluts.'"

I chewed my fourth slice of pizza thoughtfully. "Maybe the truth is . . . nothing is weird about dating in high school. Everyone is different, and we need to stop reading so many magazines giving us dated-ass relationship advice."

She held up her cup. "Hear, hear!"

"Rose. Stop saying stuff like that."

"Cheers to that."

I threw a Parmesan cheese packet at her.

# CHAPTER 17

AFTER ROSE LEFT (MAKING SURE I VERIFIED THE TIME of my date), I cleaned up lunch and took a shower. Confession: I hate taking showers. They're just so much time and effort. I have the thickest hair on the planet, and it takes hours to dry.

Once I was dressed, I swiped on some eyeliner—making a cat eye with a little swoop at the end. Then I grabbed a glittery teal eyeshadow and extended the end of the swoop. I blinked and looked in the mirror. There. Properly fancy.

I heard my dad's voice echo through the hallway. "Clara! He's here!"

Why my dad had to get home in time for my date was beyond me. Cosmic timing. I grabbed my mini black leather backpack and headed downstairs.

I stopped in my tracks. Oh boy. There was Hamlet at the front door, grasping yet another bouquet of flowers. My dad was holding the door open, and they both looked up at me at the same time.

"What is this, some teen movie?" I cracked, suddenly feeling so nervous that I almost tripped down the stairs. I saved it with a little jig, but their weird expressions confirmed that it was not a smooth move.

I stopped in front of my dad and pointed at him. "No speeches, no warnings, no anything. None of that paternalistic stuff."

My dad grinned and leaned against the doorway. "I'm paternal by biology, Shorty."

"You know what I mean," I said while pulling on my sandals, avoiding Hamlet.

Suddenly a bunch of flowers were in my line of vision and I sprang up, knocking them out of Hamlet's hands. "Sorry!" I bent over to pick them up at the same time he did, and we bonked heads. Ugh. What was *happening* to me? I was never this flustered! Hamlet managed to re-create the bouquet and held it out to me again, a lock of hair falling into his eyes.

They were a spray of white snapdragons. "Thank you. They're pretty," I said as I took them from him.

He flushed deeply, red creeping up from the collar of his crisp, white button-down shirt. The sleeves were rolled up, and the shirt fit him perfectly, paired with dark blue shorts that hit his knees. He looked like he was about to make an Asian cameo in a Nicholas Sparks movie. (Did they have Asian cameos?)

After I got the flowers in a vase, I rushed out the door with Hamlet, waving at my dad. "See you, Pai."

Before the door shut, I heard him holler, "Come home in time for breakfast!"

Now it was *my* turn to blush. What even. I couldn't make eye contact with Hamlet. I just flew down the apartment stairs.

When we reached the sidewalk, I stopped abruptly. "Did you drive?" I asked.

A car beeped in the street. "Yup," Hamlet said as he walked briskly toward the sound.

When we reached his car, I held up my hands. "Whoa, mama." The car in front of us was a slick white Lexus. "*This* is your car?!"

He held the passenger door open, pressing his lips together. "Yeah. Um, my parents overcompensate for not spending enough time with me."

As I slipped into the leather interior, I thought about how at odds Coffee Kiosk Hamlet was with this car. Who knew he was some rich kid? It annoyed me, and I felt uneasier with each passing second until he got into the driver's seat. I was never comfortable with people who had a lot of money. I knew I shouldn't care, but it was just one of those things.

"So, um, I didn't want to assume you would eat where I picked, so I made a few different reservations," Hamlet said, placing his hands on the wheel but not yet starting the car. "They are Three Leaf, Café Lola, or Hawkins & Post."

My lips curved up into a little smile. The trifecta of hipster restaurants. Hamlet trying his hardest. "Um, I guess we could try Café Lola? I haven't been to Highland Park in a while."

"All right, Café Lola it is!" he announced cheerfully as he headed toward the 110. Highland Park was north of us, between here and Pasadena, where the office park was. He tapped the steering wheel. "I've heard good things about this place."

"From who?"

"From . . . people."

I opened my window, letting in a gust of warm summer evening air. "Like real people you know or the Internet?"

He laughed, all ease. "Okay. I just read the Yelp reviews." Then I saw him shut off the AC with a near-imperceptible flick of his wrist.

"Oh, I didn't know you had the AC on, sorry," I said, rolling up the window.

"That's okay! The night air feels good!" Hamlet said, rolling down his own window.

Discomfited by his niceness, I opened my window halfway as some kind of awkward compromise. We passed the next couple of minutes in strained silence. Then Hamlet picked up his phone and swiped a few times and music blasted, startling me.

"Sorry!" He immediately lowered the volume.

After a few seconds, I felt this irritation creeping in as I watched Arroyo Park flash by my window. What in the world was annoying me so much? Then a male voice screeched.

I cringed. "Are we listening to IMAGINE DRAGONS?"

Hamlet grinned, glancing over at me. "Yeah! Aren't they great?"

"Um, yes." I tried my best to keep my voice neutral.

His smile faltered. "Well, I can change it," he said, fumbling for the phone while he kept his eyes on the road.

*You are a butt, Clara.* I took the phone from him. "Here, it's fine. You should concentrate on driving. Sorry, I've got the worst poker face." I snuck a glance at Hamlet, his profile lit from the side in two-second intervals by the streetlamps. His eyelashes were short but insanely thick, his nose straight, his mouth kind of perfect. And at the moment, he was chewing on his bottom lip, brow furrowed.

Pretty sure I was already ruining this date. "So, um, where do you live again?"

"San Gabriel." His eyes stayed on the road—the wild curves of the 110 were barely lit by the headlights.

I raised my eyebrows. "Whoa. The SGV. Pretty far out there."

"Yup."

Monosyllabic and Sullen Hamlet was unnerving. "I guess there's a lot of good Chinese food, though." *No duh, Clara.* The San Gabriel Valley had a big Asian population.

His expression basically relayed the same thing.

"We could use better Chinese food in Echo Park." The desperation was palpable. "Also Korean food. Actually, that's kind of my dad's dream—opening up a good Korean place in our neighborhood. Although, yeah, we're so close to K-Town that it seems ridiculous. But, it'll be like the KoBra, Korean with Brazilian influences." I found myself unable to stop speaking, wanting to fix the jerkiness of my behavior. Again, something I didn't usually care about, but suddenly did with Hamlet nearby.

My rambling worked.

"That sounds like a really good idea," Hamlet said, a little cautiously. "Your dad's a great cook; he could do it."

And while *I* knew my dad was good at what he did, hearing Hamlet say it out loud warmed me up from the inside. "Thanks," I said. Then flushed. "I mean, not that you were complimenting *me*, but you know what I mean . . ."

Hamlet laughed. "I love how you always have to point out awkward moments."

Jeez. "Wow, and you like to point out stuff in general."

"Yeah, I do!"

I couldn't help laughing, and he looked over at me with the biggest, most genuine grin I have ever seen on another human. Sheesh, this guy. We got to the restaurant and were greeted by the hottest woman I have ever seen in my life. I am a straight girl, and my jaw dropped as she led us to our table, her long black hair swishing above a tiny leather miniskirt. I glanced at Hamlet, expecting a drop of drool to be hanging from his mouth, but he was looking around the restaurant, oblivious to the supermodel in front of us.

Point one.

Hot Hostess sat us down at a tiny marble table, like one you'd find in a Parisian café or something. Our knees were touching. Hamlet made a few not-so-subtle attempts to space us out a bit more, but he hit the back of his chair on the one behind him— which was unfortunate because the woman in it was wearing a giant hat, which toppled off.

"Sorry!" he said, reaching down to pick it up. She yanked it out of his hands and turned around with a terse little "God!"

Hamlet flushed.

Yeah, I don't think so. The nervousness of this date melted away when faced with an opportunity to annoy someone who deserved it. I pulled a little leaf off the succulent on our table and tossed it over Hamlet's head so it landed on the brim of the woman's hat. Hamlet's eyes widened. I grabbed a small handful of leaves off the plant (sorry, guy, but you're tough, you'll recover) and tossed them one by one onto her hat. It was dark enough in there that neither she nor her friends noticed.

"Can I take your drink order?" A server popped up next to us, and I tucked my handful of leaves under the table. Hamlet let out a snort of laughter, and the server was unamused.

Hamlet fumbled for the menu. "Oh, let me see if . . ."

"I'm assuming no alcohol?" Unamused Server interrupted.

"Actually, lots of it," I said with a wink.

Still unamused. "Do you have an ID?"

"Yes, I do. I am a citizen of the United States."

Hamlet stammered, "Ah, ha-ha. Um, we'll start with water, thank you."

The server shot me a dirty look before leaving our table.

When I looked over at Hamlet, his head was dropped into his hands. I cleared my throat. "Sorry, this is what I'm like in public."

But when he looked up, I was surprised to see he was smiling. "You're so funny."

Again, just . . . announcing thoughts here. I reached for the menu so that I didn't have to respond. As I strained my eyes to read in the dimly lit room (a tiny tea candle was the only light at our table), Hamlet's phone rang.

He glanced down at it and looked up at me apologetically. "One sec, it's my grandmother."

Oh, a casual grandma call during a date. No biggie. He talked in a low voice, but I caught snippets of worried conversation.

I glanced back down at the menu. Everything was kind of expensive. I checked out the appetizers to see if they were any cheaper. Hm, the citrus salad or *literally anything else* for dinner? Choices, choices.

"Hey."

I glanced up to see Hamlet with an actual frown on his face. "What's up?" I asked uneasily.

"Sorry, but would you mind changing the date to . . . dinner at my grandparents'?"

Would I mind doing *what*? My face must have said it all, because he looked down. "Ah, never mind. Sorry, I think we'll have to do this another time. I've gotta get over there right now."

"Is everything all right?" I asked.

He sighed. "Probably. I don't know. My grandpa's grumpy because he's been sick a few days and insists on going out when he shouldn't. My grandma wants me home to distract him."

And I don't know whether it was the little smile or the worry in his eyes at odds with that smile that made me say, "Sure. Let's go there, then."

He gaped at me. "Really?"

"Yeah. This place gives me hives, anyway."

He laughed and scooted his chair out so quickly that he bonked into the lady again. Before she could say anything, he tucked his chair back in and said, "Sorry. Nice hat."

We rushed out of there, laughing.

# CHAPTER 18

WHEN WE PULLED UP TO HAMLET'S GRANDPARENTS'
house, I took in the suburban-ness of it all. The street was
wide, clean, and flanked by uniform Aleppo pines and streetlamps.
Everything glowed a bit pink and orange as the sun set, light
bouncing off the dramatic range of mountains behind the neatly
lined tract homes.

The San Gabriel Valley was almost as far east of LA as you
could get. Everywhere in this valley you saw the San Gabriel
Mountains, and it was probably the prettiest view in this otherwise concrete landscape.

Hamlet parked in the wide driveway. The yard and house
were tidy, the lawn brown and dead like every other lawn by July.
How had I even ended up here, at Hamlet's *grandparents'* house?

I didn't know what I was expecting on a first date with Hamlet, but it sure wasn't this.

As we headed toward the front door, Hamlet stopped to check the mail. Then he used his own set of keys to let us in. I looked at him curiously as we took off our shoes in the foyer. "You have the keys to your grandparents' place?"

He slipped off his Nikes. "Yeah, because I live with them?"

Oh.

"Hamlet! Hamlet, is that you?" A woman's voice echoed through the house, which smelled delicious. I sniffed the air. Sichuan peppers and sesame oil. And lamb?

"Yeah, I'm here!" he shouted back, then glanced at me. "I brought my friend!"

"Dinner's almost ready. Come over here!" Her voice came from around the corner and when we followed it, we landed right in the kitchen. His grandmother was at the stove, sautéing food in a large, nearly flat frying pan. She looked anywhere from fifty to seventy years old (Asian genes always hiding your true age!), small and sturdy with black hair tied in a low ponytail. She wore maroon track pants and a loose T-shirt that said STOP DRUNK DRIVING with an illustration of a cracked rearview mirror.

"Give me a small bowl," she said with her left arm extended, not even looking up at us.

Hamlet opened a cupboard and handed her a porcelain bowl. "Nainai, this is Clara."

She used the bowl as a ladle, scooping up some food in the

pan and sniffing it. "This is probably perfect." She looked at me. "Clara, try it and tell me if it's perfect."

Her English was precise, and her eyes shrewd as she watched me take the bowl. I glanced inside to see little pieces of meat with green onions and peppers. "Toothpick lamb?" I asked.

She looked impressed. "Yes, good job." She looked me up and down. "But you're not Chinese. Korean?"

I nodded before picking up a piece of perfectly charred lamb and popping it into my mouth. The taste of cumin and peppers instantly hit. *Mmmm.* After I finished chewing, I said, "Yes, I am. Well, my grandparents are from there. My parents grew up in Brazil."

She waved her hand in the air. "That's nice. How's the lamb?"

"So good!" I gave her a thumbs-up. "And I've had the lamb at Sichuan Dreams."

"Pft. That place sucks."

I choked. Hamlet ran across the kitchen to grab me a glass of water. I gulped it gratefully. "Sichuan Dreams doesn't suck!" I gasped. "Beloved food critic Stephen Fitch loves it, and everyone says it's the most authentic Sichuan in the city."

"Are those people *from* the Sichuan province? Because guess what, my family *is*!" She put her hands on her little hips and glared at me.

I frowned. "Well, it's *still good*."

"Clara, did your Brazilian parents not teach you to respect your elders?"

Hamlet swiveled toward her. "Oh my God. *Nainai.*"

166

She waved her hand at him dismissively. "This one's tough, she doesn't care."

I shrugged. "It's true. But also, my dad taught me to stick up for what I believe in. And I believe in Sichuan Dreams."

Hamlet's grandma rolled her eyes dramatically, turning back toward the stove. "Give me a break, that's the problem with you American kids. You think all your opinions matter. So annoying."

I laughed. "We *are* annoying." When I glanced over at Hamlet to see if he agreed, he was staring at me. A small smile hovering over his lips, eyes focused on me and only me.

Was it just me, or was this kitchen getting a bit too warm?

He glanced over at his grandmother then. "Whatever, Nai-nai. You're American, too. She was born here," he said to me.

"You think being born here seventy years ago is the same as being born here sixteen years ago, child? Stop bothering me and go check on Yeye. He wants to clean out the rain gutters with that back and those knees. Rain gutters in *July!*" She poked Hamlet with a long-handled wooden spoon. "Anyway, go tell him a story or something. He needs to rest if it kills him."

I was still giggling when I followed Hamlet upstairs. His grandfather was lying down in a spacious bedroom with high ceilings and sliding doors leading to a balcony. It was sparsely furnished, with a luxurious Persian rug and two large Chinese landscape paintings.

He was playing video games in bed when we walked in. On a huge TV that could be seen from space.

"Hi, Yeye." Hamlet bounded into the room and flopped down on the bed, making his grandfather groan and pause his game with a little *beep-boop* sound. "I brought my friend Clara to hang out."

His grandfather looked up at me with a smile. "Hi, Clara. Fun first date, huh?" Unlike Hamlet's grandma, his English was slightly accented. "Sorry you were forced to come here *unnecessarily*. I know Hamlet was looking forward to this."

Hamlet kept his eyes on his grandpa, his face a mask of *keep cool*. "Anyway. Why are you insisting on cleaning rain gutters? Nainai's about to put a tracker on you."

"You know I like to drive her crazy," he said with a wink.

Were Hamlet's grandparents *me*?

He continued, sitting up straighter. "It's not like I'm dying. Our rain gutters are *packed*. What if we have a summer rain?"

There was a second of silence before we all cracked up. Summer rain was simply not a thing here.

Hamlet and I chatted with his grandfather for a bit, then got pulled into playing a really creepy video game. It was so scary that I eventually crawled onto the bed next to Hamlet, making for some tight quarters. My knee brushed against his, and we sprang apart.

At one point Hamlet's grandma hollered at us to come down for dinner. The table was laid out with a platter of that yummy toothpick lamb (given that name because each little piece had a toothpick poked into it for easy eating), bowls of rice, a dark red soup with dumplings, and a pile of steamed pea shoots.

Needless to say, I ate a lot. His grandparents were hilarious—bickering nonstop while placing food on each other's plates. His grandpa even brushed a strand of hair out of his grandmother's face, gently and with such love, before launching into a complaint about the dumplings in the soup being too cold.

I sat next to Hamlet, but barely talked to him as I shoveled seconds, then thirds, into my mouth.

"I'm impressed by your appetite!" Hamlet's grandmother exclaimed at the end of the meal, nodding toward my absolutely pristine plate.

I looked down, a little sheepish. "I love to eat."

"Good," she said, getting up to clear our dishes. Her approval pleased me.

Hamlet jumped up from the table to take them from her. "Here, we'll do that. You guys go watch a show and relax."

"Thank you so much, everything was delicious. I'll have to share your lamb recipe with my dad," I said as I carried the dishes over to the sink.

"She never shares her recipes! Greedy," Hamlet's grandpa said with a belch.

Hamlet froze next to me at the sink so I whispered, "My dad and I have burp contests."

The chair scraped loudly against the linoleum floor when his grandpa stood up. "You're going to make your date do dishes?"

I held up a hand, already soapy. "He also said I'd have to do your laundry tonight, so . . ."

Both his grandparents cackled all the way to the family room.

"She's funny," Hamlet's grandpa declared, and I flushed with pleasure. The words to my heart.

Hamlet and I stood side by side washing the dishes, me scrubbing and Hamlet rinsing then drying.

"So, we have a dishwasher, but we never use it," he said at one point, gesturing toward it.

I nodded. "Let me guess, you use it as a dish rack?"

"Yes! I thought it was a Chinese thing?"

"It is very much a non-American thing. My dad still inspects every dish afterward, like he's trying to 'catch it' not working right."

He laughed. "Your dad's the best."

"I guess," I said, handing him a glass. "Your grandparents are pretty cool, too."

"You're probably wondering why I live with them."

I scratched my face with a soapy hand. "Oh, um, yeah, that did occur to me."

"My parents moved back to Beijing because their business was growing so much. That was a couple years ago. So now I live with these guys." He lifted his chin toward the living room. "Who aren't my real grandparents."

I looked at him. "What do you mean?"

"I mean, they're my parents' friends' parents. So, family friends, essentially."

Hm. I turned the water on a little more forcefully. "Oh, okay."

"I know that sounds weird to you. But my parents wanted me to stay here for my schooling."

"Oh, okay." It made me a little sad then, how he was working an entire summer tossing a sign up into the air, separated from his family. Driving a Lexus because his parents thought maybe that made up for the fact that they lived in separate countries.

With the last dish washed, I shut the water off. My hands were wet, but I couldn't find a dry towel.

"Here." Hamlet took one of my hands and then pulled up the bottom of his shirt to wipe it off. Then he took the other and dried that one, too.

What an incredibly sexy thing to do for a dork.

"Thank you," I muttered as I looked around at anywhere but his abs.

"You're welcome." Shirt was properly placed back in its usual position, and I felt a sharp sense of loss. RIP view of abs. "My grandparents *are* super cool, though. They're both retired NASA scientists and have lived here forever!"

I raised my eyebrows. "Wow, really? They do seem Americanized."

"Well, Nainai's from San Francisco. You know, her family's been here since like the gold-rush days."

"What!" I glanced at her small figure, hunched over as she cut pears in the living room. "That's so cool."

"Yup," he said. "And she met Yeye at Berkeley. He was there from China studying physics. After Yeye became a US citizen they moved here to work at JPL together."

JPL was the Jet Propulsion Laboratory in Pasadena. "Wow,

nerd love. That's pretty sweet," I said. I watched his grandparents sit back in their matching recliners as they started *Law & Order*.

"Yeah, it is," he said with a little smile. "Hey! Speaking of sweet, do you want to get *the best shaved ice ever*?"

I smiled. His enthusiasm was so contagious. "Sure."

We said bye to his grandparents, who sent me home with Tupperware containers full of leftovers. I was excited for my dad to taste the toothpick lamb. They waved us off from the front door.

"So, what would you pick for music, then?" Hamlet asked as we started driving.

I picked up my phone. "May I?"

He nodded, and I connected to his Bluetooth speakers. I scrolled through my music until I found what I was looking for. Some dreamy guitar and mellow electronic beats—it was a perfect match for the warm summer air whipping through the car.

I asked, "So, what's this shaved ice we're getting? Patbingsoo?" It was my favorite—Korean shaved ice topped with red beans and fruit.

"No, the Taiwanese kind, there's that new place . . . from Taipei?"

"I know that one. I've always wanted to try it!" I said with my hand out the window, feeling the wind hit my palm. Hamlet's enthusiasm *was* contagious, but also Asian desserts were my weakness.

We drove through the practically empty, wide streets of San

Gabriel, zooming by old 1960s diners-turned-Hanoi-chicken-spots and endless strip malls designed in faux Mediterranean style, landscaped with spindly palm trees. Hamlet pulled into one of the strip-mall parking lots, and we walked up to a small shop with neon lights that spelled out SNOW DAZE. There were people out the door for it.

"Whoa, busy," I said, looking around. "I didn't know the SGV had a nightlife."

He tucked his hands into his shorts pockets and puffed out his chest. "Well, a lot of us are Asian, and you know we stay up late."

I grinned. "True." People trekked here from all over LA to get the most authentic Chinese food because of the growing Chinese population in the area. There were so many regional specialties here that you couldn't get anywhere else outside of China—from northern Chinese Islamic dishes to brain-numbing Sichuan to Taiwanese desserts.

"Do you sleep before midnight? Like, ever?" Hamlet asked.

"Literally never."

He bounced from one foot to the other—I would have thought he had to go pee, except that he was doing it in this jockish way that I'd often seen him do at the office park. "Yeah, even when I had morning sparring last year, I managed to go to sleep at one a.m. every single night. Drives Nainai crazy."

"I feel you on everything but the physical activity part." My phone buzzed, and I looked down at it, surprised. I'd forgotten to check it all night.

**How's it going???** 🌚 Rose.

**We had dinner with his grandparents**

**WHAT?**

Hamlet was looking at me with that polite but kind of annoyed expression people make when you pull out your phone mid-hangout. I dropped my phone back into my purse and made a mental note to text her later. "It's Rose."

"Oh cool! Are you guys best friends?"

What a question. "Best friends. Er." I swished the skirt of my dress around a bit. "We don't actually know each other that well. We only started hanging out because of the KoBra." Our fraught history could be explained another day.

We moved forward in line so that we were standing inside the brightly lit shop. The walls were white and light blue, painted with cartoon foxes who were wearing scarves and making snowmen. A strange juxtaposition with everyone wearing shorts and flip-flops.

"So, if Rose isn't your best friend, who do you hang with at school?" Hamlet asked.

I surveyed the toppings. Mm, taro. "A few friends. These guys Felix and Patrick."

"Oh. Cool. You hang out with guys? That's awesome."

Hamlet was also studying the toppings, as if his life depended on it. I smiled. "They're just my friends. Felix has a girlfriend, and Patrick's gay."

His expression brightened considerably. "Oh, that's cool. I didn't think anything of it."

"If you say so." I admit, jealous Hamlet was kind of cute. Only because it was still the nicest, least gross male-possessive jealousy I had ever witnessed.

We ordered our shaved ice, which was served in huge tubs. Mine was flavored with cranberry syrup and topped with red bean, taro, and sesame balls. Hamlet's was plain with grass jelly. I made a face at it. "So healthy."

He shrugged. "I like it!" Then happily ate a spoonful. I got the feeling Hamlet never did anything if it wasn't out of a genuine desire to do it. Unlike most of the guys I had dated in the past, he was completely devoid of pretense.

"So who do *you* hang out with at school? A bunch of hot girls?" I asked as we sat down on the curb outside.

He guffawed. "Yeah, right. All guys. Mostly my D and D—" He stopped talking. "Um, these guys who I like to play basketball with."

"That's *not* what you were about to say."

"It was!"

I pointed my plastic spoon at him. "Dude, I know what Dungeons and Dragons is. Patrick and Felix used to be obsessed with it."

He laughed. "Okay, fine! Yeah, I mostly hang out with the D and D crew. They were the only ones who wanted to be friends with me when I first moved here. We've stuck together since."

"Were kids *mean* to you?" I asked, surprised. How anyone could be mean to Hamlet was beyond me. Did they also enjoy kicking bunny rabbits?

He shrugged. "Not exactly. But the Chinese American kids didn't connect with me; they had no interest in a FOB."

*Fresh off the boat.* A protective instinct came over me. Imagining Hamlet isolated in a totally different country made me want to walk over to his school and wreak some havoc.

"You're frowning." Hamlet interrupted my detailed revenge fantasy.

"Oh, sorry. Just . . . annoyed for you," I admitted.

His eyes met mine over his cup. "That's nice of you."

I tucked my hair behind my ear, to have something to do while he looked at me like that. "I'm just being a decent human." Hamlet had a way of making me self-conscious—at the earnestness of this conversation, at how much I found myself having to say.

But I was with King Earnest. And King Earnest was licking the ice dripping off the side of his cup, being meticulous and hot at the same time. I tore my eyes away. *Yeesh.*

"Yeah, you're decent," he said with a smile, teasing me.

I flushed but a thought suddenly occurred to me. "Are you going to go back to China after you go to college here?"

He scraped up the last of the shaved ice in his cup. "I don't know. I like America! A lot. But I also miss a lot of things back home. I don't know if I'll ever feel fully American like you guys who were born here."

A car's headlights beamed directly into my eyes, and I turned away from them, leaning in closer to Hamlet. "I get that. My dad's kind of like you . . . he's pretty Americanized now, but he also has mad Brazil and Korea pride."

"Who does he root for during the World Cup?" Hamlet asked, serious as he leaned in toward me, too. Our foreheads were almost touching.

"Oh! In this order: Korea, Brazil, then the US."

Hamlet pulled back and laughed. "That's what I thought."

I finished my shaved ice, and Hamlet took my empty cup and spoon to toss into the recycle bin. That gesture, these little things Hamlet did—they really got to me. So much so that when he walked back to me, I reached for his hand. He looked down at me in surprise as I slipped my fingers through his. The warm air blew through the parking lot, stirring up litter and dust, and we stood there for a second in the glow of neon signs. Everything felt right. I squeezed his hand. "Ready?"

We headed to his car, his steps buoyant as he kept my hand firmly clasped into his. "Thanks for the nice talk," he said, unlocking the car.

I let go of his hand, reluctantly, and smiled. "You're welcome?"

He opened my door, and when I slid into the seat, he leaned over, his arm draped on top of the door. "I just want to know everything about you." Astonished, I didn't answer, and he closed the door before I could react.

When Hamlet pulled up to the front of my apartment building, I hesitated in my seat, wondering if we should hug or something. But he put the car in Park and walked over to my side, opening the door. The little things.

"Thanks." We walked across the crunchy lawn, past the jasmine hedge. I could smell the fragrant jasmine blooms as we climbed up the stairs.

We reached my door, and I paused, the bag of leftovers bonking my leg. "Thanks for the ride and letting me meet your grandparents."

The corners of his eyes did that crinkly thing as he smiled. "Yeah, that's a rare privilege for only the most special of dates." His hands were in his pockets again. Everything about him right now was shy and unsure.

But I was sure about one thing. I wanted Hamlet Wong to kiss me.

"Have a good night, Clara." His voice was quiet. Low and sweet and real.

I glanced up from his hands to his face. That expressive, open face. "Good night," I replied.

He took a step backward but kept looking at me expectantly, as if he was waiting for me to go inside.

So I dropped the bag of food, took a step forward, and tugged him by his shirt until our hips bumped. "I want to kiss you. Is that okay?" I asked, my face tilted up toward his.

His eyes widened and his lips parted slightly. Then he placed a warm hand on my waist. "Okay," he murmured.

I got up on my tippy-toes to reach his lips, and brushed them over his. My eyes closed, I took in the scent of him—grass jelly.

His lips were soft, but they were quick to meet mine. He drew me in closer until our bodies were pressed against each other, one of my hands still clutching his shirt, the other wrapped around his neck, curled into his hair.

When we pulled apart, the blood rushed from my head into my toes.

Hamlet looked stunned. And adorable—his hair mussed and shirt wrinkled.

"Good night, for reals," I said as I grabbed the leftovers bag and unlocked my door.

I caught a glimpse of his face before I closed the door. Pink cheeks and a huge smile. "Good night!" he shouted.

"Oh my God!" I closed the door with a smile. It stayed on my face until I fell asleep that night.

# CHAPTER 19

A PERSISTENT KNOCKING WOKE ME UP THE NEXT morning.

"*What?*" I yelled from under my blanket.

"I'm coming in!" my dad said before opening the door a crack. "Are you decent?"

"No, I'm in my lace negligee," I muttered. "Since when do you care if I'm 'decent'?"

My dad stepped inside. "I don't know, you were on a date last night so . . ."

I moved the blanket off my face. "Are you implying that Hamlet might have *slept over*?"

He shrugged as he leaned against the doorway.

"Okay, I'm not *you* in high school, so . . ." I sputtered.

"Burn, Shorty," he said with a laugh. "So, how was it?"

"Pai. Seriously?"

"What!"

"I don't wanna talk to you about my date!"

"Ooh, so it *was* a *date* date. So there's something to *talk about*."

I buried myself in my blanket again. "CAN WE NOT?"

"So it went well?"

Suddenly the memory of last night's kiss came flooding back. Night air laced with jasmine. The glow of the apartment lights throwing half of Hamlet's face into shadow. The taste of grass jelly. I giggled involuntarily.

My dad gaped at me. "Whoa."

"Can you *leave*?" I yelled, tossing my stuffed sriracha bottle pillow at him.

He caught it swiftly. "All right, all right. Have a good day, Shorty."

I dragged myself out of bed to give him a hug. "You too."

He made a face. "Get out of here, Morning Breath."

"*You* get out!" I pushed him to the door.


"Clara, can you slather me?"

I squinted up at Patrick. "Can you not say 'slather,' though?"

He handed me a giant bottle of generic brand sunblock. "That's what it is. Would you rather I say 'rub'?"

I got up and tugged on my baseball cap and sunglasses. "I'd rather not have to do this task." Patrick turned his freckled and bony back to me. His shoulder blades were sharp and delicate like bird wings.

The community pool was unusually crowded today. It was in the high nineties and scorching hot on the concrete. We had spread out layers of towels, but the heat still managed to seep through and I got the distinct feeling that, from space, we looked like little rotisserie hens gathered around a blue rectangle.

"Babe! Get in the water!" Felix shouted from the edge of the pool.

Cynthia made a face from under her giant umbrella. She had alabaster skin that turned into a third-degree burn upon contact with the sun. Between that and her inability to walk more than half a mile without complaining, I was pretty sure she was meant to live in a Victorian attic.

"I just showered this morning," she said with a sniff.

"So did I—who cares?" Felix said, exasperated.

After I finished smearing sunblock on Patrick, I put in my earbuds to avoid hearing the inevitable testy couple fight ahead.

When I swiped my screen to pick my music, I noticed a few missed texts.

**Want to come over and hang out by the pool?** Rose.

And then Hamlet:

**I had fun last night. Hope you did, too.**

**What are you doing today?**

**I have the day off, too!**

Didn't even give me a chance to answer any questions. His texts were as enthusiastic and rapid-fire as real-life Hamlet.

I looked around at the kids screaming in the pool as sweat and sunblock mingled together in one delightful skin soup. Heard Felix and Cynthia shouting at each other. Saw Patrick already dozing off next to me.

Guilt about ditching these guys chipped away at me with each word I texted.

To Rose: **Yeah sounds cool. Could I invite Hamlet?**

She replied: **O M G I'm gonna need the dirt later.**

I sent her a thumbs-up emoji. Then I texted Hamlet: **Hi. I had fun too . . . I'm going to Rose's place to hang out at her pool. Want to come with?**

**COOL! Yes! For sure! And I just had practice in Chinatown, so I can be there like NOW.**

I let out a bark of laughter at his enthusiasm and woke Patrick up.

"What's up?" Patrick asked from his face-planted position as I typed away furiously on my phone, figuring out logistics with Rose and Hamlet.

I considered asking these guys if they wanted to come, but I couldn't imagine all of us hanging out. Talk about motley.

"Gonna head home. Getting too much sun, I think."

"Are you serious? We haven't hung out in weeks."

Stuffing my towel and book back into my tote, I frowned. "That's not true. I hung out with you guys a few days ago, at Taco Bell."

"Oh. Well, it's just hard to see you lately, that's all."

He was right. Not only was I busy with the KoBra, but I didn't feel like spending all my free time with them anymore. The fact that I was ditching them to hang out with *Rose* would be considered totally bizarre. Because what they knew about Rose was so limited and wrong. I should know, because that's what I used to know about her, too. And now, well. I found myself wanting to hang out with her more and more each day. "I'll see you guys soon, though. Text me this Thursday when it's my day off, okay?"

He grunted in reply, his eyes already fluttering closed.


Hamlet picked me up at the pool, and we drove toward Rose's house up in the hills, a historic neighborhood filled with old Craftsman houses.

"This place is so cool!" Hamlet exclaimed as we drove up the hilly streets. "I never knew it existed."

"That happens to me all the time, and I was *born* here," I said as we pulled up to Rose's house, which had a huge porch, giant pine trees shading the property, and pretty bright green trim against the dark wood.

We were walking up the driveway when Hamlet stopped abruptly in his tracks.

"What's up?" I asked.

His eyes were hidden behind sunglasses, so I couldn't read his expression right away. "So, I don't want to be awkward, but the thing is, I've never had a girlfriend before."

I stood there, feeling the heat rise off the concrete in warm waves onto my bare legs. How did we go from first date to girlfriend talk? I kind of felt like I was being cooked alive. "Girlfriend?" The question squeaked out of me.

He stuck his hands into his shorts pockets and then took them out. Then put them back in again. "Yeah. What I'm saying is, I'm not sure how this works?"

Hm. I fanned myself with my hand. "Well, uh, we don't have to put a label on it or anything . . ."

"Oh. Okay. So you don't want to date *just* me?" He was smiling, but I could hear the hurt.

"No, I didn't say that," I said in a rush. Wait, did I want to date other people? Did I want to be *exclusive* with Hamlet?

Maybe. I wasn't sure. I just knew that the way he was looking at me right now was special, and I couldn't really handle the idea of him looking at anyone else that way.

I walked up to him and poked his arm. "I like you."

His smile transformed from forced to genuine, and I felt the wall of emotional defense so carefully constructed inside me start to chip away. "I like you, too," he said before poking me back.

"Okay then," I said, returning the smile. "Can we start from there?" Would he be all right with this? Something about Hamlet destabilized my usual assurance, which was built on my willingness to walk away. That willingness gave you power. With Hamlet, I wasn't sure if I could walk away.

And to my relief, he said, "Sure." Then he pulled me in quickly and kissed me on the tip of my nose. "Sorry, I've been distracted by your cute nose the entire car ride."

*Oof.* My heart fluttered as we walked up to Rose's front door.

She answered the door before we even knocked, wearing a long, gauzy, floral-pattern dress over a bathing suit. "Took you guys long enough to make it up the driveway."

Hamlet's telltale flush crept up his neck again, and I reached out for his hand instinctively. Rose glanced down at our clasped hands and smiled. "Well, well, *well*!"

I slipped past her, pulling Hamlet in behind me. "Calm down."

She closed the door. "I am calm. I'm so calm that I'm a clam."

Hamlet laughed, and I looked at him. "Are you going to encourage that kind of joke?"

"It's funny," he insisted.

I pointed at Rose and said, "Don't get excited. He thinks everything I say is funny."

We stood in her living room, which was bright and sunny—big windows; white walls; and soft, neutral-colored furniture set against gleaming hardwood floors. There was art everywhere, from oversize paintings with abstract shapes and bright color to little watercolors in delicate gold frames.

"Wow, your house looks like Pinterest," said Hamlet.

Rose laughed as she handed us towels. "Thanks, I think? That'll make my mom happy."

She led us out of the living room into the kitchen, which had a big open floor plan and more windows. You could see the pool from in here, sparkling and surrounded by colorful chairs and lush native landscaping. "My dad works from home nowadays, so he's upstairs. FYI, in case you guys were planning on doing it in the pool."

"Are you ten years old?" I screeched while Hamlet chuckled nervously. The words "doing it" being said with both of us so fresh in our dating made me feel queasy. I glanced at Hamlet to make sure he hadn't fainted. He was just the color of a tomato, was all.

My usual pool time consisted of dozing off and reading gossip rags, but with Rose and Hamlet, they wanted to be *in* the pool. Playing games.

"Marco Polo? Are you serious?" I asked as I stood in the shallow end, on my tippy-toes to prevent the water from touching my torso.

"Yes! And also, it's ninety degrees out, are you actually *cold*?" Rose asked, treading water in the deep end.

"This water is *freezing*!" I protested.

Hamlet swam over (shirtless Hamlet was always . . . well . . . just *well*) and stood up so that he was directly in front of me. Water poured off his shoulders, and I was so distracted that I didn't even pay attention when he said, "Sorry about this." A second later, he had hoisted me under the arms and dragged me out into the deeper part of the pool so that my body was now completely submerged.

I screeched, like a total wuss. But after three seconds, the water was warm and I stopped flailing.

"You are such a baby," Rose scoffed before dipping under the water to do a little backflip, as if to highlight the difference between us.

Hamlet kept one hand supporting my back. My bare back. "You good?" he asked.

I nodded. "Yeah." Then I touched his hip underwater, grazing it gently with my fingers. His eyes met mine, and this time his smile was slow.

"EH-HEM!" Rose splashed us.

We played Marco Polo with Hamlet as the seeker first. I hadn't played since I was a kid, and it was hard to get into at the start. I tried to escape out of the pool a few times, but Rose dragged me back in. She was about one thousand times stronger than me in every way. But when Hamlet, as Marco, found me and grasped my shoulder, I screamed and felt that very real competitive thrill. After that, it was *game on*.

By the time our third round was finished, we were starving so we padded into Rose's kitchen, dripping water on the tile floor. Rose pulled out cans of sparkling water, fruit, and cheese. "Admit it, you had fun, Clara."

I grabbed an apple and bit into it. "It wasn't the worst."

Hamlet immediately went into helpful mode, pulling out a cutting board and knife to start slicing apples and pears. This pleased me. One of my pet peeves was people standing around asking, "Can I help?" when they were secretly hoping they could just watch TV in the other room. Like those bums Felix and Patrick.

Rose and Hamlet, on the other hand, were a flurry of activity. I joined them, grabbing some glasses and ice for the drinks.

"Clara, have you told Hamlet about the food truck competition?" Rose asked as she sliced a large hunk of cheese.

The sparkling water hissed as it hit the ice. "I'm not sure . . ."

"No, you haven't! What is it?" he asked, his eyes on the fruit, careful in his deft and precise chopping.

"There's a big food truck competition in August with a *one hundred thousand dollar* prize," I answered.

His hand stilled as he looked up at me. "What?"

"I know, right?" Rose said. "So Clara, did you actually enter us?"

"Yup."

Hamlet was so excited he abandoned his fruit and walked over to me. "This is so so cool. Adrian hadn't mentioned it to me!"

Rose and I glanced at each other. I bit my lip. "Well, that's because he doesn't know."

"Whoa, why not?" Hamlet asked, his voice immediately dropping an octave.

I took a sip of one of the drinks. "Because I want it to be a surprise! Plus, I don't want him to stress. Worry about losing, you know?"

Rose said, "Well, I mean, there's a chance you can lose when you do anything. He's an adult. I'm sure he could handle the pressure."

I exhaled in irritation. "It's hard to explain to overachievers like you guys. Some people don't have confidence running through their veins since birth."

Rose frowned. "Yeah, that must be it. Not a highly effective combination of hard work and growing tough to failure."

I stared at her. "Are you saying my dad doesn't work hard?"

"No! I'm just saying that people who are 'fearless' have actually just failed a lot. It's not some preternatural characteristic I was born with." She looked for validation to Hamlet, who hesitated before nodding in agreement. "To me, that totally undermines all the work I've done to build this confidence."

Normally this kind of lecture from Rose would have annoyed me—having to be so serious about everything. But I had to admit that I had grown to care about the truck and wanted to succeed in this one thing, too. And was willing to take that risk of failing for once. Ugh, had Rose Carver's can-do-itness rubbed off on me?

I held up my hands. "Okay, okay. Remind me to never call you confident again."

A deep voice interrupted us. "Well, if it isn't a bunch of hardworking teenagers in the service industry!" Rose's dad walked in with a grin. He was wearing a blue T-shirt, jeans, and glasses, his imposing height instantly filling up the sprawling kitchen.

"Hey, Dad," Rose said with an embarrassed giggle. He gave her a kiss on the top of her head, then walked to the island and peered over Hamlet's shoulder. "Ooh, pears." He grabbed a slice, then looked at Hamlet. "Who are *you*?"

"Dad!" Rose exclaimed. "That is so rude."

"What! I'm being straightforward." His eyes twinkled with

humor before he turned toward Hamlet again. "I'm Jon, Rose's dad, in case you couldn't tell by her embarrassment."

Hamlet wiped his hands on his shorts. Which were damp. He didn't seem to notice, as he held out his hand to shake Jon's. "Hi! I'm Hamlet. I'm Clara's boyfriend."

The ice tray I was holding fell onto the counter. Rose gaped at Hamlet then at me. "What! ALREADY? You had *one date*!"

I took a deep breath. Dating Hamlet Wong was going to be a freaking trial for my chill.

# CHAPTER 20

HAMLET WAS A FORCE TO BE RECKONED WITH. FOR THE next couple of weeks, he leveled all my normal boy barriers—texting me about everything (from making plans to sea otter gifs), showing up at the truck, and inviting himself to meals with my dad and me. That arm's length I required with boys was shrunk down to a millimeter.

Normally, I would have seen this as obnoxious behavior. In fact, I should have been running for the hills.

But no one had ever blown through my defenses like this. In my other relationships, I'd always had the upper hand. Even the most macho and controlling of dudes had never managed to push me out of my comfort zone. The only person on planet Earth who could get away with it was Hamlet. Because with him it wasn't entitled or pushy—it was just . . . Hamlet. Earnest and genuine in his interest in me.

That's how I found myself walking across a hot parking lot to the Chinatown gym where Hamlet boxed on Saturday mornings. It was a large space in an old warehouse—all concrete and sweat. The bay doors were open, and Hamlet was directly in my line of vision. Punching a heavy bag, his strong shoulders swinging, an intense expression of concentration on his face.

My thirst for Hamlet came in waves. And right now, it was a straight-up tsunami. Why was I so attracted to him in this state? I tried to override the archaic sexist wiring in my brain. The second he saw me, he stopped moving and grinned, the bag narrowly missing his face as it came swinging back at him.

"Hi." I pushed the black bag with the tip of one finger.

He leaned over, his thin cotton shirt stuck to him with sweat, and gave me a quick kiss on the cheek. "Hi." His lips hovered by my jaw, and I felt the hairs on my neck stand on end. "I'm just gonna take a quick shower, and I'll meet you outside?"

"Sure," I said, acting cool and feeling hot. I skirted the piles of shoes and boxing gloves as I left the gym and sat down on the hood of Hamlet's car, which was parked in the shade of an oak tree. A few minutes later he came out, shouldering his gym bag, hair damp and clothes crisp and sparkling clean.

"Ready for tacos?" he asked as he pulled on his sunglasses and stood in front of me.

I hooked my legs around his. "Always." Some whoops and hollers came out of the gym, and he blushed.

"All right, that's our cue to leave." He reached for my hand to help me down from the hood.

Hamlet and I were going to do a "taco walko," a walking tour of eastside taco trucks patented by my dad and me. Hamlet had admitted to Chipotle being his Mexican restaurant of choice and, when I'd finally recovered, I made a plan to remedy that.

At our third truck in Echo Park, he was shoveling a monstrous carnitas taco into his mouth and I was trying to capture it on my camera when a text from Rose popped up.

**Hey, do you have plans today?**

**Taco walko hellloooo**

**Oh, whoops. Ok, nevermind!**

I stared at the text for a second before texting back: **Why what's up**

**Oh, nothing, no big deal.**

Something about that nagged at me while Hamlet and I finished up our tacos.

"Who's texting you?" he asked as we dumped our greasy paper plates into the trash.

Hamlet had the ability to tell when I was agitated even when I was silent. Something that probably made his life really pleasant.

"Rose. I think she wants to hang out," I said apologetically.

He took out a little Wet-Nap from his wallet and handed it to me. "Cool, tell her to meet us for the movie tonight."

I took the Wet-Nap with nary a smart-ass remark. Hamlet's pockets were like a mom's purse. "Are you sure?"

"Sure, I'm sure. Unless you don't want to? I don't really

understand how close you guys actually are." He wiped his fingers off fastidiously with the Wet-Nap.

Good observation. I wasn't so sure either. Our friendship was so, for lack of a better word, organic. I shrugged. "Well, we're friends. And I don't hate hanging out with her."

Hamlet laughed. "That's Clara-speak for 'I like her.'"

I flushed because it was true and said, "Well, then let's invite her. Watching a movie in a cemetery will creep her out!"

**We're going to watch The Exorcist at Hollywood Forever wanna come?**

**Not how I thought I'd spend my birthday, but why not!**

Birthday! "Hamlet, it's her *birthday* today!"

His entire face lit up—he was Christmas Day and Disneyland all rolled into one. "Her *birthday*? I'm so glad we invited her then! We have to prepare!"

I pulled my dad's black Dodgers cap down lower over my head, avoiding the sun. "All right, calm down. Let me respond to her first."

I wished her happy birthday with some dumb bitmojis that were sure to infuriate her, then told her where to meet us.

A few minutes later, Hamlet and I were in a dollar store ransacking the aisles for the worst possible party favors.

I held up a tiara with tiny baby bottles attached. "What in God's name do you think this is for?"

Hamlet tilted his head, which was currently wearing a pink cowboy hat. "I have this *wild* suspicion that it's related to princess baby showers."

"What is wrong with people?" I put it back on the rack, frowning.

"We need to get this," Hamlet announced, holding up a SpongeBob piñata.

"What about SpongeBob SquarePants screams Rose to you? I am really curious."

He shrugged. "It doesn't. That's why it's funny?"

I laughed. "Actually, that's a good idea except we can't really do piñata stuff at the cemetery." We were headed to Hollywood Forever, an old cemetery where a bunch of golden-age movie stars were buried, like Judy Garland. Every summer they showed movies—their whole motto was "Watch the stars under and OVER the stars." Pretty messed up. And rad. Hamlet had never been before and neither had Rose, and I was excited to share it with them. That's the thing about having new friends—everything you like and do feels fresh again.

Again, I felt a flash of guilt for not inviting Felix and Patrick. Hollywood Forever was usually our thing. But I knew it would be awkward, and I didn't want to worry about everyone getting along. It'd been getting harder and harder to separate my social life between the two groups. Hamlet never said anything, but I'm sure he was wondering why I hadn't introduced them to him yet. But when I told Patrick and Felix about dating Hamlet, they didn't take it seriously at all ("TO BE OR NOT TO BE!") and thought I was just working a lot.

After the dollar store, we grabbed a cake at the grocery and some sandwiches at the deli counter. The best part of the cemetery movie screenings was that you got there early, staked out a spot, and had a picnic. Hamlet didn't need to know that this would be my sixth time going with a boyfriend. Sixth different guy. And when he insisted on blasting some dated pop music in the car, I couldn't help but marvel at how different from the others he was. How I didn't care that he had kinda bad music taste. How I liked how confident and assured he was in the things he liked because he was so free of judgment himself.

He tapped his hands on the steering wheel and sang along.

"Hamlet."

"Yes?" Without tearing his eyes off the road, he slid his hand up the back of my neck, his fingers pushing into my hair.

See, one second Hamlet's singing some dorky pop song and the next he's doing sexy stuff like this, and the juxtaposition of it all really got to a person. That person being me. Only me.

Before I could truly savor the moment, my phone buzzed. A text. I wriggled a little so that Hamlet would let go of my neck. He glanced over at me with a questioning smile. I smiled back and his eyes returned to the road and he continued singing. The text was from my mom.

**Get a load of the hotel where we'll be staying in Tulum!** 🌴😀📇☀️🏢

It was accompanying a link to a hotel website. I scrolled through the photos and groaned.

"What?" Hamlet asked.

I held up my phone to him, but of course he kept his eyes on the road. "My mom just sent me a link to the resort in Tulum. It's *killer.*"

"Tulum?"

"Oh! I'm going to see my mom in Mexico next month!"

He lowered the volume of the music. "Cool, that should be fun." Hamlet knew the lowdown on my parents and, without his saying anything, I could tell he had some chilly feelings about my mom. Loyalty to my dad and all. It both annoyed and pleased me.

"I plan on flying out early enough to get back in time for the food truck contest. Best reward *ever* for my summer of the KoBra."

We turned into the parking lot for the screening, driving by the sidewalk filled with people waiting in line for the movie. Hamlet reached for the parking ticket at the entrance. "Do you really think your dad's gonna let you go since your punishment was for the *entire* summer?"

I texted my mom back with the heart-eyed emoji then slipped my phone into my pocket. "I have zero doubt in my mind. My dad always caves."

Hamlet grinned. "Well, you've got a way."

My heart flipped in my chest, and I resisted rolling my eyes at myself.

# CHAPTER 21

THE SUN WAS STARTING TO SET, AND THE SKY WAS A pale lavender and pink that I always felt was specific to a certain kind of hot day in LA—when the sun had been so brutal for hours on end that even the sky needed a minute to chill. So the sunset took its sweet time, letting the light blue fade at a lazy pace under the thick blanket of ever-present smog, and turning the sky into a palette of hazy, desaturated pastels.

It was against this backdrop that we found Rose, an elegant silhouette, waiting at the front of the line and clutching a lawn chair.

"Finally!" she exclaimed when she saw us. "It's been murder trying to hold this spot." Her eyes darted over to a group of men behind her. "Do you think they'll be pissed if you guys get in?"

I assessed them in less than half a second. Not a threat. "It's just the two of us, and you were holding a place in line. We're not *cutting*." I raised my voice, challenging the bespectacled and short-shorted to have a problem with that. None of them said a word. Sometimes teenagers really scared the crap out of hipsters. It was like their tenuous hold on "cool" was exposed around the truly young.

Hamlet hastily stepped into line, then gave Rose a bear hug. "Happy birthday!"

She smiled, a little sheepish. "Thanks. Sorry to crash your date." Both of us protested with scoffs and waving hands, and it was a bit much.

"I had no idea you'd be here like an hour early to get a spot in line," I said, poking fun to mask feeling guilty about it.

"Did you actually think I would be able to relax knowing this was a first-come first-served deal?" Rose asked, her voice harried. "I'd rather be here yesterday than have to wonder if we'd get a good spot!"

I put my hand on her shoulder and replied, "I'm sorry for your life." Then I held up a huge shopping bag. "Despite that, we have some birthday goodies for you. Get excited."

Her eyes lit up. "You didn't have to! My family already did this whole birthday extravaganza earlier."

"What's a birthday extravaganza? Americans take birthdays

so seriously," Hamlet said while reaching out for my hand. Instinctively and comfortably. There was some movement at the gate, and Rose craned her neck to check it out before responding. "Oh, we went to get crepes at my favorite brunch spot and then my mom took me shopping. Then we got home to . . ." She trailed off for a second. "To uh, watch the Rose Birthday Movie."

I stopped chewing my gum. "What? What is the *Rose Birthday Movie?*"

The line moved ahead and I handed the tickets to the agent, still looking expectantly at Rose.

"Calm down, Clara. It's just a little movie my parents make every year—they make one for my brother, too—a compilation of videos taken of me over the years."

Hamlet took Rose's unwieldy lawn chair from her, a tiny chivalrous move that would normally irritate me, but I knew Hamlet would do that for a fellow male, too. For anyone. He said, "That sounds amazing. You guys are like a TV family."

"Thanks," she said. "For holding the chair, I mean. We're not a TV family, but I know it always sounds like that."

"To be honest, I was expecting something worse," I said as I shifted the shopping bag on my shoulder. "Two points to the Carver family for not being more embarrassing. In fact, that sounds sorta great." Rose looked pleased, and I was pleased she was pleased.

We moved into the cemetery, currently the only place in the

city with lush green grass. There was a winding path that took us to our destination, lit in intervals by torches. We wove between various tombstones—some modest brass plates laid into the earth, others ostentatious sculptures made of shiny black marble, and even the occasional cherub fountain marking the final resting place of some old rich person or another.

Rose glanced around. "This is really strange, you know. Watching movies around all these dead people."

"Hey, the dead need to be entertained, too," I said.

We arrived at a big grassy lawn spread out in front of a giant wall where the movie would be projected. I beelined for a good spot in the center and tossed a couple of blankets down. People started mad-dashing around us for spots. These movie screenings were like Black Friday sales for movie buffs—sometimes I feared for my life. If I died by Converse stampede, I'd be one pissed-off ghost.

I pulled out some miniature party hats the size of shot glasses. "We have to wear these."

Rose laughed and picked a mint green one with gold glitter trim. "Yes!"

I put a purple one on Hamlet, adjusting the gold elastic behind his ears. "So handsome."

"Wait, I want to wear the pink one," he said, reaching for it in the bag. "It matches my outfit better." He was wearing an oatmeal-colored shirt flecked with pastel fibers and dark brown shorts. I was learning that Hamlet was quite the fussy dresser.

Unlike me. I gestured down at my black denim cutoffs and ratty striped tank. "Give me that one, then. Purple will be stunning on me."

Once we were properly outfitted with tiny hats, I held up party blowers. "We have to get this out of our system now, or people will kill us during the movie." After handing them to Rose and Hamlet, I blew so hard into mine that the honk echoed throughout the lawn. People threw dirty looks at us.

"You love it!" I blew again.

Rose hid her face behind her hand. "Oh my God."

Hamlet blew into his, but at a moderate volume. "I don't want to get in trouble," he said apologetically.

I blew hard again. Rose flinched and sank down into her chair, separating her entire being from me. Hamlet laughed, and I honked and hummed in rapid succession along to "Happy Birthday."

Rose sank lower and lower into her chair, but Hamlet was laughing so hard his face matched the color of his tiny pink hat.

While he was recovering, I pulled out a small cake that had Transformers toys all over it. It said "Happy Birthday, Son!" on it. This time Rose burst out laughing. "What the heck?"

Hamlet placed candles in it, methodical and thoughtful in their placement so that they complemented the tiny robots and cars and things. I took out a lighter and lit the candles. "It's not like there weren't more appropriate cakes, but we thought this one provided the most entertainment."

"Good call," she said, a grin still plastered on her face.

We sang "Happy Birthday" to her, Hamlet in a low voice, kind of embarrassed the entire time. I, of course, sang with vibrato in a volume so loud that people around us starting joining in. By the end of it, there were, like, thirty voices wishing Rose a happy birthday.

She couldn't stop smiling after she blew out the candles. "Thanks, guys."

"You're very welcome," Hamlet said, already slicing the cake expertly. He handed her a slice on a My Little Pony paper plate with a plastic fork.

Although we were sitting there eating a Transformers cake off of paper plates with colorful ponies on them, there was a conspicuous lack of irony in this moment. It was something I noticed every time I hung out with these guys because I had become so used to a certain behavior with Patrick and Felix. Where everything was a joke, a mockery, a way to separate ourselves from feeling stuff for real. It was easier not to feel the real stuff— and Patrick the slacker was all about easy. Felix, he was so preoccupied with being cool all the time. And Rose and Hamlet? I watched them set up the Connect 4 we had purchased at the dollar store and immediately throw themselves into it, competitive and serious within seconds.

They were the opposite of that. They were all in.

When the movie ended, we headed to Hamlet's car. I held his hand in one hand and a lawn chair in the other.

Rose stayed close to us as we walked down the dark paths

toward the parking lot. She glanced around the headstones nervously. "I can't believe I just watched that movie in the cemetery. I'm *never* going to fall asleep tonight."

That night, at two a.m., I texted her a gif of Linda Blair's head spinning. I could practically hear her scream from miles away.

# CHAPTER 22

THE NEXT WEEKEND, I STOOD IN FRONT OF THE FAN IN the living room, letting it cool off my face. Summer in our apartment was the pits. We only had one of those window air conditioners, and it barely kept the living room cool, let alone the whole apartment.

As we got more and more experienced with the truck, my dad let Rose and me each have some solo Sundays, since we only had one routine stop. And today, Rose was manning the KoBra. It was a rare day off together for my dad and me, and being hot and miserable was how we were spending it.

My dad was draped across the sofa like a rag doll, trying not to move. Flo hadn't left the cool porcelain of the bathtub in hours. We were like a Renaissance painting. Suddenly, my dad sprang up. "Ooh, let's get naengmyeon!" Cold Korean buckwheat noodles, often served with slushy, icy beef broth. The best and only thing to eat on a hot summer day.

My dad started to do an excited-for-food dance: pulling his cap down low and making weird, wobbly moves with his legs, while keeping his arms up at chest level.

I hated it so much that I loved it. He stopped dancing long enough to ask, "Hey, do you mind if Kody comes along?"

Yes.

But my dad's hopeful and nervous expression made me bite my tongue. And I never hung out with his girlfriends, so I knew it must be somewhat important. I plastered on a smile and said, "No, that's cool."

A half hour later, we were all piled into my dad's old rear-wheel-drive Nissan, still souped up from his racing days. You could hear us coming from a mile away. Kody had politely offered me shotgun, but my dad's quick warning glance stopped me from taking it. "No, you go ahead." I crammed myself into the tiny back seat instead, cursing her with every bump—my dad did not believe in suspension.

We pulled into a packed strip mall—storefronts crowded with neon lettering in both Korean and English, the parking lot manned by two valet guys who somehow made sense of the automobile Tetris. The icy-cold AC hit us when we opened the glass double doors into the restaurant. I shivered instantly and noticed the patrons huddled over their big metal bowls, also shivering in their shorts and tanks.

The smiling yet gruff hostess led us to our table, which was under a floating flat-screen TV playing K-pop videos. The table-tops were laid with paper place mats emblazoned with beer advertisements. "Hey, isn't this the actress you have the hots for?" I asked Pai, pointing at the dewy face on the mat, being a brat in front of his girlfriend. Maybe it was the hot day or the pressure of meeting Kody, but I couldn't stop myself.

He peered down at it. "Nah."

"Plastic surgery confuses all."

Kody laughed and I allowed myself to be pleased for .5 seconds. My dad threw the little paper packaging for the metal chopsticks at me. "Hey! Not everyone gets plastic surgery."

"Maybe not, but probably every *actress*!" This was a common argument between us. Because I was one step further removed from Korea, my dad always felt super defensive about Korean culture. I liked to tease him about it to rile him up—especially about plastic surgery.

Before my dad could answer, the server came over and asked for our orders. You had about thirty seconds to review a menu at K-Town restaurants.

"We'll get three mul naengmyeon," my dad said, pointing at the menu just in case his Korean wasn't quite up to snuff. "And one galbi." A meal with my dad was never complete unless we added *more* meat. In this case, grilled beef short ribs that would come out sizzling on a stone plate.

"Did you want to ask your *girlfriend* if that's what she wants?" I asked pointedly. Sometimes my dad could be such a dude.

He looked chastised for a second, but Kody put her hand on his arm. "Oh, it's fine. Adrian always orders at Korean places. And I order the sushi," she said with a wink at him. They exchanged this intimate look that made me wrinkle my nose involuntarily.

"You're a sushi expert?" I asked politely, taking a swig of some of the cold barley tea the server handed us.

Kody shrugged, her long brass earrings shaped like crescent moons jangling. "Kind of. I lived in Japan for a few years."

"She's fluent in Japanese!" my dad bragged.

Something about my dad's pride made my stomach clench a little. The only time he talked like that was when it was about *me*.

Our side dishes arrived—small bowls of white radish kimchi, regular cabbage kimchi, some potato salad with apple slices, and little marinated black beans. My dad and I dug into them, me going straight for the potato salad and my dad for the radish kimchi. "You can tell the quality of a Korean restaurant by its side dishes," my dad often said. Side dishes were always free, so it was impressive when a restaurant took care to make them tasty.

Kody picked up a slice of the cabbage kimchi. "So, Clara. Adrian tells me you're doing a great job on the truck."

"Yeah, we've been killing it," I said as I poked around the potato salad with my chopsticks until I found a slice of apple. I glanced at Kody. Maybe I could use her presence to my advantage. Pai might be in better spirits, or at the very least want to look nicer around her. "That reminds me, considering how well we've been doing, could I still meet Mãe in Tulum?" I opened my eyes as wide as they would go.

Pai looked at me, annoyed. "Really? You want to bring that up now?"

I had to give Kody credit, she was cool as a cucumber. We might as well have been talking about the weather, poking around the side dishes.

"Why not? I've proven my worthiness, blah blah blah."

Pai made a face. "Are you kidding me?"

Before I could answer, the server arrived with a tray holding three metal bowls of noodles, frosted over with the cold. Also on the tray was vinegar in a squeeze bottle and a little glass jar of Korean mustard. Before handing us our bowls, the server took out a pair of scissors from his apron pocket and cut the noodles— first left to right, then top to bottom.

To avoid my dad, I took the mustard and spooned a tiny dollop into the icy beef broth. If you put more than that, there was the danger of lighting your entire brain on fire. Then I squeezed a healthy amount of vinegar in and mixed everything around with my chopsticks. We were silent for a few minutes as we dug into our food, and when the plate of sizzling galbi arrived we attacked that too without speaking. For all my chattiness, I had been taught to respect good food and give it my full attention. When I was able to catch my breath after inhaling my noodles, I looked up at my dad. "I think I've proven myself. It only seems fair to let me go."

Kody slurped her noodles.

Pai put his chopsticks down. "That's the problem, Shorty. You were supposed to learn something from this—not just get it over with to meet your mom at some resort."

I couldn't believe it. He wanted to give me a lecture right now, in front of Kody. Who finally looked uncomfortable, by the way—picking up the bowl to take a sip of the soup so that her face was obscured from us. "I *did* learn something!"

"Oh yeah? What?"

Why was he being such a jerk right now? His combative tone immediately put me on the defensive. "I learned how to make a stupid pastel."

Pai was silent, his clean-shaven jaw clenched, his body very still. Kody moved toward him, and he immediately relaxed. Watching this interaction made me want to throw my bowl of noodles at them. Why did they suddenly feel so close together and me so far away? The table between us felt like an ocean.

He eventually spoke. "Yeah. So no, you're not going to Tulum."

*"Pai!"* The whine came out before I could stop it.

Leaning forward, Pai pointed a chopstick at me. "It's not just because you're being a little butthole right now. It's because your mom has *nothing* planned. Did she already book your flight? Because it would be really expensive this late in the game. No, she wouldn't even think about that. She has no concept of money or responsibility."

My face burned. Pai's feelings about my mom weren't a surprise, but I didn't want to hear them laid out in front of Kody, of all people. Suddenly I hated everything about her—starting with her shaggy haircut and ending with her on-trend black clogs.

"We didn't *plan* anything because you've been a total drag all summer, and I haven't had a *minute*," I said, keeping my voice low but feeling my anger build.

Kody paled, and my dad pushed himself away from the table. "I'm getting the check."

The ride home was silent, and as soon as we parked, I muttered a good-bye to Kody, jumped out of the car, and ran up the stairs to the apartment. When I got to my room, I pulled my curtains aside and watched Kody hug my dad good-bye and then get into her own car. The need to talk to my mom was overwhelming. When I called her, it went to her voice mail. I didn't do voice mail, so I texted her.

**Pai is a hard NOPE on Tulum**

I paced the room as I waited for her response. Minutes went by, the phone slippery in my sweaty palm. Phantom vibrations kept me checking it for a response.

Eventually my dad knocked on my door. "Clara."

I ignored him.

Another knock. "Open the door."

Dragging myself over to the door, I took a deep breath before opening it. "What?" I didn't look him in the eye.

He made a face. "Excuse me? You think you can be rude to *me* right now?"

"Why not? You were rude earlier!"

He raked a hand through his hair, agitated. "I'm sorry I called you a butthole."

"In front of Kody."

"Yes, in front of Kody."

"Butthole is reserved for family fights only."

He laughed, quick and low. "Yes, butthole is reserved for family."

I pulled at a piece of splintering wood in the doorjamb. "And I didn't like you talking crap about Mãe in front of her, either."

"Understood." He crossed his arms over his chest. "But you pushed me to it, Shorty. I wanted you and Kody to get to know each other, but you wouldn't let it happen. Instead, you kept insisting on this Tulum thing."

A tiny crumb of remorse rattled through me, but it wasn't enough to change my feelings. "Well, you've made your position clear. I texted Mãe to tell her I'm not going."

For a second, it looked like he wanted to apologize. But his mouth formed a line, the expression that made him look like a serious frog. "Listen, at the end of the summer, let's go somewhere. Someplace way more fun than a bougie beach. It'll be your reward for working hard all summer."

The sliver of wood I was pulling at pierced my skin and I hissed, pulling my finger back. My dad reached out and held my hand up toward the hallway light to get a better look. "Splinter. Let's pull it out before it gets infected."

I sat on the edge of the tub as my dad picked at the splinter with a pair of tweezers that he dipped in alcohol. As we both stared intently at the tiny line of wood under the translucent layer of skin on my index finger, my phone vibrated next to me. I glanced down and saw it was my mom, finally.

It was a simple, succinct 💀.

# CHAPTER 23

"WHAT'S THE DEAL? YOUR BOYFRIEND'S A MILLIONAIRE?"

I flipped down the visor in Patrick's car so the sun wasn't blinding me. It was Tuesday and I had the day off, so I'd invited Felix, Patrick, and Cynthia to a waterpark. That Hamlet's mom happened to own. It was going to be *real fun* having them all meet for the first time. Rose included.

I looked back at Felix to answer his question. "No. I mean, I don't know. But his mom bought this totally bizarro bankrupt water park a couple years ago and it's going to reopen next week. And we're allowed to try out the rides before it does."

Cynthia's frown was visible in the rearview mirror. "Didn't you say his parents lived in China or something?"

I pinched the bridge of my nose. CYNTHIA. "Yeah. They do. They bought it as an investment. Even Hamlet acknowledges it was weird, but apparently his mom always has these hare-brained schemes." I giggled, thinking about the last story he'd told me. "One time, she bought an American customer-service telemarketing office in Beijing but didn't realize until weeks into it that it was for sex toys." After a few seconds, I realized I was the only one laughing.

The water park was about two hours inland from LA, so it was going to be a long ride. Hamlet and Rose were meeting us there. Initially I was going to drive with them, but I'd felt guilty and told these guys I would ride with them instead.

The dead air in the car was making me have serious regrets.

But then we blasted Prince and all was well as we drove on the desolate 210 freeway, passing brown hills, tract homes, and endless gas stations and fast-food stops. At one point, we stopped for In-N-Out because no road trip was complete without it.

"So, is Rose your new bestie now?" Felix asked in a teasing tone as we dug into our burgers. I caught a hint of something else in there—a little hurt.

Normally I would have denied it in a heartbeat, paired with a grade-A scoff. But it wasn't really something I could deny. I'd hung out with Rose for about 80 percent of my summer break. And I liked doing it. I grabbed a fry off Felix's tray, earning me a glare from Cynthia. "Rose is cool."

"Are you serious?" Cynthia asked, her cat-eye sunglasses lifting on her face as she wrinkled her nose.

I sighed. "Yes. I'm serious."

Patrick shook his head. "That's messed up. Who's going to be your mortal enemy now?" Patrick was making light of it, too. But like with Felix, I detected some bitterness underneath. I took a bite of my burger, fending off that nagging feeling I'd had for weeks—that I wasn't sure how much I enjoyed hanging out with these guys anymore.

"Your mom," I replied with my mouth full. He laughed, and the awkwardness dissipated.

Full of burgers, fries, and milk shakes, we pulled up to the water park an hour later.

"Oh. My. God," I said as I stepped out of the car, pushing my sunglasses onto my head so that I could get a better look.

We were in the middle of absolutely nowhere. The desert. A scrubby mountain range loomed in the distance, shrouded by the smoggy curtain that took up permanent residence here during the hot months. We were in a giant parking lot that could fit an entire city's worth of cars. And spread out before us was an oasis.

Kind of.

A huge turquoise retro sign declared this place AQUA-TROPICA. A neat row of palm trees flanked either side, and behind the ticket booth you could see giant waterslides rising and dipping like pastel-colored snakes. Everything was very "Americana"—from the 1950s lettering on the signs to the paintings of happy blond families.

Hamlet and Rose were waiting for us out front. Rose was hovering under the awning, fanning herself. The heat here in the inland empire was no joke. It must have been triple digits, easy.

But my eyes were on Hamlet. And his on mine, with an easy smile matching his relaxed stance.

He had no idea he was entering the lion's den.

Wearing a robin's-egg blue baseball cap, white T-shirt, and navy swim trunks, Hamlet extended a hand to Felix first. "Hey, nice to meet you guys finally. I'm Hamlet."

Felix looked at the hand for a second. Raised an eyebrow. "Hey. I'm Felix." An almost imperceptible look of recognition passed across Hamlet's face. He knew Felix was an ex. But he kept his hand out, and Felix reluctantly shook it. My shoulders relaxed a little—this whole interaction was making me so tense.

Everyone else introduced themselves, and then we entered the park. A sense of foreboding followed me inside while Hamlet talked to some maintenance workers. He eventually waved us over.

"Okay, we're good to go," he said. "There are some rides we're not allowed to go on because they're not quite ready, but the rest should be fine. Our jobs are to test everything at least once to make sure it's going well." He grinned, waiting for an excited reaction that never came, except from Rose, who whooped.

Rose was sticking to Hamlet like glue, barely talking to everyone else. "So, there are workers at each ride? Just waiting for us?"

He nodded. "Yeah, I guess?"

"Like slaves," Patrick said as he snapped his gum.

*What the heck, Patrick!*

Hamlet laughed. "Wow, never thought of it that way since they're paid, but yeah, whatever." I squeezed his hand. One point Hamlet.

"Yeah, so no, not like slaves," Rose said drily. Patrick had the grace to blush.

I looked around. "Where do we even start?"

Hamlet stopped walking and let go of my hand to rummage around in his back pocket. He pulled out a colorful laminated map with various attractions and landmarks illustrated in a cartoony style. "Well, we're here," he said, pointing at the bottom middle of the map. "We could go in a circle, starting at the Rocky Rapids?"

"Sounds good," Rose said after a few seconds of scrutinizing the map. "That way we can make sure we don't miss anything."

"Wouldn't want to *miss* anything," Cynthia said, her red lips curved up into a smirk.

Before I could react, Rose leveled her sunglass-covered gaze onto Cynthia. "Excuse me?" Normally, I would have loved to see Cynthia wither under a Rose freeze, but I was hoping everyone would actually get along today. Hamlet, ever the diplomat, strode ahead, taking Rose with him. "All right, Rocky Rapids it is!"

There was a particular thrill in not having to wait in lines to go on a ride. A childlike giddiness took over everyone. For a few minutes as we ran laughing through the grounds, hopping over barricades, it felt like we were little kids again.

With the assistance of a stocky, barrel-chested Aqua-Tropica worker, we climbed into a large circular raft. "Thanks, Rodney," Hamlet said as Rodney pushed us off.

Patrick had both of his arms spread out on either side of him, the picture of ease. "Do you know *everyone's* names?"

"Pretty much. I've had to visit here a few times to help out since my parents are out of the country," Hamlet said with a shrug.

"That's nice," Patrick said. And he wasn't being sarcastic. I think it was becoming clear to him that Hamlet *was* nice. That he wasn't faking it, that—surprise, Patrick—sometimes people were genuine!

The raft tilted to the side a bit when I bounced hard on the seat, making everyone squeal and grab hold of the handles. Cynthia glared at me and I smiled, teeth showing.

Rocky Rapids wasn't as rocky as the name promised. It was mostly us floating along a "river" that snaked past various plasticky islands and real palm trees. Every once in a while, we passed through a waterfall, which made us scream as if it was unexpected each time.

By the time we finished, every single one of us was properly soaked. Cynthia looked irritated by it, her mascara running down her face.

Rose pointed at her eyes. "Waterproof. It's all about the waterproof." Cynthia furiously pulled out a compact and wiped at the streaks under her eyes.

We went on some more rides: Tsunami Bay, which had us

crashing around so hard in a giant pool that both Felix and I almost threw up; Death Drop, which was exactly what it sounded like, a huge slide that went down, almost completely vertically, into a "lagoon" with fake sharks floating around in it; and Battle Cove, a pool of calm water where we floated in doughnuts and bonked each other with foam noodles.

All of us were a little sunburned and soaking wet after a few rides. Cynthia was reapplying sunblock on Felix's neck, and Rose and I had ducked into the shade of a bushy palm. Hamlet pulled out his map. (I now understood why it was laminated.) "Okay, so next is Dueling Devils. Oh, this ride is *amazing*, two people can race each other!"

We followed him down one of the paths and stopped when Hamlet slapped his forehead. "Oh crap, this is one of the closed ones."

"What? That looks *awesome*, though," Felix said.

We looked over at the ride, which had yellow tape draped across the entrance and a sign that read Closed Temporarily. The look that appeared on Patrick's face set off alarm bells. "Hey, I bet we could still sneak on."

Rose shook her head adamantly. "No. We are *not* doing that."

Hamlet pushed his sunglasses up onto his head and peered over at the ride. "Yeah. I don't think that's a good idea. It's cool. The next ride is the Beast, which is like a roller coaster—"

But Patrick was already scrambling over the fence with Felix and Cynthia close behind.

"Hey!" I yelled. But they ignored me, making their way to the other side of the fence in seconds. The one athletic activity we all excelled in.

Rose ran over to me. "Get your friends in order!"

Hamlet was already at their heels, and he nimbly hopped up onto the fence, leaning over the top. "You guys! Come on, it's not safe!" he yelled.

If I was being honest, there was a part of me that wanted to jump the fence with them, but one glance at Hamlet's worried expression squelched that compulsion. So instead I jogged over to the fence and hollered, "You *better* not get on that ride! I swear to God!"

Hamlet helped me up so that I could see them on the other side.

The three of them were already running to the top of the stairs that led to the giant tubular slides. "Come *on*, Clara! You know you want to!" Patrick shouted.

Felix was pushing Cynthia into one of the slides. Before he hopped in right after her, he pointed at me. "See you at the bottom!" Then he and Patrick jumped into their respective slides—their whoops audible as they whooshed through the pastel green and blue tubes, hidden from view.

"I'm sorry, Hamlet." I glanced at him

But Hamlet was already over the fence, running. "I'm serious—it's *not* safe!" he shouted as he headed toward the end of the ride, his legs moving so fast they were almost a blur. *Crapcrapcrap.*

In a few seconds, Rose was on the other side, too. She looked up at me and held out her clasped hands as a sort of stirrup. "Here!"

I used the stirrup as I hopped down, landing a little low and scraping my knee. Rose pulled me up. "Are you okay?"

"I'm fine! Follow Hamlet!" Both of us booked it, the hundred-degree sun scorching us as we sprinted after him.

We were stopped by an ear-piercing scream. Rose and I looked at each other in alarm, then ran even faster.

When we reached the end of the ride, I gasped. The slide ended at a giant pool, where it jettisoned people. A giant pool that was currently only half-filled.

"Oh *no*," Rose muttered. Hamlet was already in the pool, and I saw him bent over someone—Felix. Cynthia was sobbing, and Patrick was sitting waist-deep in the pool, looking dazed.

I ran over, and my heart hammered in my chest when I noticed the blood spreading like ink through the water. Surrounding Felix.

"Is he okay?" I asked, my voice shrill and unrecognizable.

Rose immediately jumped into the pool and helped Hamlet—grabbing the other side of Felix, who was limp but had his eyes open, dazed. There was a wound on his head, the source of the blood.

"Go get help," Hamlet said to me in a low voice.

"But, I—I don't have my phone!" None of us did; we'd left them in our lockers at the entrance.

"One of the workers can call," he replied, pointing at the exit gate. Then he looked over at Patrick. "Are you all right?"

Patrick nodded, but he was clutching his left arm, which was bent at an unnatural angle. I felt vomit rising in my throat.

"Clara." Hamlet looked at me again. I nodded and ran to the gate, finding one of the workers. After he called 911, I ran back to everyone, hoping that somehow when I returned everything would be different. That my friends were pulling another prank.

But Rose and Hamlet were sitting next to Felix, keeping his head out of the water. The sight of Cynthia holding her bundled-up tank top to Felix's head, soaked red with his blood, made me woozy.

Nope, it was all very real.

"Don't close your eyes," Rose said firmly. "Unless you want to die."

Cynthia sobbed, and Hamlet threw Rose an exasperated look. She frowned. "Well, it's a possibility!"

Patrick stood next to them, still cradling his arm. When he started to sway, I ran over and steadied him. "Hey, how about you get out of the water and sit down," I said.

He followed me, nary a wisecrack for once, and I helped him climb the stairs out of the pool. As I set him down on a bench, I heard sirens. Shortly after that, a group of medics were running in, some of the park's employees close behind.

Everything happened in a blur—Felix was lifted onto a

stretcher. Cynthia was okay but wanted to ride in the ambulance with Felix. After some inspection, a medic told Patrick he'd probably broken his arm and needed to go to the hospital, too.

Hamlet, Rose, and I followed them out into the parking lot. I walked alongside Patrick for a few seconds. I didn't know what I was expecting, contrition or an apology? But when they got into the ambulances without a word to Hamlet and Rose—both of whom had done everything to help them—I had to say something.

"Hey!" I shouted.

Other than Felix who was lying down, everyone looked at me. I took a deep breath. "I hope you guys feel better soon, but after this is all done, you owe Hamlet an apology."

Hamlet tugged at me. "It's okay, Clara. They're hurt—"

"Are you seriously asking for an apology *right now*?" Cynthia cried from the ambulance bench.

Felix put a hand on her arm. "It's fine, Cyn. She's right. Sorry about this, Hamlet."

"Don't even worry about it," Hamlet said with a grim smile. "Just take care of yourself, man."

Then the doors shut, and Felix's ambulance wailed off into the distance. Patrick's ambulance was idling, his injury not as serious. I walked over to him and he gave me a small smile. "Best summer ever." I didn't laugh. He sighed. "You're right, we were being jerks." He looked down at his lap. "But, I mean, it kind of sucks. Being ditched, you know?"

I bit down on my lip, suddenly feeling like I wanted to cry. "I didn't ditch you guys."

He glanced behind me at Rose and Hamlet, who were talking to the EMTs. "Maybe not. But you're going to."

Before I could respond, the medics closed up the doors and drove off, the ambulance growing smaller in the distance, leaving me caught between its receding lights and Hamlet and Rose.

# CHAPTER 24

"CLARA, LOOK ALIVE!"

I startled and looked up at the TV. My player had just fallen off a cliff.

Hamlet's grandma threw her controller down in disgust. "I want to be on a different team!"

It was a few days after the water-park catastrophe and I was sitting on the carpet at Hamlet's, playing our usual Friday night *Space Pineapple Death Match*. Early on in this new Friday routine, his grandpa reluctantly moved the video-game console downstairs so that we could play group matches. I was distracted, and Hamlet's grandmother pulled herself off the carpet with a groan. "I'm going to get some snacks." She pointed at me. "You. Practice some more while I'm gone." Hamlet's grandpa heaved himself off a chair to follow her. "You're going to pick bad snacks," he complained after her.

We paused the game, and the second his grandparents had scuttled into the kitchen, Hamlet reached over and pulled me closer to him—both of our backs pressed against the sofa. He touched the tip of my nose. "What's up?"

"Your grandpa's kicking my butt, as per usual."

"No, I mean you seem off today. Is everything okay?"

I took a second to appreciate this Hamlet quality of checking on me. He was good at honing in on my feelings, and right now it was guilt about my friends ruining his parents' grand opening. My shoulder bumped his as I scooted closer. "Yeah, I'm all right. Did your mom pick a new grand opening date yet?"

He shrugged. "No, my parents have to figure out the lawsuit first."

Shame seeped into me. After the accident, Hamlet's mom had to decide whether to delay the grand opening since the accident was bad press—you know, "Teenagers Almost Die in Water Park." Before she could figure that out, however, Felix's parents were threatening to file a lawsuit against the park. Felix had reached out to me to apologize because his parents weren't backing down. I cursed Past Clara for not endearing herself more to Felix's parents when we'd dated.

And in the middle of all this, I couldn't get Patrick's voice out of my head: *But you're going to.* Everyone around me seemed to be noticing some sort of shift in me that I wasn't sure I was ready for.

Here I was spending a Friday night with my debate-club-president boyfriend at his grandparents' house. My debate-club-president boyfriend. And I already knew my weekend plans: I was going to get Ethiopian food with Pai and Kody (my idea—an olive branch after naengmyeon-gone-wrong) and *go on a hike* with Hamlet. And then work the KoBra on Sunday.

Over the course of the summer, my life really had become unrecognizable.

"Why do you like me?" The words came out before my brain could stop them—its squishy brain arms reaching out frantically while its "Noooooooo!" became an echo as the words flew farther away from its grasp.

I expected silence, the normal reaction to such a random and naked question. But Hamlet just chuckled and said, "Because!"

"Because why?" I couldn't stop. The need to see myself through Hamlet's eyes was overwhelming. I didn't feel like myself lately, and I needed someone else to confirm that I was, indeed, the same person. Or confirm that I wasn't.

He pulled his knees up into his chest. "Well, you're really funny."

What else was new. "So you're into clowns."

The joke got a belly laugh from Hamlet that it did not deserve. "Actually, I'm scared of clowns."

"Who *isn't*? The person who feels no fear in their heart when seeing a freaking clown in the flesh is probably a serial killer!"

Hamlet threw his head back and the laugh that came out of

his body immediately made me crack up with him. When he finally calmed down, he was wiping away tears. Tears. I smiled at him, and the tenderness that flooded out of my chest and into all my extremities caught me off guard.

*I don't deserve him.*

I blinked. "Okay, so what else?"

"Jeez. You're being so bossy about this."

"Your grandparents are going to take three hours making a fruit platter for us. We need to fill the time."

His head was still leaning back on the edge of the sofa, his arm draped casually behind me. But when he looked over, not smiling for a second, his eyes were serious and intense. They cut through me, blazing hot, and I was completely disarmed.

Keeping his eyes on mine, his fingers grazed my bare shoulder. "I like your freckles. The way you chew on your lips when you're annoyed." I rubbed them together self-consciously and he smiled. "And I like . . . how you dress. Especially when you wear your Docs with your little shorts."

I rolled my eyes. "Okay, pervo." But I was pleased—I always felt so sloppy and unkempt next to Hamlet. Whenever I first saw Rose in her carefully coordinated outfits, I wished that I dressed more like her.

"But I think what I like most," he said almost sleepily, his fingers playing with my tank-top strap, "is how you're different from me."

It should have been sweet, comforting—something like that. But instead, I could only think of how that chasm of difference between us had shrunk over the summer. How that bothered me for some reason. "Different how?" My needling knew no bounds.

"You know how. Everything! I like how sure of yourself you are. You don't do things to please other people."

"But you're confident, too!"

He scoffed. "Kind of. I'm always worried about, I don't know, being nice or something." He seemed a little embarrassed by that admission. But it was one of the reasons I liked him so much, too.

"You're kind," I said quietly, resting my face on his hand. "I'm not."

"What?"

I shrugged. "It's fine, one human being cannot exemplify all the good things in the world."

Instead of laughing, he frowned. "You are kind. You just don't like to show it. Like a cranky old man in a village."

I released a bark of laughter. "Get out!"

He sat up and ran a hand through his hair. Hair so thick I imagined combs shattered upon touch. "You are! You're like that cranky man who yells at children but then secretly mends their shoes."

"*What!*" I couldn't stop laughing.

"You're . . ." he paused. "You're all tough candy shell. When inside—"

"I'm oozy chocolate? Please."

Instead of responding, he leaned over, pulling me in so close that our eyelashes practically touched. His lips grazed my jaw and then moved up toward my ear. "Yeah, chocolate. Melted."

Every bone in my body turned into liquid as I turned my lips to his. He cradled my head gently and kissed me softly. And then. Then he said, "I love you."

I stilled. My blood stopped coursing through my veins, my heart froze midbeat, my cells were suspended. I couldn't move.

Uncertainty passed over his face, his eyes still on mine. When I didn't react, he moved back a little, his body no longer touching mine.

*Hamlet loves me. Hamlet LOVES me? Hamlet loves ME?* My brain was malfunctioning, wires being crossed, indecipherable signals being passed back and forth, and I couldn't speak. I didn't know what to say.

"Don't let *me* interrupt."

Both of our heads swiveled to see Hamlet's grandma holding a tray of fruit in front of the TV. His grandpa was right behind, with a giant bowl of popcorn.

Hamlet blushed. "We were just—"

"Give me a break," his grandmother grumbled as she tottered back over to the sofa, walking between us and plopping herself down, the tray rattling on her lap. She glanced over at me. "This one is a bad influence, huh?"

I stammered, "What, why . . ."

"Eat some fruit. Cool off," she said, shoving the tray onto the coffee table in front of us. We both reached for the tiny forks poked into the pears and ate silently, not making eye contact with each other while the video game started up again.

That night, I looked through some old photos of Felix and me from when we dated. There was one of us hanging out in some parking lot. Felix with his arm draped lazily around me, both of us smiling in the harsh glare of the lights. I didn't remember that day, because days with Felix and Patrick always ran together into one indistinct blur.

Felix never said he loved me. Even though we cared for each other, and still did, it never got to that level. We liked a lot of the same things and were attracted to each other at the time. But Felix didn't dig past a certain depth, and neither did I. Hamlet, though? He was fearless in his digging, in his pursuit of something more meaningful.

Looking at these photos with Felix was bittersweet. The chasm between us from the water-park incident felt unbridgeable, and I wondered if Patrick was right. Were they being replaced?

I texted Patrick and Felix: **How are you guys?**

The conversation bubbles were immediate. But took forever. I frowned. It wasn't like them to take that much time drafting texts to me.

Patrick replied first: **Good. I requested a child's neon green cast.**

I laughed.

Felix replied soon after: **Okay. My parents are being over the top and keep checking up on me in the middle of the night to make sure I haven't died.**

I texted back: **Do they know you're past the danger zone??**

**They think Jesus was punishing them for letting me date you.**

The laughter felt good, and for just one evening, it was like old times.

# CHAPTER 25

WHAT 😮 😱

I could feel the force of Rose's enthusiasm through her texts. For once, my energy level matched hers, my fingers flying on my phone as I texted back: RIGHT??????????!!!!!

I need to process this. Are you home? Can I come over?

It was Monday afternoon and both of us were off KoBra duty.

Yeah, come over

An hour later, we were sitting in my room, Flo in my lap while the fan rattled inches away from us.

"Nothing? You said nothing," she said, her voice flat.

I fiddled with Flo's collar, irritating her. One paw pushed my hand away. "Well, I was *shocked*. And then his grandparents came in the room!"

She groaned. "Hamlet, what the heck? Why would he say that with his *grandparents* around?"

"I don't think he was planning it. It just seemed to slip out."

"Either way, terrible timing."

"Agreed." I let go of Flo, plopping down backward onto the bed.

Rose propped her chin on the edge of my bed. "Do you feel the same way?" she asked.

I stared at the ceiling. "I don't know. I mean, yes, I like him. But . . . *love?*"

"I know. So serious."

"SO serious!"

The breeze from the fan lifted my tank top off my belly, making the fabric flutter for a second. "I feel like that guy in a rom-com who freaks out over the obviously perfect-catch girl having feelings for him. Like, why am I obsessing over a love declaration from a nice guy?"

"Rom-com main characters are old. You're sixteen. Love declarations are weird."

This was stressing me out, and my room started to feel oppressive. Rose seemed to pick up on this and said, "Let's do something fun today."

"Yes and yes."

Her eyes narrowed in concentration. "You know, there's a list of all the trucks entering the competition on the website."

I sat up. "And?"

"Maybe we can check them out. See what we're up against."

My mind took that suggestion and spun through other ways to make it more interesting, like prank roulette. By the time it landed on an idea, I was brainstorming.

"Is a wig completely necessary?" Rose asked, her voice low and skeptical.

I browsed through the wig bin at my favorite thrift store. "Is *anything* ever necessary?"

"Hi, Clara!" The woman behind the counter waved at me, her eyebrows drawn high and dramatically, her fake mole shifting on her upper lip as she smiled widely at me.

I waved back. "Hey, Erin!" I glanced at Rose next to me. "I've purchased many a disguise here."

"I am very much *not* surprised," she said, wrinkling her nose as she picked up a neon orange bob with her fingertips.

"We're spies today. We need to be fully covert," I said, eyeing an electric blue pixie wig.

She lifted an eyebrow. "Aren't we going for inconspicuous here?"

"No way. Just *unrecognizable*." I pulled the blue wig on and looked at her. She grinned and gave me two thumbs up.

Rose picked a long, wavy, blond-streaked wig with bangs. She looked amazing in it and I made her take a billion photos. As we sorted through the racks for clothes, she got more and more into it. Clothes were definitely her forte.

When we left the store, I was wearing a short polyester shift dress with geometric patterns. Very 1960s go-go girl. Rose was decked out in a long white caftan with little laced-up booties straight out of *Little House on the Prairie.* We both wore large sunglasses that obscured our faces.

Rose couldn't stop giggling, self-conscious as she drove us to the first stop: No Pain No Grain, a grain-bowl truck in Hollywood. Rose parked her car at a metered spot, and the sun beat down relentlessly on the tops of our wigged heads when we stepped out.

I tugged at my dress. "Ugh, should have considered the weather before choosing this piece o' crap unbreathable fabric!"

Rose was scrolling through an iPad. She had, of course, mapped out all the trucks and made a very thorough checklist. "Okay, so their specialty is making healthy, 'clean' bowls full of obscure veggies and various free-range or grass-fed meats."

"Sounds like the worst." I peered at the truck through my sunglasses. Their line was minuscule, and it was full of Hollywood's finest clean-eaters—mostly thin and most likely wealthy as well, judging from the menu pricing. Before Rose could protest, I jumped into line and targeted a young white woman with wavy red hair who was wearing a crop top and loose linen pants. "What's your favorite thing here?" I asked with a heavy vocal fry.

She glanced at my hair and then my outfit, visibly startled. Probably not the usual clientele she found at her ol' reliable grain truck. "Well, I usually go for farro topped with okra, black beans, and a sprinkling of gomasio."

"Interesting. Are you a vegetarian?" I asked.

Glancing around quickly, she leaned in a bit and whispered, "No. Between you and me, I don't actually think their chicken is free-range." Her eyebrows lifted.

I raised my own. Quelle horreur. "Are you for real?"

"For real." A firm, knowing nod. "But their veggies are grown in their own garden, and they're heavenly." I stored that fact away. Strengths: veggies. Weaknesses: chicken. We bailed before it was our turn to order, already moving on to our next destination, the Frank 'n' Frank truck, which served, you guessed it, fancy hot dogs. My dad and I both loved this truck, so I braced myself for some stiff competition. We surveyed the long line before us. It was peak lunch hour, so that wasn't surprising.

"Hm . . . this truck doesn't even give you options," Rose pondered as she glanced at the menu scrawled on the side of the shiny white truck in neon green. "There's, like, one hot dog, and you get grilled onions on it with various condiments."

I nodded. "Their hot dogs are freaking delicious, that's why. Why dilute the product?"

Rose stood there looking like a serious cult leader in her caftan. "Not too different from the KoBra, we keep it minimal, too."

"My dad knows his strengths," I said. Because we were both hungry, we grabbed a couple of hot dogs (Rose discovered she could actually get a vegan one, bleh) and sat down at a nearby bus stop bench shaded by a large magnolia tree.

"This is fun," Rose said between bites.

"You sound surprised."

She shrugged. "I never know what I'm getting into with you. And . . . I still don't get why we need to wear costumes, but whatever."

I pointed my hot dog at her. "Aha! You say 'whatever' because you know the costumes are purely for fun. And could it be that you're embracing *hijinks* right now?"

"Calm down, Clara," she said. "You're so annoying."

"I know," I said with a laugh. A bus pulled up, and we watched some people unload before it drove off, the exhaust fumes spewing some debris up into the air. I waved it away from my face. "Thanks for hanging out with me today." It was getting easier and easier to say things like that to Rose without having to crack a joke, too.

"Of course." She wiped the corner of her mouth with a napkin. "I know what it's like to need a distraction when you're worried about stuff."

I was hesitant before I asked, "So, is that how you cope with your anxiety?"

And to my surprise, Rose didn't shut it down. She fiddled with her straw. "Kind of. Sometimes I think it's just me being a worry-wart? I've always been this way. I worry about *everything*. And sometimes the dumbest stuff keeps worrying me, days and weeks after." A breeze hit us then, and it felt so good. She lifted her face up to it. "It's like this pitch-black field where I'm forced to walk, and I know there's a giant hole somewhere waiting for me. So I'm constantly thinking about it, when I'm going to drop into this pit."

That sounded like a literal nightmare, and it hit me then how seemingly perfect people were just as messed up as everyone else. I stayed quiet so she would keep talking.

"Sometimes, I can't . . . live in the moment. I'm always thinking of what-ifs and the terrible things people could be thinking about me." She looked up at me. "I always think everyone's mad at me. All the time. And it's like, I don't really care? But I do. It's hard to explain."

"You mean, like your parents?" I asked.

She shook her head. "No. I mean, yeah, of course I worry about what they think. But literally *everyone*. Like a stranger on the street. If I say something dumb to a barista, it bothers me for weeks. If someone doesn't respond to a text or e-mail right away, I'm convinced I did something wrong. I feel as if my brain's *trolling* me."

"Your brain is a jerk."

She laughed, the sound filled with relief. "It is."

"Do you want me to give your brain a talking-to?" I joked, but inside I felt a flare of sympathy and frustration for her. Rose's shallow breathing—it was a way for her to calm that troll brain down. I knew that dealing with something like this wasn't as simple as hanging out with friends to forget your worries, but I was glad to be that friend for her these days.

We finished up our hot dogs and headed to our next destination, a lobster-roll truck in Glendale. As far from the ocean as you could get in LA, but I guess things didn't always make sense.

# CHAPTER 26

A FEW DAYS LATER, MY DAD HOPPED INTO THE TRUCK, where Rose and I were setting up for the day. "Ladies," he said, giving each of us a nod.

"Man," I said with an exaggerated bow.

Wearing a stiff new Dodgers cap, my dad rubbed his hands together. "All right, how did yesterday go?"

Rose grinned. "Great. We ran out of pork, so we stopped by the store and got more ingredients on the way back."

He gave me a little sideways hug in greeting. "Good job, my ladies."

"Please stop saying 'ladies.' Blech." I elbowed him in the side.

"And!" Rose exclaimed, holding up a finger. "We had our best day ever, money-wise!" She and I bumped fists, then did a little dance.

I looked at my dad for his equally celebratory reaction, but instead he had this strained expression on his face.

"Hello? Pai? Aren't congratulations in order?"

He ducked into the driver's seat before answering. "Yeah, definitely! All right, let's head over to Mid-City before traffic gets bad."

I glanced at the clock. It was almost five. Fat chance.

Nearly an hour later, we arrived at a craft fair set up on a big parking lot off Wilshire.

As my dad and I prepped the food, I glanced at him. "So, what's up?"

My dad kept his eyes on the green bell pepper he was chopping. "What do you mean?"

"Why are you acting all weird?"

He made a face but didn't look at me. "I'm not?"

"Yeah, you are."

He sighed. "Sorry. I just have a lot on my mind right now."

"What is it?" I asked, a little nervous. My dad rarely stressed out in front of me, and it only really happened when things were serious.

My dad finally looked at me. "The investor I was counting on for the restaurant just backed out."

I felt a knot form in my stomach. Growing up without much money, it was still an instant reaction—a wave of dread passing over me every time my dad worried about finances. "Oh no. What does that mean?"

"It just means that after all my work and planning this summer, everything may have to be put on hold."

I blinked. "Sorry, Pai. That sucks."

"What about the competition?" Rose piped up from the order window.

I whipped my head around and stared at Rose with huge eyes, telepathically telling her to shut up.

"What competition?" My dad glanced over at me.

Rose looked at me apologetically. "Sorry, I know you wanted to keep it a secret, but it could solve everything, right?"

A tiny flare of hope shot up into my chest. Maybe Rose was right. "Well, I wanted it to be a surprise, but . . ."

"Clara." My dad's voice was short with impatience. "What's this about?"

I looked at Rose and she nodded, her eyes supportive. I took a deep breath. "Well, there's this food truck competition on August eleventh—"

"I know what competition you're talking about," my dad interrupted, his voice clipped. "And no, I don't want to enter that."

"Why not?" both Rose and I yelped.

He tossed the bell pepper scraps into a compost bowl. "Because. It's a circus. I don't have time for it."

Since when did my dad have this attitude? I frowned at him. "What? What do you mean? What could possibly be the risk? If you win, you win ONE HUNDRED THOUSAND DOLLARS!"

"So what, Clara? Do you know how many trucks enter that thing? It's nuts, the chances of winning are so slim, and I don't want to go through that headache. Plus, the deadline to enter probably passed."

I felt Rose's eyeballs digging into my skull. "I already entered us," I whispered.

"What!" Pai yelled, making me startle and drop the spoon I was using onto the floor.

Rose immediately tried to de-escalate the situation. Something she probably learned in the Young UN Club or something. "Clara wanted it to be a nice surprise if we won, Adrian! It was—"

"I don't care! You did this *without my permission*! Are you two out of your minds?"

The silence that followed was like a vacuum—the air sucked out of the truck, my ears ringing with the absolute voidness of it all. Betrayal and disappointment were so heavy in my chest that I could barely breathe. It was unfamiliar, and I didn't like it.

"You okay, Clara?" Rose asked quietly, putting a hand on my shoulder.

I wasn't sure how to answer. No, I wasn't okay. And I wasn't okay with not being okay. My emotional investment in this truck came crashing down on me, as if to say, "Ha-ha, this is what happens when you care." I felt suffocated. By my dad's reaction to me trying to do something nice. By Rose's concern. By this stupid truck.

I tossed my cap onto the counter. "See you guys later." My voice shook, and it took all my willpower to not burst into tears as I stepped out of the truck.

"Clara!"

I ignored my dad's voice and walked rapidly toward the craft fair exit, and kept walking until the fair was far behind me, my face hot with tears.

Feeling disoriented, I looked around and noticed that I was headed west on Wilshire. My feet kept moving—past traffic and the big office buildings.

Before I knew it, I was at the La Brea Tar Pits. I hadn't been here since I was a kid. There had been more than one field trip to this ancient, bubbling mass of tar sitting smack in the middle of the city. I entered the museum grounds, the scent of sulfur hitting me as I walked by the lake of tar and the expansive lawns. When I stepped inside the museum itself, the cool, circulated air hit me. Air-conditioning in LA was almost healing; it made every place feel the same, a guarantee of something familiar.

I didn't move for a few minutes, letting the air cool off the fine layer of sweat on my face. Letting time slow everything down—my thoughts, my pulse, my anger.

After a few seconds, I paid for a ticket and entered the main exhibit hall. There were big informational displays about the last

Ice Age, showing dire-wolf skulls and animatronic woolly mammoths roaming the earth. Reading about long-extinct animals made me feel insignificant, which calmed me down.

My phone vibrated. I'd been getting texts since I started walking, but this time it was a phone call.

Hamlet. I picked it up.

"Hi."

"Clara? Are you okay?"

"Sure."

There was a pause. "Well, your dad told me about what happened. Where are you right now?"

I stood in the middle of a dark room, a timeline of ancient animals circling me on the walls, lit dimly. "I'm looking at ancient history."

"Huh? They said you guys were in Mid-City somewhere."

"Yeah, I ended up at the Tar Pits."

I heard a car turning on. "Please stay there. I'm coming."

"Hamlet. I don't need saving." I watched a group of little girls press their faces up against the timeline on the wall, gaping at the illustrations of saber-toothed cats being sucked into the tar.

"It's a billion degrees out. Are you going to *walk* home?"

Good point. "I can get a car."

"That would cost fifty bucks or something, give me a break. I'm coming—I'm actually not that far. Don't leave, okay?"

I sighed. "Fine. I'll be here."

We hung up, and suddenly I was very tired. I stepped outside into the lush atrium, found a bench next to a small waterfall, and lay down. Kids' voices mingled with the sound of tumbling water, and I took a deep breath. My eyelids fluttered once, twice.

"Clara?"

I woke up with a start. My neck hurt, and I was totally disoriented.

Hamlet's face appeared over me. "Hey."

Right. I sat up slowly, my legs stiff. "Hey."

He sat down next to me, his shoulder hitting mine. "Good nap?"

"Yeah, I give this Airbnb four stars."

He smiled. "I don't think you give stars for Airbnbs."

"Oh God, whatever."

His expression more serious, Hamlet looked at me. "What happened? Your dad didn't really tell me much."

"It's not a big deal."

"Kind of seems like a big deal. Like, this was very *drama*." He held up jazz hands.

"Well, you know how I entered us in the food truck competition?" He nodded. I continued, "Rose told my dad about it because he was bummed that an investor backed out of his restaurant plans. She thought he'd be excited, and instead he was a *total dick*."

"How so?"

Anger built up inside me, seeping out in tiny, toxic increments. "He got *mad* I entered the truck and said he didn't want to do it!"

Hamlet was quiet for a second. "Did he say why?"

248

"Just something about it being a hassle. I was so freaking disappointed." My voice trembled, and my eyes filled with tears.

He tucked a strand of my hair behind my ear, a gesture that instantly soothed me. "I understand."

The tears fell before I could wipe them. "Do you, though? He got me to care about this stupid truck, this stupid job—and then he let me down. So hard."

Holding my hand, he said, "Well, I don't think he meant to let you down. He must have his reasons . . ."

"He got me invested in this, and now I've wasted my entire summer." I thought of all my time on the KoBra with Rose, my summer spent away from my other friends to be with Hamlet. All these little threads holding this new version of me in place. A line appeared between his eyes, on top of his nose. His voice was quiet. "*Wasted* seems a little harsh."

And even though I knew why it stung for him, I felt a flare of frustration where compassion should be and I pulled my hand out from his grasp. This was just *so much*.

And then, I knew what I wanted to do.

"I'm going to Mexico."

His head snapped up. "What?"

"Screw my dad. Screw the competition. My mom wants me there so I'm going."

Hamlet's expression was incredulous. "Are you kidding me? How . . . And what about your punishment? Don't you have to work the entire summer to avoid suspension?"

"Who cares?" I felt the weight of the past couple of months

lifting off me in big chunks, making it easier to breathe, to be myself again. The threads loosening.

"Who *cares*?" His voice was loud now.

All around me, a thin, invisible barrier formed—a translucent thing covering every inch of my skin. I felt my expression slacken, my eyes turn into two cold stones. "You're being a drag, Hamlet."

Hamlet looked at me, his expression hardening as well. "You know what? You've asked me why I like you. I've given you reasons. I've even told you I *love* you." I flinched. He kept going. "And while you've never told me why you like me, I have my own theories—the main one being that you've surrounded yourself with people who enable this side of you, and I don't."

"What side of me?" My voice was acid.

"The side of you that can't handle being real, that thinks it's special not to care." He stood up and put his hands into his shorts pockets. "But, Clara, it's the least special thing about you. It's the exception."

There were so many comebacks that flew to my mouth, so many mean things I wanted to throw at him. But his words cut straight through my chest and into my heart. Before I could recover, he walked away from me, leaving me alone with a bunch of ferns and aimless koi fish.

# CHAPTER 27

I EVENTUALLY GOT HOME AFTER THE MOST EXPENSIVE cab ride of my life and ran straight up to my dad's room. Ignoring Flo rubbing on my legs and still wearing my shoes like an animal, I grabbed the laptop off his desk and took it to my room.

During the ride home, I had stalked my mom's Instagram account, looking through her Stories to make sure I had her location right. She was staying at the Lotus Hotel and had arrived today. Perfect.

I opened the laptop and Googled "flights to Tulum."

The part of me that wanted to run after Hamlet, to call my dad—it was overshadowed by that familiar need to escape, to have some breathing room away from everything.

By the time my dad came home, I had purchased a one-way flight to Mexico for the next morning with my dad's credit card. I felt only a slight pitter-patter in my chest when I hit Finalize Purchase.

Consider it my summer bonus, Pai.

A few minutes after he got home, there was a knock at my door. This time, I ignored it. Flo meowed and I shushed her.

There was another knock. I turned up my music—lots of incoherent screaming with clanging piano. I let that do the talking.

I only turned it down when I heard his footsteps fade away.

To avoid feeling whatever it was I was feeling about my dad, I packed, focusing on how surprised my mom was going to be instead. I threw several bathing suits, shorts, and tanks into a duffel bag.

While I was loading up my phone with podcasts, there was another knock at the door.

"Clara."

Hearing him say my name almost shattered my resolve. I closed my eyes and concentrated on Mexico. The beach. Mãe.

"Clara, please. Let's talk."

I couldn't ignore him forever, so I spoke through the door. "Can we talk tomorrow? I need time." If I saw his face, I knew I would cave.

He was quiet for a moment. "Okay. Tomorrow. Did you eat?"

My stomach grumbled at the mention of it. "I'm fine."

"You should eat."

I smelled it then—kimchi stew. I took another sniff. And an omelet. "Maybe later."

"I'm not going to leave you a tray of food. No one died."

I almost laughed. "Whatever."

"I'll leave it on the stove for later so you don't have to look at my monstrous face." I heard him go downstairs shortly after that.

Later that night, when my dad was asleep, I crept downstairs and saw the stove light left on for me. The rice cooker was full and warm, and there was a small stone pot filled with kimchi stew, sitting next to a chunk of omelet wrapped in plastic.

I ate my food in silence, and in the dark.

The closest airport to Tulum was Cancún, and there had been no direct flights left that were affordable. So, after getting up long before the crack of dawn for a seven a.m. flight and taking an airport shuttle to LAX, many, many hours later I finally landed in Mexico at eight p.m. My phone was dead, so I could avoid hearing any voice mails or seeing any texts from my dad for now. He would have found the note I left on the counter for him hours ago.

I wondered if he would have contacted my mom. Probably. Would she be at the airport to pick me up?

Feeling like a shriveled corpse with greasy hair, I made it out of customs and into the fairly small but busy airport. Although I had met up with my mom plenty of times in various cities, this was my first time traveling to another country alone.

There was no sign of my mom. Okay, so maybe she didn't know I was coming after all.

Luckily, I had saved New Year's cash from my grandparents, so I had some money on hand for a cab ride. I went to the currency exchange desk and switched out my American dollars for pesos. *Next, get a taxi.*

Nervous, I walked to an information booth. My Spanish wasn't the best, but between growing up in LA and speaking some Portuguese, I'd survive. "Perdón," I said to the man behind the counter in a quiet voice, embarrassed already. "¿Dónde están los taxis?"

With a friendly smile, the young dude with short wavy hair and thick glasses pointed to my right and directed me in accented English. I nodded and said, "Gracias!" As I walked to the taxi stand, I glanced out the bank of windows to my left and stopped in my tracks.

*What.*

There was a storm raging outside—the palm trees bent, rain pouring in a slant, and everything blanketed in gray mist.

It had *not* been raining when we landed. The storm must have just started. What *was* this? My summer getaway hurricane?

After I grabbed a receipt at the taxi stand and waited in line outside, a cab was pulled up for me.

I slipped inside and took out a scrap of paper from my pocket. It had the hotel address, which I showed to the driver, an older man wearing a fedora and sporting a soccer jersey. He nodded and gave me a thumbs-up. "Okay!" he said.

"Gracias," I said in my quiet foreign-language voice, and settled back into the seat, the rhythm of the windshield wipers lulling me.

After a few minutes, the driver held out a phone charger. "¿Necesitas?" he asked.

"Oh, sí. Por favor." I hooked up my phone. "Gracias."

After a few seconds, my phone buzzed to life—alight with a flurry of texts from my dad, Rose, and Hamlet. I didn't open them.

We headed into the storm, and my stomach felt as tumultuous as the weather surrounding us.

# CHAPTER 28

WE GOT ON THE HIGHWAY AND PASSED THROUGH
Cancún—full of large, looming resorts that gave off eerily
empty vibes during this storm. But after about an hour and a
half, we turned onto a road that transported us from the busy,
touristy, spring-break vibes of Cancún onto a more remote,
low-key thoroughfare. There were people on bikes, even in the
rain. Everyone looked less spring break and more yoga retreat.
One side of the main road was jungle, and the other, just across
the street, was beach. No large resorts here, just tucked-away
"eco hotels" with discreet entrances off the main road. We pulled
up to the Lotus Hotel—a small but elegant thatched-roof, two-
story building with rustic wood columns. Despite the weather,

the windows and doors were thrown open, with only gauzy white curtains separating the lobby from the elements. The driver helped me with my bag, and I thanked him.

As I hoisted the duffel onto my shoulder, I saw a figure run out from the entrance with a large white umbrella. It was a young guy wearing a polo shirt and khaki shorts. "Señorita, let me help you," he said as he took my bag.

"Oh, thank you."

He held the umbrella over me as we walked toward the hotel. The second we stepped inside, the stormy weather was muffled, even though we were basically standing in a glorified gazebo. Soothing music played, all flutes and chimes. Scattered between plush white furnishings were various bronze sculptures of elephants and tigers. Candles flickered everywhere, and I had the distinct feeling that someone was about to massage me right there in that lobby.

"Good evening. Do you need to check in?" a woman behind the front desk asked me. To her credit, she gave me and my dirty jeans and sweatshirt only the quickest once-over and managed to stay polite. Who knows how many children of celebrities had rolled in here looking as ratty as me?

"I'm here as a guest of Juliana Choi," I said.

The woman nodded. "Ah, are you the DJ for the party tonight?"

My eyes darted around. Was I being *Punk'd*? "DJ? Uh, no. I'm her daughter."

"Oh!" Her thick, sculpted eyebrows jumped in surprise. "Please excuse me. I wasn't told there was a daughter arriving . . ."

"It's a surprise," I said, beginning to feel nervous about this whole plan.

As she typed away, I wondered about this party. Did I pick a bad night to visit? She was hiring a *DJ*? My anxiety mounted with every tap of her keyboard, and I was about to drop my bag on the floor and text Mãe when I heard a shriek.

"Clara?"

I turned to see my mom running toward me, her arms raised and a huge smile on her face. And like every time I saw my mom, I was startled by how pretty and young she was. Petite in height, like me, but small-boned and delicate. Her long, highlighted brown hair was wavy and artfully tousled, spilling over onto a coral crop top that she wore with matching high-waisted shorts. A long, fringed, cream-colored robe was thrown over it all, and she resembled an exotic bird.

She embraced me in a tight bear hug as soon as she reached me. "I can't *believe* it!" she shrieked. I caught a whiff of some spicy perfume as she crushed her hair against my face.

"Surprise, Mãe," I said, laughing at her excitement.

Clutching my arms as she stood back, she asked, "What happened? Did your dad cave as you predicted? He texted me this morning, saying you were coming, but he wouldn't elaborate!"

I was about to answer when I realized something. "Wait, you knew I was coming?"

She pushed aside a lock of my hair and peered at my face, distracted when she answered. "Yeah, but I had no info on when you'd get here. I texted you to ask, but you didn't respond. I would have sent a car for you, silly." It's true—I had told my dad my plans but had purposely left out the flight info so he wouldn't try to catch me before I could get on the plane.

I also noticed that she said "sent a car" not "picked you up." I guess it wasn't surprising. My mom was *not* the kind of person to schlep over to the airport. She paid someone to fold her laundry for her. Macrobiotic meals were delivered to her home—her refrigerator was empty save for a few cans of sparkling water and iced coffee.

She nodded at one of the bellhops in the lobby and he came over, taking my duffel bag from me. There was something ludicrous about a well-groomed young man in a polo shirt holding my ten-year-old nylon black duffel with a giant rainbow-patterned patch that said DIE on it in huge letters.

"First, let's get you settled into your villa. It's *amazing*. You're basically *on the beach*, and the whole place is done up in *sheepskin*," Mãe said as she clip-clopped out of the lobby in her Greek sandals. My mother excelled at speaking in italics.

I followed her and the bellhop out into a courtyard, my wet Vans squeaking on the floors. "Wait, I get my own *villa*?"

Mãe looked back at me, winking over her shoulder. "Of course, do you think I'd make you share a room with me?"

259

While the idea of having my own "villa" was exciting, I was surprised by the simultaneous disappointment I felt—I had imagined spending tonight with my mom cozied into a giant bed watching *Real Housewives* and ordering room service, our usual hotel combo.

Instead, we approached a little hut with a thatched roof like the rest of the hotel, petite palm trees planted around its perimeter, a hammock swaying in the wind on a closed-off balcony. The bellhop opened the door, and we entered a room that was simply but stylishly furnished—all boho textiles and sheepskins tossed over rough-hewn wood pieces. There was a canopy bed tucked into a corner by a large window, the mosquito netting pulled aside, and a small sitting area with a love seat and coffee table. Another gauzy white curtain separated the room from the small bathroom with its bamboo-and-granite sink and rain showerhead.

It was probably the nicest room I would ever sleep in.

The bellhop left after my mom tipped him, and we were alone, finally. Unexpectedly, I felt shy. But my mom plopped onto my bed and pulled out her phone. "I'm gonna Story this, okay?" Pointing the phone at herself, her chin expertly tilted at a flattering angle as she lay down on the bed with her hair spread around her, she started speaking. "Guys. I had the BEST surprise of my life!" Then suddenly her face turned to its normal expression, and I knew the camera was pointed at me.

It's not like I wasn't used to this—my mom had been recording every minute of her life for the past few years—but I still felt ambushed. I pretty much knew what I looked like—a bedraggled mop with half my makeup rubbed off. My hands flew to cover my face instinctively.

Mãe laughed and went back into selfie mode. "That's my daughter, Clara, and she's feeling *uncharacteristically* shy. Best surprise EVER!" The words echoed back as she watched the video a few times before uploading it. She sprang up from the bed. "So, I gotta get ready for this poolside party thing. Meet me out there in a few?"

"What poolside party thing?" I asked, already staring longingly at my bed.

Her hands fluttered dismissively. "Oh, it's part of this whole tastemaker retreat."

"Wait, what? What retreat?"

She made a face and laughed. "Clara. That's what all of this is. I'm here as part of a retreat with other social media tastemakers."

My heart thudded down into my feet. "Oh. I guess I didn't know."

"Didn't I mention it?"

The fatigue from the travel hit me so hard then that I almost fell over. "Maybe you did? I don't remember."

"We'll still have fun! I'll just have to do a few events here and there."

The idea of being trapped in a resort full of social media

tastemakers made me want to scream, but I forced a smile. "Cool. Give me a sec and I'll meet you out there."

As soon as she left, I pulled out my phone, connected to the hotel's Wi-Fi, and took a deep breath. I had avoided this long enough.

After a couple of rings, my dad answered. "Clara?"

Out of *nowhere*, a tidal wave of homesickness rushed over me, filling my lungs. I couldn't breathe.

"Clara? Can you hear me?" he repeated.

I nodded, stupidly. Realizing he couldn't see me, I cleared my throat. "Yeah. Hi."

"HI?! IS THAT ALL YOU HAVE TO SAY RIGHT NOW?"

Something about his yelling calmed me down. I understood this; this was familiar.

"YOU WENT TO ANOTHER COUNTRY WITHOUT MY PERMISSION!"

Pause.

"HOW IS THAT LEGAL? WHAT HAS THIS COUNTRY COME TO? OH, BETTER NOT LET IN REFUGEES, BUT SURE, HEY, LET A MINOR FLY TO CENTRAL AMERICA!"

Pause.

"ARE YOU LISTENING TO ME?!"

I cringed. "Yes, I'm listening."

His breath came out in angry huffs. "Well? What do you have to say for yourself?"

"Young lady."

"What?!"

"You forgot to add 'young lady.'"

Another pause.

"Clara, I swear to God, I'm going to—"

"Kill me?"

"You know. Maybe. Maybe I'd murder you. My own child."

I started to laugh then, but then the laugh got weird and garbled and filled with tears. I managed to say, "I was so mad at you."

Pai's silence made me squirm. Finally, he responded, his voice tired. "I know. But, you have to wonder, was this reaction perhaps a *tad* disproportionate?"

"Nah. Seemed about right."

He sighed. "Clara. This is insane. You're in deep trouble when you get home, you realize this, right? Like, this is *way* worse than the fight with Rose. You're going to have to work on the truck your entire senior year to make it up to me."

The mosquito net got caught in my hair as I paced in my room, and I tried to pull it out with one hand. "I know. And I'll pay you back for this ticket. And everything else. But, I just . . ." With a quick yank, my hair was released. I straightened out. "I needed to see Mãe."

"You needed to see Mãe, or get away from us?"

He didn't have to clarify who "us" was. Hamlet's and Rose's unread texts practically weighed my hand down. I didn't answer, and when enough seconds had passed, my dad changed the subject. "Well, Shorty, how are you? How was the flight? How's *Tulum*?" The last word dripped with a faux frou-frou accent.

I sat down on the bed, my back against the fluffy pillows. "The flight was fine. I watched three movies."

"Whoa, which ones? Wait, let me guess. The new Marvel thing, the new Pixar thing, and a documentary about the financial crisis of 2007."

"Are you *psychic*?!"

We both laughed, then an awkward silence settled between us. "So, how's your mom?" he asked.

I stared at a large spider that was making its way across the wall next to the window. "She's good!" Could he hear the effort it took for me to be chipper? "And this hotel is, as you would say, *the bomb*. My villa is on the beach."

"*Your* villa?"

"Yeah, I get my own. Isn't that cool?"

The judgy pause on the other end made it clear that *no*, it was not cool. But he replied with, "Yeah! So what have you guys got planned?"

I turned on the ceiling fan when I realized how hot and sticky I was. "Well, I just got here, so not sure. There's a party tonight or something, so we're going to that."

"A *party*?"

"Pai. Calm down. It's one of the events for this retreat thing."

"Oh. So she told you about that?"

My dad's relief didn't go unnoticed. "You knew about it?"

I felt his shrug over the phone. "Yeah. Jules told me about it a while back." *Jules*. It was moments like this that reminded me that my parents had actually known each other at one point in their lives. Really well.

"Wait," he said. "Did *you* know?"

Ugh. When you were a kid with parents who were divorced or separated or whatever it was my parents were, you were stuck in this annoying diplomatic purgatory—always wondering if you were saying something to get the other parent in trouble. "Yeah, I knew," I lied again.

"I'm surprised you were still hell-bent on going, then."

I took my time responding because, had I known, maybe I wouldn't have been so quick to hop on a plane to get here. With my dad's credit card. In the middle of a fight with my boyfriend. "It's going to be fun. Once the storm passes, I'm going to work on my tan."

"Right, that storm. I saw that when I checked the weather report. Did your flight get in all right? When did you land?"

My dad and I talked for a bit longer—I told him the details of my flight, which he actually wanted to hear. Suddenly, I realized the rain had stopped. And that there was live music playing outside.

"I think I should go now," I said, reluctant to interrupt our conversation. "Party's in full effect."

"Okay. Well, enjoy yourself, because you're grounded forever once you get back."

I would have laughed except I knew he wasn't joking. "I will. I'll buy you a puka-shell necklace."

He laughed then. "Looking forward to it." A beat of silence. "I told Hamlet and Rose where you were."

Another wave of homesickness hit me. "I'm pretty sure I broke up with Hamlet. And Rose is probably mad, too."

"I don't think so. They were both worried about you."

I blinked, my eyes tired. "Is it okay if we don't talk about them right now?"

"Sure." He sighed. "Can you do me a solid, though, and call Hamlet? Or text him? Or something?"

The room was growing warmer. I fanned my face with my hand. "Maybe. I don't know."

"And, I noticed in my lovely airline receipt that you didn't buy a ticket back home yet. How long are you going to stay there?"

I stood up and moved the phone to my other ear so I could examine the thermostat. "I don't know."

"Lot of thought went into this plan of yours."

"Well, I mean, it's not *forever*."

"Oh good!" I heard Flo mew in the background, and I missed her so much.

"Talk to you later, Pai."

"Later, Shorty. Also: one week max, got it? You need some downtime before school starts."

A week. That seemed like forever and not enough at the same time. "Okay."

A pause. "Love you, little girl."

I swallowed the lump in my throat. "Love you, too, Pai."

When we hung up, I stared out the window at the beautiful people who had started to gather in the courtyard. Time to put my game face on.

# CHAPTER 29

WHEN I STEPPED OUTSIDE, THE AIR WAS COOL AND THE sky was filled with stars. The storm had left everything drenched and sparkling—palm trees, the woven hammocks in everyone's villas, and the slick stone paths leading from the rooms to the lit-up courtyard.

Strings of twinkly lights and torches made everything glow. Perfect Instagram lighting, apparently—every single person out there seemed to be snapping Stories or photos on their phones. Beautiful moments never happened unless you uploaded them first.

I'd been to plenty of these kinds of events with my mom, and I'd dressed for the occasion. Knowing that I couldn't match these people with their outrageous clothing budgets, I went with "teenage minimalist": black cutoffs, my Docs with black ankle socks peeking out, and a white cotton T with the sleeves rolled up. I hadn't had time to shower, so I leaned into my dirty hair by adding more product to push it back from my face, the tousled strands tucked behind my ears.

Eyes appraised me as I wove through the crowd—everyone was probably wondering if I was that teen fashion blogger, or a YouTube star.

I found my mom pouring some kind of bubbly drink into a delicate wineglass, surrounded by people. She'd had a wardrobe change, too. Still wearing the fringy robe, she had switched into a long, silky black dress with a leg slit a mile high. She was barefoot and her hair was done up in an artfully messy topknot. What glammed up the entire outfit were her bright pink lips on a glowing, otherwise makeup-free face. When I noticed these things about my mom, I couldn't tell if it was admiration I felt or irritation.

She looked up with the glass and her eyes met mine. "Clara! Finally!" she exclaimed. "Everyone, meet my perfect daughter. I mean, *look* at her."

Gazes zeroed in on me. You could see some faces registering my age and doing the math. Others skimmed over me, head to toe, trying to figure out what I was trying to do with my outfit. Some smiled warmly at me.

"Cool intro, Mãe," I said drily before smiling at everyone. "Hi, I'm Clara."

Here's the thing: when you act confident, even when you're nervous, people relax and stop scrutinizing you.

"I didn't know you had a *child*, Jules!" A Latino man wearing the tightest shorts I'd ever seen pushed my mom playfully on the shoulder.

She handed me the drink, and I happily accepted it. "Well, I do, Jeremy. She's my one and only." Pouring another drink for herself, she looked up at the mini crowd held in her thrall with a huge grin. "And Clara is *amazing*. She flew out here and surprised me!"

"Get *out*!" This time Jeremy pushed me, and I had to laugh.

"It's not a big deal," I said before taking a sip of the drink, the fizziness pleasantly traveling down my throat.

A blond white woman wearing a tropical-print romper pointed her drink at me. "Said like a true cool teenager. How old are you?"

I glanced at my mom before answering. "Sixteen. Seventeen in a couple months."

Her eyes widened, metallic blue eyeliner meeting meticulous eyebrows. "Wow! Jules, when did you get pregnant?"

The familiarity didn't seem to faze my mom. She rolled her eyes. "Kendra, I was so young. God . . . I was basically *her* age. Can you even?"

"Babies having babies," Jeremy said with a disapproving cluck. Everyone cracked up, and the music thrummed through the night air, making everything feel funny and good and clever. Or maybe it was the champagne.

"Who's the dad?" Kendra asked.

Mãe perched herself on the edge of an armchair, the twinkly

lights creating a soft halo around her. "He was my high school boyfriend, Adrian. Meu Deus, Adrian was *so hot* back then."

I groaned. "Grossss."

She laughed and pulled me over to her. "Sorry, filha, but it's true. He was good at *break dancing*." Everyone laughed, but it wasn't unkind. Like a nostalgic we-get-it kinda laugh. "Anyway, I got pregnant, and the rest is history. Adrian's done a fantastic job helping raise this daughter of mine in LA."

*Helping raise?* Something needed to be corrected there, but I felt like it would be awkward to react, so instead I took another sip.

And I continued to drink—people kept offering me shots and various frosty cupped drinks with fruit in them. At one point, my mom and I did a near-perfect choreographed dance to "Baby One More Time." When Jeremy claimed that he was swim team captain in high school, I pushed him into the pool, only to dive in soon after. Soaking wet, I peeled off my shirt and wore it as a turban.

And I knew all this because people there recorded every single moment.

Sunlight streamed through the mosquito net, and I blinked. My mouth felt like it was filled with cotton, my head was throbbing, and there was something happening in my stomach that I had to stay very still to ignore.

There was a vibration near my leg. I grasped for my phone with the most minimal movement possible. *Do not barf. Do not barf. Do not barf.*

When I peered at the screen, the clock said eleven a.m. And there were about a billion texts from Rose and Hamlet. Now a prisoner in my hungover body, I finally decided to read them. I opened the ones from Rose first.

Yesterday:

**Adrian told me you left for Tulum. He's kidding right?**

**HOLY CRAP YOU DID IT**

**How could you do this to your dad? TO US? The whole deal was we had to work all summer or get suspended when we get back. You BETTER not have messed this up for us.**

**Clearly we were never friends.**

**I hope you drown in the ocean.**

This morning:

**You know, for some reason I lost sleep over that last text to you. I don't want you to die but I wouldn't mind some severe injuries.**

My head throbbed behind my eyes as if in response, but I still had to smile at these texts.

I wanted to read Hamlet's next, but first I needed some water. There was a bottle of Perrier in a gift basket from the hotel and I chugged it, almost choking in the process. Stupid sparkling water. I managed to drag myself to the bathroom, splashing my face. When I glanced in the mirror, I startled. If a raccoon became a ghost and then dipped its head in grease, it would have looked like me.

Feeling like The Worst, I picked up my phone again to read Hamlet's texts.

Yesterday:

I'm sorry about our fight. Can we talk?

Ok, I understand if you need time.

Wait. Adrian told me you went to TULUM???????

Because of our fight? Or your dad?

Either way, WTF CLARA! Can you please text me when you land? I just checked the weather for Tulum and there's a storm coming??

All right looks like there were no plane crashes today. But I also checked to see if anyone was abducted or murdered in Cancun and its surrounding areas and looks like no. So that means you're alive. I guess I'm relieved.

Today:

Uh. Have you seen your mom's IG? Who is that guy in the tight shorts?

I almost dropped my phone. Last night came back to me in quick flashes. *Ugggghhhhh social media influencers!* I wanted to respond to Rose and Hamlet, but I needed to shower. To clear my head.

An hour later, I managed to make it to the hotel café, essentially a long balcony filled with tables lined alongside the beach. My mom was already there, wearing a large straw hat and sunglasses, nursing a giant cup of coffee. I sat down between her and Kendra, who was drinking a *Bloody Mary* of all things. I held back a gag.

"Morning, filha," Mãe said, giving me a kiss on the cheek. "Want some coffee?"

I took her mug gratefully. "Yes, please."

Kendra clinked my mug with her Bloody Mary. "You were a total star last night. My DMs are *crazy* this morning. Everyone wants to know who you are!"

That made me cringe. "Oh God."

"Oh, yes. I got an earful from Adrian this morning," my mom said with an eye roll. "Thanks for getting me in trouble, friends."

Kendra laughed. "You're always welcome. Anyway, Clara, you have to join us for the *activities* today," she said, her round, mirrored sunglasses showing my grimacing expression reflected back at me.

I looked at my mom, who grinned and dug into a plate of eggs. "Oh yeah. You're coming."

"What are these *activities*?"

Kendra answered, "First, we're going shopping. There are a few sponsored posts we have to do with local boutiques. Then we're hitting up a spa. Lunch at a resort later. Then back here for a yoga class and chill before dinner."

I shrugged. "Cool, I'm in."

Mãe squealed. "I'm so glad you're here!"

With my headache subsiding and the sun shining, I couldn't help but smile and agree.

# CHAPTER 30

TULUM HAS ONE LONG MAIN STREET, AND IT'S WHERE
you can find a lot of the boutiques, cafés, and restaurants. It
was a very sleepy town that had somehow, in the past few
years, become wildly popular.

Riding a sleek new beach cruiser, I glanced at the squad I was
with. Jeremy and Kendra had joined us, along with a few others:
a photographer who traveled the world taking photos of fancy
hotels, a stylist for celebs, someone who ate a lot of fancy food,
and an interior designer. My mom and Kendra were both fashion influencers—meaning they wore free designer clothes and
took lots of photos and collaborated with designers sometimes.
Jeremy was an architect who also happened to be a model.

The day was sunny, but there were dark clouds on the horizon. Apparently, it was the rainy season, so the weather was temperamental. We had already hit up a few boutiques where everyone had gotten free stuff (including me! A pair of insanely overpriced leather sandals and a straw hat—both of which I decided to wear immediately) and taken a thousand and one photos.

We were on our way to the spa at yet another eco resort. I found a lot of this stuff really over-the-top, but at the same time I couldn't deny that it was a pretty sweet deal. Getting paid to shop and relax? To eat fancy food and stay at posh boutique hotels? Okay!

"That hat looks fab, Clara Shin!" Kendra shouted to me from her bike, snapping a photo and making her bike teeter precariously for a few seconds while doing so. I couldn't believe none of them had eaten it while filming and riding. It was bound to happen, right? Bonus points if caught on camera. I was almost willing to do it for them.

While everyone else had been glued to their phones all afternoon, I decided to leave mine back in my room. One, international roaming charges were no joke. Two, avoiding Hamlet and Rose.

I popped a wheelie, making someone behind me scream with fear. My mom called out, "You better not hurt yourself on this trip, or Adrian will kill me!" He would, but it was my dad who taught me all the tricks on my eighth birthday. I felt another wave of homesickness, but the kind where I wished my dad could be here to experience this with me. I couldn't remember the last time he traveled anywhere by plane. He would have foodie-fainted over the ceviche we'd had at the party last night.

A couple of spa staff were waiting for us at the entrance that was shaded by tall palms. They took our bikes (bike *valet?*), and we entered the white adobe-style building. After getting signed in and bundled up in plush robes, we got our various treatments—everything was planned out for us: first, a dip in the various pools. I stayed in the cold one, sweaty from the bike ride. Then we got hot stone massages in individual huts outside. I made sure to stick close to my mom. I didn't want to be rubbed down while naked next to a stranger. Then it was time for a facial. My face was glowing afterward, and I felt like an angel. When everyone was in the saunas and steam rooms, I went poolside and took a nap. Throughout everything, we were served bottled water with slices of lemon and various fruits. My mom took a Story of me with an orange slice covering my teeth as she asked me a bunch of questions, cracking up the entire time. I also let her take photos of me with cucumbers on my eyes, even though apparently that was a spa cliché and no one really did that anymore.

By the time we got back to the hotel, I was pooped from pampering. Everyone seemed to feel the same and went off to their villas to relax until the yoga class.

My mom and I lay back in lounge chairs facing the Caribbean Sea, each with a coconut in hand. People actually did that here. I was hoping for a sunset, but Mãe told me we were facing east. She said we could have dinner on the jungle side tomorrow to watch it to the west. As a warm breeze drifted lazily over us, I glanced at my mom and smiled. "Today was fun."

She rolled over onto her side to look at me. "Right? I'm so glad you made it, meu bem." When my mom wasn't around her posse, she used Portuguese mom-expressions like "meu bem."

"Me too." And I was.

"How's everything going, then?" she asked, taking a sip.

I shrugged. "Fine."

"Really? Then how come Adrian was totally panicked when he called me yesterday?"

My head swiveled toward her. "What! You told me . . ."

"Girl. I was lying. Where do you think you get your skills from?" She flipped her hair to punctuate the point.

I shook my head. "Of course." The sky darkened, and someone lit the tiki torches around us. "Well, I kind of . . . left without telling Pai."

*"What?"*

"Yeah."

"How did you pay for your ticket?" Incredulity made her eyes huge.

Picking at the lemon yellow cushion on my chair, I took my time answering. "I know Pai's credit card number by heart."

"Meu Deus," she breathed, making the sign of the cross on herself. "I can't believe you're still alive."

"I know. It was . . . impulsive."

"Ya think?" she said with an exaggerated American accent.

"What made you do it? You wanted to come here that badly? *I* could have convinced your dad!"

Someone came by to offer us mango slices. We dutifully took some. So delicious, it hurt. After chewing, I responded, "Well, see, I entered the KoBra in a food truck competition. It was supposed to be a surprise for Pai because the reward is *one hundred thousand dollars*." Mãe whistled. "Yeah. Exactly. But then Rose accidentally told him about it—"

"Who's Rose?"

I exhaled impatiently. "My friend from school who had to work with me on the truck."

"Wait, your *friend*? Adrian told me you guys got into a huge fight and that's why you had to work on the truck in the first place?"

My hand fluttered between us. "Yeah, we hated each other, but it's cool now. *Anyway*. She told him about the contest, and he *freaked out* and got mad. At *me*!" I looked to her for confirmation on how horribly unfair it was.

She frowned. "Why?"

"I have no clue! I mean, he was in a bad mood because an investor backed out for his restaurant."

"Clara." My mom looked at me with exasperation. "Maybe he was just in a bad mood, and it wasn't the right time to tell him the news about the contest?"

I ate another slice of mango. "Maybe. Either way, he got mad and that made me mad." Suddenly my words sounded absurd coming out of my mouth. The monumentalness of my dad's offense became so small as I sat here on a beach in Tulum. I tried to figure out why, at the time, it felt so big. "It made me mad because . . . I finally cared about this stupid truck. And I was trying to help—that money could be the final piece he needs to open his dream restaurant! And, and . . ."

"You were disappointed?" my mom asked. She was stirring her coconut water, the question casual. Perfunctory, even. But it zeroed in on everything.

The ocean and sky were the same color now. I stared at the reflection of the moon on the water. "Yeah. I was disappointed." And it was the first time I had been that thoroughly disappointed. It's easy not to be disappointed when you're always wading in the shallow end of feelings. Patrick and Felix never disappointed me. I glanced at my mom.

Neither did she.

"Hey, so your dad also told me you were dating someone new?"

The subject change caught me off guard. "Oh. Yeah . . . I mean, I was? I'm not sure what the deal is now. I fought with him, too, before I left," I said sheepishly.

"Wow, Clara. Burning everything *down*," she said, spraying herself with some mosquito repellent. "What's his deal?"

Hm, Hamlet's deal. How to explain this guy? "Well, he works at this coffee kiosk at one of our stops. Which he doesn't really have to do because his parents are rich. Like, they own skyscrapers in China rich." My mom nodded knowingly. I'm sure she knew every variety of wealth in her line of work. I continued, "He was born in Beijing and moved to LA when he was little, but his parents moved back for work, so he lives with some family friends. They're cool. And he goes to a different school but is the same grade as me. And . . . that's where our similarities end." I had to laugh.

"What does he look like? Is he cute?" Right down to business, my mother.

"He's your basic . . . hot."

"Basic hot?"

I squinted. "No, he's more than that. I mean, he's definitely hot. But there's nothing basic about him." I swallowed the lump that was forming in my throat talking about him. A buildup of guilt, remorse, and *missing*. "He's driven and kind. A boxer."

"Ooh."

"Yeah. There's a lot of 'ooh.'"

My mom whipped her phone out. "Can I find him on your Insta?"

"Yeah. He's there."

I craned my neck to watch as she scrolled through my feed. "Oh!" she exclaimed, pointing to a photo of him holding Flo up like a prize fish. "Is that *him*?"

A surge of happiness coursed through me just seeing his face. "Yeah, that's him! Hamlet."

She glanced up at me. "Excuse me?"

"Don't ask."

"Well, he's *cute*. What's the problem? Why did you fight?"

*It's the least special thing about you.* The words still hurt days later. "Oh. You know. The stuff people fight about."

Before she could respond, Kendra and Jeremy were running down the beach waving to us with big, sweeping arm gestures. My mom waved back. "Looks like yoga's starting," she said, getting up. She held out her hands to help me up. "Well, don't be too sad, Clara. High school romances, who needs them, right? There are so many guys out there, and they'd be lucky to date you."

It was the nice, mom thing to say. But a small part of me wanted her to push me, to challenge my reasons for wanting to end things with Hamlet. But I knew, for my mom, high school romances didn't work out. And she'd been keeping herself at arm's reach from those kinds of intense feelings ever since.

I trailed behind her as she ran toward her friends. A reminder of teenage mistakes, of the ephemeral nature of love.

# CHAPTER 31

DAYS PASSED IN A RELAXED AND PAMPERED HAZE.

I'd wake up, take a morning yoga class with my mom or Kendra or someone on the beach, have a super-late brunch at the hotel, then spend the afternoon helping my mom take photos of herself at some destination. One day it was ancient ruins (which was rad until someone almost fell off a ledge taking a selfie); another day it was sailing to an island where we had a picnic spread out for us with, like, antique flatware. Evenings were always spent back at the hotel—dinner, drinks, hot tub. Repeat.

And in all that time, I had sent one text to Hamlet: **Thanks for checking in. I'm good. I just need time. Talk soon.**

He had responded with a thumbs-up emoji, which in Hamlet-speak was a low-key "F-you."

I had apologized to Rose but I hadn't heard back yet. It would have worried me more, except it was easy to bury that stuff deep in the back of my brain, prioritized way below the sand in my bathing-suit bottom or the mosquito bites on my ankles.

But one morning I woke up and just didn't feel like doing yoga. Instead I wondered what Rose, Hamlet, and my dad were doing. Because my dad was respecting my time with Mãe, I hadn't really talked to him, either. How was the KoBra doing? Was Rose still working on it? Did Hamlet win his boxing tournament last weekend? Was it still hot in LA? Did Flo miss me?

So I told my mom I was going to take the day for myself. I borrowed her iPad because I had dropped my phone into the ocean yesterday, and it was on the fritz. I slathered on sunscreen even though the day was overcast, packed my backpack with water and the iPad, then hopped on my bike.

Shuttled off from one activity to the next since the day I arrived, I hadn't had time to explore on my own. I was pretty tired of all the restaurants and businesses on the main drag, so I decided to explore the small side streets today.

The instant I turned left onto the first random street, the vibe completely changed. Everything was slower, quieter. I saw actual children playing in the road. There were homes and businesses, but spread far apart, and the buildings were older, less finished.

Time passed as I rode leisurely around these little roads and soon the sun came out—beating down on my new straw hat. Sweat trickled down my temple, and I pulled over to have some water. As I guzzled out of my bottle, I noticed a small wooden sign with an arrow pointing down a sandy path shaded by over-grown tropical greenery. Vines and ropey limbs tangled up to create a dense corridor.

Well, why not? I walked my bike down the path, swatting at the occasional mosquito. After a few minutes, the plants gave way, and I was standing on a pristine white beach. But in the middle of it was a tiny hut and plastic tables scattered with chairs. Nothing matched, everything looked like it came from someone's porch.

I loved it.

"Hola," a woman greeted me warmly as I walked up to the hut. There was a counter, and I could smell food cooking in the back.

I smiled and waved. "Hola." Then I glanced around to see if there was a menu.

Catching my searching expression, the woman said, "No menu here. We cook what we have!"

Sniffing the air, I was down to eat whatever they were serving. "Okay, sounds good." She told me to seat myself, and I sat down at the table closest to the ocean. There were some people in the water. It seemed like you could plop down at the beach here and eat or just hang out.

The setting was perfect and quiet and peaceful. And yet . . . the antsiness I'd woken up to was still there. I pulled my mom's iPad out of my backpack, slipping it from its designer leather sleeve. I really wanted to see what was going on with the KoBra.

Opening up the browser, I planned on stalking the Twitter

account first, but my mom's e-mail popped up. I was about to close out of it until I noticed a folder labeled CLARA on the sidebar.

Probably all of our e-mail correspondence archived. Oh boy, there would definitely be some hilarious gems in there—like the epic diary entries I'd sent her in middle school when I hated all my friends. I clicked on it, excited to go down memory lane.

But the e-mails weren't from me. They were from Pai.

What? Were these, like, child-custody-related e-mails? I knew I shouldn't, but I clicked on the latest one, which was from a few weeks ago.

**July 24**
**To: Juliana Choi**
**From: Adrian Shin**

Jules,
Does Clara know this Tulum trip is for work? She seems to think it's just a vacation for you two. Mind clearing that up so she's not so pissed about not being able to go?
-Adrian

I frowned. Okay, clearly my dad was waiting for my mom to tell me. Which she never had. I scrolled down and skimmed the e-mail subjects. My dad had been sending them regularly for years, it seemed. I clicked one from six months ago, in February.

To: Juliana Choi
From: Adrian Shin

Jules,

Clara's sad about her breakup with that loser
whatshisname. Thought she could use some Mom time
when Valentine's Day comes around. Probably less
awkward than me talking to her. Give her a call, okay?
-Adrian

Whatshisname. My dad's least favorite boyfriend of mine,
Leo, he of the no teeth-brushing. He always called my dad "bro."
Although he wasn't the love of my life, I had been pretty bummed
when we broke it off. So it was nice when my mom called. We
had Skyped while watching the least romantic movie we could
think of on Valentine's Day. (*Blackfish*—nothing kills romance
like a documentary about animal cruelty!) I had chalked up the
timing to Mom instincts.

I went even further back, to two years ago.

September 3
To: Juliana Choi
From: Adrian Shin

Jules,

Hey, I didn't hear back about whether or not you can make
it to Clara's birthday this year. Here's the wish list I promised

of things she wants. She's going through a spectacular phase in puberty of hating everything, so this was a serious undertaking.

- *The Bell Jar* by Sylvia Plath
- A Venus flytrap
- A neon sign shaped like a cat
- New pair of Vans, high-top black ones
- Colored pencils
- Something called "primer." I think it's makeup??
- Pasta maker

True mystery, our daughter.

-Adrian

My breath caught in my throat. I got every single thing on my birthday list that year. From my mom. My dad took me to the beach, and I remember thinking my mom was so much cooler than him. How she was so good at knowing exactly what I liked. He had let her take all the glory for the presents.

Always.

I went as far back as ten years ago in e-mails and found birthday lists then, too. From my dad to my mom, every time. Dozens, hundreds of e-mails. Reminders for my mom about school recitals and upcoming visits. Photos of me on the first day of school in slightly bizarre outfits. Horrible class pictures. Holiday and birthday photos when she couldn't make it—posing with the gifts she sent. Updates on my health, including medications I was taking when I got sick. Every lost tooth noted. The first day of my period and the sheer panic that came with it. Questions about birth control and makeup and clothes.

This folder was a record of my entire life.

My food arrived: a whole grilled fish with buttery rice, beans, and a fresh salad. I looked up and the same woman from behind the counter looked concerned. "¿Estas bien?" she asked.

I touched my face; it was wet with tears. Good God. Crying in public was my new thing now? "Yes, I'm fine! Just allergies." She gave my shoulder a little pat, and I stared at the screen for a few seconds before shutting it off.

When I took a bite of the food, I immediately thought of how much Pai would like the seasoning. Sitting there eating fish on a white sand beach with a cool breeze drifting over me, more than ever I wished I were on the KoBra—enclosed in an over-heated truck with my dad and my best friend.

# CHAPTER 32

WHEN I GOT BACK TO THE HOTEL, MY MOM WAS GETTING her hair and makeup done in her villa.

"Clara! You're just in time. I'm about to start this interview for *Pleat and Gather*," she said as a stylist tugged viciously on her hair with a curling iron.

I plopped onto her bed. "What's *Pleat and Gather*?"

"You don't know *PLEAT AND GATHER*?" she yelped, whether from incredulity or pain, I couldn't tell. "It's only the biggest fashion website, kiddo. Anyway, wanna stick around?"

"I have no life obligations, so sure." I was a little dazed from my afternoon snooping, and passively watching my mom get interviewed seemed like a great idea at the moment.

The interview took place outside, where my mom lounged on

a pale pink sofa, the white sand beach and sparkling blue ocean as her backdrop. Her hair fell in waves over her tanned shoulders, and she wore a long white linen dress with thin spaghetti straps, her legs tucked under her casually. She looked like a fancy mermaid.

With a camerawoman behind her, the interviewer—a young Mexican blogger with a bleached-blond bob named Teresa—started asking Mãe questions.

"We're here with influencer and tastemaker Juliana Choi in gorgeous *it* destination Lotus Hotel in Tulum." *Gotta get that product placement.* "Jules, as her fans like to call her, does it all with her four million followers—travels the world, sits in the front row of every major fashion event, and collaborates with designers to add that *extra*. She's also a mom to a very chill teenage daughter who's here with us. Can you *even*?"

Luckily, I was sitting in a chair behind the camera woman, so they couldn't swing the camera over to me or anything. Nonetheless, I still felt uneasy being discussed. My mom winked at me, and I was sure her fans would love that authentic private moment between mother and daughter.

"So Jules, tell us about your creative journey."

I resisted laughing.

Mãe settled back into the patterned cushions. "Well, since I was a child, I was always drawn to beautiful things. I grew up in Brazil, surrounded by lush tropical landscapes, and that sensibility still informs me." I couldn't help but wonder—informs *what*? Social media people always talked about "creating content."

It seemed like a catchall to legitimize careers built on taking photos of yourself in aspirational settings. But people loved it, so who was I to judge? Also? My mom grew up in São Paulo, a huge city that I wouldn't exactly describe as "lush." She continued, "Not to mention the cultural influences—Catholic icons, the people, the food, the rich layers of diversity."

Teresa nodded intensely. "*Yes*, girl. So inspiring." Huh? She barely said anything! Didn't "journey" mean talk about actual events? But Teresa moved ahead. "What was your childhood in Brazil like?"

I knew what it was like. Her parents struggled financially running a small grocery store and were so strict and religious that my mother grew up feeling stifled and alone.

"Wild and free," Mãe said with a laugh. *Huh?* "You couldn't ask for a more magical childhood. Children played on the streets. I'd be fed by the street vendors and I ran amok. It was just so *liberating*."

It was hard for me to keep a straight face as she kept talking about this magical childhood of hers. My mom had *hated* her childhood—it was what drew her to my dad, their common ground. I knew my mom was probably lying because the reality was so depressing, and this wasn't exactly a probing profile by the *New Yorker*, but still . . . It was so disingenuous it made me itchy.

"Speaking of liberation, do you have any plans to 'settle down' and work for a designer? You'd be great at branding," Teresa said.

A little wrinkle appeared between my mom's eyebrows. "I

*adore* all the designers I've collaborated with. But I'm not sure if I could ever pick a city in the world to live in for that long, you know?" Teresa nodded in firm agreement. "I love . . . *the world.* Discovery. I get to meet different people every month or week. I guess if most people are trees—putting down deep roots—I'm like an air plant?"

*"Amaaazing,"* Teresa declared, her eyes closing worshipfully. I was trying not to laugh. Leave it to my mom to pick an of-the-moment hipster plant to compare herself to.

Suddenly Teresa was looking at me. "Let's get real and talk about being a mother! How did you find time to raise such a great kid *and* follow your dreams?"

My skin tingled waiting for her answer. Because for sixteen years I had managed to gloss over, in my own memories, how absent my mom was. It felt like she was there because my dad made sure of it. She never missed a birthday call, gift, or holiday. But she wasn't actually there.

"I was really young when I had Clara," Mãe said. She took a long pause. "Obviously, right?" she said with a little laugh. Teresa laughed. She had a way, my mother.

"When I moved to LA with her dad, I was so lost," she said. And there it was. A genuine moment. "I thought that if I was a teen mom, I had to give up on my dreams. But, with Clara's dad's support, I was able to strike out on my own."

If I was being resentful, I would say that was an understatement. My dad's support? He raised me.

But everything about my mom—her uncomplicated ambitions,

the superficial friendships, never leaving her comfort zone—it all reminded me of . . . well, me. And I understood her.

I just didn't want to *be* her anymore.

As she continued the interview, a rosy revisionist history of our past, I snuck back to my villa and booked a flight home.

# CHAPTER 33

"DID I DO SOMETHING WRONG?"

I looked up at my mom while I packed a few hours after the interview. "No! You didn't. I promise. It's just time for me to go back home. I left a lot of things hanging."

She sat down on the edge of my bed and nodded. "I got that feeling. Is it about that boy, Hamlet?"

I smiled. Hearing his name said by my mom was sweet. I liked her being in the loop. "Yes. But also the KoBra. Pai. Rose. I let people down." I willed my voice not to waver as I threw my new sandals into the duffel.

Mãe was quiet as she watched me pack. "I'll miss you." And even though my mom could be astonishingly clueless and self-absorbed sometimes, I knew I would also miss her.

"Me too."

"You'll miss you, too?" she joked.

I cracked a smile. "Good one."

"I know." She crossed her legs, turning herself into a tidy, folded little mermaid person. "So, why are you in such a rush?" I was catching a red-eye tonight to make it to LA by morning.

"Because the food truck competition is tomorrow." I wasn't sure if I could pull it off—I had e-mailed Rose and she'd responded immediately, saying she'd figure out a way to get the truck and meet me at the competition. I could tell she was still a little mad, but she seemed as invested in this contest as I was.

"Whoa. Bold move. Adrian was against it, right?"

Ignoring the nervous flutter against my ribs, I nodded. "Yep. But I still want to go through with it."

She squinted at me. "That's new."

"What, this?" My hand drifted up to the little silver hoop in my left ear cartilage, pierced a few months ago.

"No. This . . . drive." She paused and I was self-conscious. I hated that I wanted my mom to think that I was cool. "I like it," she said. "It suits you." The second person to say these words.

I tried to hide my pleasure by making a face, crossing my eyes. "I have so much drive. The *best* drive. Huge."

Mãe cracked up. "Well, good luck, minha filha." It was both optimistic and ominous.

After saying my good-byes to the social media squad that I had grown rather fond of, I got into a car headed to the airport.

My mom popped inside to give me one last hug. "See you soon, filha. Te amo."

"Love you, too, Mãe." I was usually so sad when we said our good-byes—never knowing when it would be that I'd see her next. And it wasn't that I wasn't sad this time. It was just that there was a lot for me to look forward to outside of this good-bye. Real life.

As the car drove away from the hotel, the sky rumbled and fat raindrops splashed onto the windshield. I tried not to read too much into the timing.

The flight back home wasn't too bad, even though the grandma next to me farted steadily the entire time. At least it was direct.

Bright eyed and bushy tailed after two hours of sleep, I swept through customs in record time and ran down the long LAX corridor lined with colorful subway tile.

I only had a few hours until the food truck competition started. It was going to be nuts since my phone was still broken and I would have to grab a cab and hope Rose was all set up.

The international terminal exit had a row of people waiting for their loved ones.

A very large, very neon yellow poster caught my eye. It said: MY GIRLFRIEND. And the person holding it was flipping it around his head, much to the annoyance of everyone near him.

My smile hurt my face it was so intense, and I ran toward

Hamlet. When I reached him, jostling people and apologizing along the way, he dropped the sign and closed the distance between us in two big steps.

We were so close that I could see the bit of sunblock left smudged and white on his cheek.

"I'm sorry," I blurted out.

He frowned, and for half a second my heart stopped. Then he leaned over and kissed me. Kissing Hamlet felt like coming home, for real. I stood up on my toes to deepen the kiss, my duffel smashed between us. When we finally broke apart, he smiled down at me, all tenderness. "I forgive you." Just like that. Hamlet was the least complicated thing in my life.

"That's it?"

He picked up the poster and tapped my butt with it. "Lucky you."

Suddenly it occurred to me—"How'd you know I was coming?"

He turned red. "Well, I might have talked to your mom."

"What?"

He took my bag from me, trying to distract me from what he was about to say. "Well, when you left I started following her on Instagram and, uh, well, she messaged me yesterday to tell me you were coming home. She wanted someone to be here to pick you up."

That's when I noticed Hamlet was wearing a KoBra T-shirt. "What's that?"

He grinned. "I'm going to help at the competition today."

Something warm bloomed in my chest. "You are?"

"Yeah. Why do you think I'm here? We have to *haul*."

Minutes later, we were sprinting toward Hamlet's car in the parking garage. "We still have three hours before the competition!" he yelled, glancing back at me as he ran with my duffel carried easily over his shoulder.

We threw everything into the car, slammed on our seat belts, and peeled out of the parking lot. I braced myself against the dashboard and laughed. "Dang, James Bond."

He immediately slowed down and glanced over at me sheepishly. "Sorry, I just got caught up in the moment."

"I'm not complaining!"

"Well, it's not safe," he grumbled, pulling on his sunglasses primly. I shook my head but couldn't keep the smile off my face.

We got onto the freeway, starting our long trek to the competition. At the moment, we were on the westernmost side of town, near the beach, and the competition was a good twenty miles away at Griffith Park. I looked at the time nervously. "I hope the traffic gods are on our side today."

"Don't worry, I know all the best ways to avoid traffic," he said firmly. "The question is, what the heck was your plan? You were going to steal the truck and take it to the competition? Just you and Rose?"

"Well. Yes."

"Oh my God."

"What?" I stuck my chin out.

"It's just . . . the worst plan, that's all."

Hamlet drove across three lanes until we landed in the Express-Lane. I looked at him in surprise. "You have a FasTrak?"

"No."

"I'm really into this Jason Bourne side of you."

Again, he slowed down. "Don't get used to it. Is your seat belt on?" he barked.

"Yes, sir," I said with a wink, which only flustered him further.

We flew by some gridlock, but I kept my glee to myself. There's this LA curse—if you actually express your smugness at passing traffic, you will immediately hit some. It happens every single time.

*"This is going to be the best surprise!"* Hamlet exclaimed, slapping his hands on the steering wheel happily. "Rose kind of hates you right now, though. Just FYI."

"I'm counting on it." The thought of being stuck in that stuffy truck bickering with Rose filled me with the most intense relief. I found myself missing the weirdest stuff lately.

And, like with Hamlet, I knew the first thing I needed to do when I saw her was apologize.

We were quiet for a few seconds, long enough for the car to be filled with a huge elephant. His love confession and my non-reciprocation. I chewed my lip down to bits trying to decide if this was the right time to bring it up.

Hamlet's phone buzzed with a barrage of texts. THANK GOD! I picked it up gratefully. "Rose is freaking out."

"Ignore it," he said, speeding up again.

"You got it, Bryan Mills."

"Who's *that*?"

"You know, Liam Neeson's character from the *Taken* movies?"

He shook his head and turned on the radio. Loud.

The rest of the drive was quick—there was no traffic, and we found a parking spot in a secret lot that Hamlet knew about. I found this competence very attractive.

Taking a few trails off the main path shaded by ancient live oak trees, I could hear and smell the trucks before we arrived. They were parked in a giant lot bordered by the gnarled old trees and gently sloping hills of brush. As we got closer, my nerves finally caught up with me and I was filled with trepidation.

When I saw the KoBra, I took a deep breath. *Here we go.*

# CHAPTER 34

ROSE STARED AT ME, FROWNING.

For normal friends, it would have been a moment ripe for a hug. But I was me and she was Rose. So we stood there awkwardly without speaking. I punched her arm. "Hi."

She punched my arm back. Hard. "Hi."

"Sorry for leaving you," I said, the words whooshing out of me. And I was surprised by how easy and natural it was. Words that usually had to be yanked out of my insides with a crowbar.

Her delicate chin quivered. I was mortified. Seeing Rose cry would be like breaking the seventh seal to bring on the apocalypse or something.

"We can talk about that later," she said, her voice steady. Before I could answer, I spotted my dad in the doorway of the truck.

What! What was he doing here? The happiness that flooded me in that moment almost knocked me off my feet. Never had I been happier to see that lucky Dodgers cap.

I looked over at Rose and she smiled. "Surprise!"

"Adrian?" Hamlet exclaimed from behind me.

But my dad kept it cool. He leaned against the truck's doorframe and crossed his arms—the birthday tattoo visible on his forearm. "Well, well, well."

Looking at my dad in his truck—a culmination of decades of blood, sweat, and tears—the e-mails I'd read yesterday flashed through my mind, paired with the strongest memories of my childhood.

The day my mom left, the feeling of her hair pressed against my face and the wetness of her tears immediately forgotten when my dad scooped me up in his arms and took me down to this very park we were standing in. Putting me on the little train that traversed through creeks, horse stables, and trees. The worst day turned into a magical one.

My first day of kindergarten, the first time I'd been truly apart from my dad and left with strangers. He let me wear his old Bone Thugs-N-Harmony T-shirt, tied into a knot at the waist, and the animal charm bracelet my mom had mailed me for good luck. When I wouldn't stop crying, he stayed parked outside the school, within view of the window all day—missing his first day at a new job and getting fired.

Being picked up from a sleepover in fifth grade when all the girls circled around me and asked me why my dad was so young and was he really my brother and where were my *real* parents. My dad pounded on the front door of Lily Callihan-Wang's house so hard that the entire family woke up. He bought me a McDonald's hot fudge sundae on the midnight drive home and we sang along to TLC's "No Scrubs."

My dad's expression as he sat in the doctor's office with me as I got a shot for a bacterial infection, wailing. Not being able to tell if it was his palm that was sweaty or mine as he grasped my hand, so tight.

My dad's expression, again, as he read the instructions on the back of a tampon box out loud to me as I lay curled up in fetal position on my bed, torn between laughter and tears.

And his expression, now. I realized right then—how disappointed you could be when you were all in with someone. When you cared so deeply. How your heart could break, so precisely and quickly.

But I'd always known that. Ever since my mom left my dad, left us. And everything since then had been an attempt to keep myself so far away from all that. Anything real, anything difficult to hold on to.

As I stood there surrounded by three people who had the ability to do just that—crack my chest open to all the disappointment and difficulty and grief—I knew I still wanted it. The risk of the bad stuff was so worth the good stuff. People who would be there for you even when you messed up and behaved like a little jerk? They were the good stuff.

My fear that my dad would move on without me, with Kody or whoever else, seemed so absurd then.

It was hard to keep the emotion out of my voice. "I'm back."

"I see," Pai said, cool and distant.

I took a deep breath. "And I'm the worst person. Do you still want me as your daughter?" The words came out choked, garbled.

His posture relaxed and he smiled, somehow sad and happy at the same time. "Sure, Shorty." He stepped down from the truck and when he reached me, I hugged him fiercely.

"I'm sorry," I said into his shirt, the tears dropping rapidly— they'd been at the ready since the second I saw him. I heard Rose and Hamlet tactfully walk away from us.

His chin rested on the top of my head, and he wrapped his arms around me, too. "I know."

"I'll never do anything like that again."

"I canceled my credit card, for one thing."

I laughed a little, snot running down my face. "I overreacted. I was just disappointed and it was hard and Mãe was easy."

He pulled back and rubbed the snot off my face with the dish towel from his back pocket. "Yeah, she has a way of making everything seem simple."

I looked at my dad's face—the one that resembled mine, but with a straighter nose and darker eyes. "The thing is, I didn't like it? It was fun at first but, ultimately . . ."

He smiled that crooked, knowing smile. "Unsatisfying?"

That was it. "Yeah. Missing something."

I heard a sniffle from somewhere inside the truck. Whether it was Rose or Hamlet, I really couldn't say.

"Don't ever do that again. Got it?" He poked my forehead.

I scowled but nodded. "I won't. I don't want to let you down again. Ever."

"Well, you will." He tucked the towel back into his pocket. "But that's okay. I'll be here."

There were two faces looking out at me from the windows on the KoBra. Rose wiped her eyes, and Hamlet was openly crying. Oh my God, we were a freaking mess!

My dad rubbed his hands together. "Ready to do this?"

"Yes! But wait, why did you change your mind?"

"You have a persuasive, annoying friend," he said drily, glancing at the truck.

As if on cue, Rose stuck her head out the window, her eyes miraculously dry. "Okay, cool! Everyone's happy and made-up— we only have an hour and a half until judging!"

My eyes widened at my dad. "Can we do it?"

He nodded, jaw slightly clenched. "Yeah, let's do this."

We scrambled into the truck. My dad tossed a KoBra T-shirt at me, and I started unbuttoning my flannel to put it on.

"CLARA!" Three voices shouted at me. I looked up to see everyone with their backs turned toward me.

"Calm down, puritans," I said while pulling on the T-shirt. "Hamlet, don't pretend like you don't love it."

There might as well have been a giant anime sweat drop over his head. He laughed nervously, looking at my dad. Pai made a strangled noise and banged the pots and pans around. "When Clara's done stripping, let's make our game plan," he said.

We immediately kicked into gear. Pai and I were in charge of meats, Rose was in charge of rice and sides, and Hamlet was tasked with drinks and assembly. The truck grew warm once we had the grill and burners on, and an unpleasant sense of panic washed over everything as we scrambled.

And then suddenly: "Ten minutes until judging!" Hamlet yelled.

My dad and I looked at each other. I'd never seen him so nervous. I tried to distract him as I stirred the sauce with a whisk. "So, do you know how the judging works?"

He nodded. "I did my research while you were gone. In ten minutes, they'll be coming up to the trucks, one by one, and trying our food. Did you know Stephen Fitch is a judge?" His voice almost squeaked.

"I did. That's why I entered us. We're basically custom-made for that man. Inventive cuisine unique to the LA immigrant experience? Check and *check*."

And then our ten minutes were up. My dad rushed around to make sure the dishes looked perfect, adding touches here and there. Wiping off the edges of the plates with a towel and peering down at each one with hawk eyes. I went over to where Hamlet was pouring drinks and moved a cup closer to his ladle so it wouldn't drip. He looked at me, his cheeks flushed from the heat and the excitement. "Thanks."

I winked at him. He turned redder, and I gave him a quick kiss, pressing my cool lips to his hot mouth.

"Hey, you two! No kissing while handling food!" my dad shouted.

And then an air horn blared somewhere outside, making me cover my ears with both hands. Someone spoke into a megaphone: "Time's up! Judges will be coming by."

We looked at one another nervously. I fanned my face with a plate. Rose smoothed her hair repeatedly. Hamlet picked up a pen and spun it on his fingers. My dad took a long swig of water from a Tupperware container.

After a few minutes, I stuck my head out the window to see where the judges were. There were about twenty trucks in this competition so this was going to take *forever*.

My dad cleared his throat. "Well, everyone. I just wanted to say thanks. Thanks for helping me this entire summer, even if you were forced. And thanks so much for this." He glanced at me. "I never would have done it if Clara hadn't signed me up. She was right about that."

I fanned myself with a paper plate. "I'm always right."

"And humble," added Rose.

Hamlet threw an arm around my dad. "You're welcome, Adrian, although all I did was help today."

My dad threw me a sly look. "You've helped in other ways."

For Pete's sake.

Suddenly, there was a rap on the window. We froze and Rose came to her senses first, rushing over with a huge smile, ready to charm. "Hi there!"

I scrambled to the stove and took the food out of the oven where we had stuck it to stay warm. My dad and Hamlet ferried the plates over to the window, and Rose handed them drinks.

"Here you go," my dad said. "I'm gonna hop out to explain what you're eating there." We watched as my dad stepped out of the truck and shook hands with the three judges. One was the food editor for a local magazine, one a restaurateur from France, and the other was food critic Stephen Fitch. I held in a squeal at seeing him in person. Pai gave them the rundown on the menu, then stepped back to let them eat the food.

The food editor, a tall Japanese American woman in her fifties, took a bite out of the pastel, and her eyes lit up. The muscular, bearded Frenchman ate a forkful of the lombo and chewed thoughtfully, giving nothing away with his expression. And Stephen Fitch dug into the picanha with gusto, his eyebrows raised as soon as the spice hit him.

A pool of sweat was practically gathered at my feet. I turned away and drank some water to distract myself. Rose did the same. Hamlet kept his head close to the window, watching everything.

Finally, we heard them thank my dad and move on. We got out of the truck and joined him outside. The afternoon sun was dropping lower into the sky, and the hottest part of the day had passed. A jazz band was playing not too far off and a breeze rustled the leaves of the eucalyptus trees.

We sat down, tired and relieved to be done. With the judges still making the rounds of the next few trucks, we had a minute to cool off and catch our breath. It was then that I realized I was starving. I went into the truck to plate some food, and we ate in amiable silence. The last twenty-four hours of emotional turmoil had caught up to all of us, it seemed.

Another air horn blare startled us. The voice came over the megaphone again, "We have a winner! All contestants please meet in the middle of the lot for the announcement!"

Gah! We ran to where everyone was gathered. The crowd was filled with nervous energy, and I looked over at the line of people next to me and squeezed Hamlet's hand really hard. *Please, please, please. For my dad. He deserves it. Please.* I didn't even know who I was pleading with.

The hopeful expression on my dad's face was unbearable, so I looked at the judges lined up in front of us instead. Stephen Fitch picked up the megaphone and cleared his throat before speaking. "Thank you so much to the contestants this year. As predicted, this was a really difficult task. The food of this city is better than ANY OTHER CITY in the world!" Everyone cheered. "It represents the beating heart of LA: the people." I felt myself choking up—thinking about how my dad's love for me had always been tied to food. How I identified with my city through the different flavors of the cultures brought over here by families around the world. By brave people like my dad.

And it hit me then—how much home mattered to me and my dad. How it had kept us anchored through so much uncertainty.

"And so let me just cut to the chase. The winner of this year's LA food truck competition is—Chili Today, Hot Tamale!"

# CHAPTER 35

I DROPPED HAMLET'S HAND.

The winners were screaming and jumping up and down. Some were in tears. I'd be in tears, too. That was a boatload of money.

My dad took off his cap, ran a hand through his hair, then walked toward the truck. Rose cried, "What! That hunk of junk won over *us*! Completely unfair!" Several people looked over at us. Oh my God, Rose was the sorest loser on this *planet*.

My dad came over, put a hand on her shoulder, and said, "Hey. That's enough, Rose." She looked like she wanted to argue, but one look at my dad's crestfallen expression made her stop. When he walked to the truck, she followed him.

My chest hurt witnessing this sadness, and I turned to talk

to Hamlet. But he was a few feet away talking to Stephen Fitch. When Hamlet caught my eye, he waved me over.

"Are you Adrian Shin's daughter?" Stephen asked me, his wire-rimmed glasses sliding down his nose a bit.

I nodded, not able to speak for a second. "Yeah. Yes. I am."

"Your dad's food is just excellent," he said enthusiastically, reaching out for my hand. "I want to talk to him. Can you introduce us?"

Trying to remain cool and collected, I brushed a lock of hair away from my face. "Oh sure. Uh, he's in the truck. Follow me, please." Out of view, I shot Hamlet a *look*. His eyes were wide and he mouthed, *What's happening?*

I shrugged and hurried ahead of Stephen to warn my dad.

"Pai!" I hollered as soon as I got to the truck.

He looked up from wiping down the counter, his expression grim and irritated. "What?" he snapped.

"Stephen Fitch would like to speak to you," I said. "That's *all*," I hissed quietly, nudging him in the ribs.

"What?" Confusion clouded his features as he peered outside. Then he paled. Wiping his hand hastily on a towel, he stepped outside and I followed.

Rose, Hamlet, and I stood off to the side as they talked.

"Hi, Adrian. I'm really sorry you didn't win the competition," Stephen started. My dad held up a hand like, like "No problemo!" Please.

"But I wanted to say, you're doing something really special here. That pastel, the combination of flavors! Truly inventive."

"Thank you," Pai said, rubbing the back of his neck, suddenly shy.

Stephen handed him a business card. "If you're still interested in opening up a restaurant, I'd love to talk about investing. What you said about your Brazilian and Korean cultures—that was fantastic, and it's exactly the sort of thing that is integral to the food scene here. I'd love to set up a time to talk."

A very quiet, very long squeak came out of Rose, and I held back from dragging my hands down my face and screaming.

"Yes! Of course! Thanks, man," he said, holding out his fist. Stephen glanced down at it, then smiled, giving him a bump.

When he left, we remained cool for about .5 seconds. Then jumped up and down. Hamlet ran over to my dad and lifted him up.

"Ohmygodohmygod!" I screeched. I had zero chill and zero cares about it.

Rose paced in circles, beside herself. "Your investor problems are solved! Just like that! And what if he features you on *The Weekend Feast*?"

"What's that?" Hamlet asked, excited before knowing why.

"An NPR show about food!" she exclaimed.

My dad held his hands up. "All right, you guys. Let's remain calm. You don't know if he'll invest yet!"

But hope was making me buoyant. "Don't say that! Think positively!"

The three of them stopped moving. They exchanged glances then laughed. As one. One laugh unit.

"What?!" I asked, testy and defensive.

My dad shook his head. "You sound like . . ."

"Me," Rose finished for him. "You sound like a total try-hard." Her tone was like mine, flat and rude.

I flushed. "So?"

"It's a good look," Hamlet said with a wink. My own moves being used against me made me flustered, but I couldn't help but smile. So big my cheeks hurt.

We went back to the truck and cleaned up, everyone considerably less glum than before. When I noticed that the sun was setting, I had an idea. I hopped into the driver's seat. "Grab a hold of something," I announced as I lurched the truck out of the lot, finding the main road in the park.

"Clara! The four of us can't ride in this thing," my dad said, bracing himself against my headrest.

"It'll just be a few minutes, hide yourselves from cops," I said as I adjusted the rearview mirror. Rose threw herself into the passenger seat and put on her seat belt frantically. "Where are we going?"

"You'll see."

We followed a road that led us out of the park and up into the hills. A few minutes later, Hamlet popped up next to me, leaning against my headrest. Squinting into the tunnel we were headed toward, he asked, "Are we going to the observatory?"

Ugh, Google Maps boyfriend! I didn't answer, instead taking

us up the hills until we reached the parking lot for the Griffith Observatory. Since it was a Saturday evening, it was completely packed. I drove by the lot and instead went farther up the hill, to an area I knew we weren't really allowed to drive into—it was more of a hiking trail.

Rose sniffed out disobedience quicker than a cop. "Clara, we're not supposed to drive here."

Again, I ignored her. There was nothing obstructing us from driving on the dirt path. It was just wide enough. And finally, we reached the spot I was looking for. An old stomping ground of mine—a dirt lookout with the hillside behind us, and a view of the city in its entirety in front of us.

I parked and got out of the truck, climbing onto the hood and then the roof. I called down, "Come up!"

They joined me one by one. And by the time we were lined up on the roof, the sun was very low in the sky. To the left was the observatory—my favorite place in the entire city. Most people knew it from *Rebel Without a Cause*, the beautiful art deco architecture with the three domed buildings, the middle one housing a telescope that could view distant planets. It had a planetarium and exhibits inside, but my favorite thing about the observatory was the view. You could see all of LA from here.

What tourists usually came to see was the Hollywood sign, which was directly to the right of us, larger than life. Iconic but completely meaningless to me, to be honest. People who were born and raised here didn't see LA with the same starry eyes. It was just home, and the Hollywood sign did little to stir any feelings in me. But I did feel something when I looked down at the city stretched below us.

From this vantage point, you could see downtown to the left, Dodger Stadium a little farther north of it, a sprawl of suburban areas, the main drags that crisscrossed the entire city—Wilshire, La Brea, Santa Monica. And on a clear day like today, you could see a glimmering strip of the Pacific Ocean to the very west of us.

When you saw the city like this, everything inside you slowed down. Relaxed. It wasn't that LA was perfect, or some immigrant utopia. Like other good things in the world, it was deeply flawed, and on some days you sat parked on the 110 surrounded by buildings you couldn't see because of the smog, and you hated it here. It could be relentless and lonely. But it was also where my dad had built his life, where so many people had. It was a place where you could grab Brazilian Korean food in the park where Walt Disney dreamed up Disneyland. But more important, it was home. And I related, deeply, to a home that was a little messed up, but ever-evolving.

And as the sky turned a light lavender on the edges, pale pink in the middle, and then a deep orange near the horizon, you, gratefully, felt your littleness in the universe.

I looked over at the KoBra crew and felt so grateful for the small part of the universe I had.

We watched the sun set, quiet with our own thoughts. My head tilted back and my eyes closed as a cool breeze drifted over us. Summer was ending, I guess. It felt good, and it felt sad. I knew that things wouldn't be the same with Patrick and Felix, and I was okay with that. I glanced at Hamlet and Rose, their gazes straight ahead, the last of the day's light shining on them. It was startling how I felt about them now, how fiercely they mattered to me.

Yeah, I was okay with a lot of things.

When the sun dipped behind the hills, my dad jumped off the hood. "We should go before we actually get into trouble." At the word *trouble*, Rose booked it after him.

I grabbed Hamlet's hand before he could follow. "Wait a sec." I watched Rose disappear into the truck, then looked up at Hamlet. It was dark, but my eyes adjusted and I could see his features perfectly. I had his face pretty well memorized now. Like the streets in my neighborhood, the pages of my favorite books. "We need to talk about what you said to me last week, before I left. Um, how you love me." I was grateful for the darkness, hiding my blushing cheeks.

He took a deep breath. "You don't have to—"

"I know. And I'm not ready to say it back." Relief poured out of me, a weight that had been filling the parts between my bones finally lifting. "Is that okay?"

He blinked a couple of times, looking down at our feet. I held his hands firmly, and my palms were dry for once. After a while he looked at me and, while there was some sadness in his eyes, I believed him when he smiled and said, "Yeah, that's okay."

I squeezed his hand. "But you have to know . . . I've never said that to anyone before. Except my parents."

"Really? What about *all* those ex-boyfriends?"

I lifted my hand up to the base of his neck and wound my fingers into his thick hair. "I never loved them. In fact, I never liked any of them as much as I like you. I think that's why I freaked out. Not because you said you loved me. Just understanding the extent of my actual feelings for you. It's really new."

His eyes softened. His whole face, the edges of his body— they softened. Everything. "You like me more than them?"

I leaned my forehead against his. "Yeah. So much more."

Catching my belt loops with his fingers, he drew me closer to him and said, "All right. I guess I'll have to be patient. We'll live on Clara Time. Not Hamlet Time."

And then he lifted my chin, gently, touching his lips to mine. The kiss was sweet and full of promise. Like him. When he let go, I felt a lurch in my chest that told me Clara Time was going to catch up to Hamlet Time real fast. And when he climbed down from the roof, I took one last glance at the view—lights sparkling in the inky-blue night.

In this huge city, there were three people in this truck who mattered a lot to me. I'd protect that little part of the universe for as long as possible.

# ACKNOWLEDGMENTS

MY FIRST THANK-YOU ALWAYS GOES TO MY AGENT, Judith Hansen, fiercest champion for any creator lucky enough to have her in their corner. I'm so grateful for your guidance and wisdom.

Endless gratitude to my editor, Janine O'Malley, and to Melissa Warten for their expertise and good humor while forming an actual book from this pile of swear words. Thank you to Margaret Ferguson for helping me shape this story in the very beginning and for everything before that. Thanks to the FSG/Macmillan team, including Elizabeth Clark, Brittany Pearlman, Joy Peskin, Jodie Chester Lowe, and Karen Ninnis.

For the research and eyeballs needed on this book, I'd like to thank Lisa McCune of Scratch, Louis Quezada of Border Grill,

Suzy Yu, Alice Fanchiang, Cat Fanchiang, Chengzhe Zhou, Sophie Xiao, Charmaine Ou, Ben Zhu, Adi Alsaid, Lilliam Rivera, Nemuel DePaula, Nina Khatibi, Fernando Encarnacao, and Jennifer Li.

Thank you to Derick Tsai for being the Josh Lyman of my book life. Thanks to Willard Ford and everyone at SSG for turning me into someone who can fight with more than just her words. Thanks to #RetreatYoSelf. Bless our frosé and In-N-Out. Thank you to Rilo Kiley for letting me use your perfect words.

Thanks to all the librarians, booksellers, festival organizers, and lovely readers whom I've met over the years. Your support and kind words have meant the world to me.

So much gratitude to early readers Brandy Colbert, Sarah Enni, Morgan Matson, and Amy Spalding. You weren't just readers but my lifeline during the wildest year ever. Keeping with this metaphor—thank you to Robin Benway, Anna Carey, Kirsten Hubbard, Alex Kahler, Elissa Sussman, and Zan Romanoff for keeping me afloat in our fair city.

Infinite ♥ to the Bog: Leila Austin, Alexis Bass, Lindsey Roth Culli, Debra Driza, Kristin Halbrook, Kate Hart, Michelle Krys, Amy Lukavics, Samantha Mabry, Phoebe North, Veronica Roth, Steph Sinkhorn, Courtney Summers, Kara Thomas, and Kaitlin Ward. Special shout-outs to Somaiya Daud, Laurie Devore, Kody Keplinger, and Stephanie Kuehn for the #accountability on this book. Thank you, hags.

It's no surprise that families matter a whole lot in my books.

Because mine is always there, filling the pages, even when you can't see them.

For all the love and support, thank you to Kristi Appelhans, Tony Appelhans, Kira Appelhans, Tom Watson, Oliver Appelhans-Watson, Leah Appelhans, and Nate Petersen.

Thanks to my sister, Christine, for being the most reliable person in my life. I couldn't have done anything this year without your help. Even if I had to hear *Frasier* at midnight. Thanks to my parents for doing so many things right that I've only noticed and appreciated with time. For supporting everything I've ever wanted to do, minus going to sleepovers.

And thank you to my husband, Christopher Appelhans. I wrote about falling in love in LA because of you. I write everything because of you.